Shane Brown was born in 1974 and lives in Norwich, UK. He received a doctorate in Film, Television and Media from the University of East Anglia in 2014. He is the author of the young adult *Breaking Point* series of novels, as well as *Elvis Presley: A Listener's Guide* and *Bobby Darin: A Listener's Guide.*

.

Follow the author on Twitter @shanebrown74.

BREAKING POINT
Shane Brown

CHAPTER ONE

1

The knock on the bedroom door brought James Marsh's mind away from the film he was watching on his laptop and back to reality. He paused the film as his mother opened the bedroom door a little.

"Are you decent?" she asked.

"Decent enough," he replied.

She came into the room and looked dismayed at the fact that he was still in bed and watching the film.

"Come on," she said. "It's a quarter to eight. You can't be watching films at this time in the morning."

She walked over to the bed and peered at the laptop screen that was in front of him.

"What is it today?" she asked. "Another film from Uncle David?"

"Yeah. It came in the post before you got up. I thought I'd give it a look before I have a shower. I must have got carried away."

"There's a surprise! You're always getting carried away. Now, get in the shower!"

James's mum left the room and he reluctantly shut down the laptop. James knew that his mother wasn't too sure if the influence of his Uncle David was a good one or not. He thought it confused her how a boy of sixteen had somehow got interested with the one-hundred-year-old movies that his uncle watched and talked about far too much. It didn't seem natural to James's mother. In fact, it seemed more than just a little unhealthy to her. But James knew that, if she was more honest with herself, she would admit that it was her brother David that concerned her more. He knew she would never say it out loud, but James had a feeling that she was uneasy about her son idolising a man that she had always thought of as a little eccentric, even if he was her own flesh and blood.

Nearly twenty years her senior, he lived in the middle of nowhere with three cats; generally wore clothes that had, to put it mildly, seen better days; and apparently spent most of his time doing research for a book on a long-dead film star that most people had never heard of – a book which, everyone seemed to be certain, would never be finished. In fact, James's mum had more than once questioned whether the whole project was a figment of her brother's imagination. He, meanwhile, insisted it was going to the definitive biography of the long-forgotten actress. Despite all of that, Uncle David had become something of a father figure for James since his parents' less-than-amicable divorce, and that was something James's mum *did* at least appreciate.

James, meanwhile, would freely admit that watching, and reading about, these films was becoming a habit that he would find hard to break. An addiction. While other kids his age were watching big-budget films about superheroes, James spent his time watching Buster Keaton, Clara Bow, and Lon Chaney. But something about them fascinated him, and he also liked the fact that these films were somehow *his*. None of the other kids at school knew anything about them. This was his own private little world in which he could somehow hide away from anything and everything that bothered him.

But it was an expensive hobby and, sadly, he didn't have much money to spend on it - the Marsh household was certainly not a wealthy one - but what money he *did* have was spent at a second-hand shop in town that stocked records, old film posters and other memorabilia. He had been going there every Saturday for more than a year, and he enjoyed spending time with Alfred, the shop's aging owner, who was more than happy to have someone to pass his music and movie knowledge and anecdotes on to. Meanwhile, Uncle David sent him DVDs on an almost weekly basis as well, and the latest arrival, a film called *Noah's Ark* from 1928 that so far had nothing to do with Noah's Ark, was what James had been watching when his mum had interrupted him.

If he had a choice, James would have watched the film until the end, but he didn't have time for such luxuries. He needed to leave early for school, just like he did every day. It was safer that way. Bearing that in mind, he got out of bed before he had much time to think about it, stripped out of the T-shirt and boxer shorts he had been sleeping in, and wrapped a towel around his waist before padding down the hallway to the bathroom. He turned the shower on while he brushed his teeth so that the water was hot enough when he stepped under it.

He saw showering as something of a necessity rather than a pleasure, and so kept the process as short as possible. If nothing else, it kept things moving along nicely in the Marsh household in the mornings. Sometimes, he would take a bath in the evening, and that was when he would hog the bathroom for an hour or longer, just soaking and relaxing while listening to some music until either his sister or his mother started hammering on the door, telling him it was about time he got out.

When he stepped out of the shower (less than three minutes after he stepped in), he wiped the steam from the mirror to see if he needed a shave, but decided that the one he'd had a couple of days earlier would do for a while yet. Then he turned around, so that he could get a look at the bruises on his back. He was relieved to see that they had finally started to fade. It had taken long enough. Almost two weeks. At least they had stopped hurting a few days earlier. As he wrapped the towel around his waist again and walked back to his bedroom, he wondered how long it would be before he was covered in fresh ones.

For the last few months, the bruises on his back had become as much a part of his life as the films he adored so much. He always made sure his mum and his sister never saw them. He knew it was safe to walk along the hallway in just a towel when he came out of the shower in the morning because his mum was downstairs, and his sister had already left for work. But he wouldn't do it at another time of day when they might see him. And, no matter what the time of year or how hot it was, James would never sit around the house half-dressed. Not anymore. There would be too many questions asked about where he had got his cuts and bruises (and, indeed, scars) from. They were his secret and had to remain that way, no matter how much he would have loved to have blurted out everything and told someone exactly what had been happening to him.

When James had dried off and got dressed, he went downstairs and made himself a mug of tea and a couple of slices of toast before going into the lounge. He wasn't someone who liked to eat a big breakfast. In fact, even the toast was something of a struggle, but his mother wouldn't let him go to school on an empty stomach, although she didn't realise that it was school itself that made him feel more than a little sick each morning. Also, if there was a choice between a hearty breakfast and an extra quarter of an hour in bed, then bed was always going to win.

When he went into the lounge, he saw his mother sitting there, still in her dressing gown.

"No work today?" he asked, sitting down on the sofa.

"The temp agency said they didn't have anything for me this week," Alice Marsh replied.

"We'll manage," James said, forcing a smile and trying to make her feel better.

"We won't have much choice."

Money had been a struggle for some time. Alice Marsh had lost her job as a classroom assistant nearly a year earlier, and had tried to find work since, but had fallen into the unenviable trap of temp work. It paid well enough when she had work, but sometimes there simply wasn't any. The benefits system hardly helped those people who relied on temporary work. Alice would sign on when she was without work, but by the time her claim had been processed she was, more often than not, working again. It meant that there was no regular money, and that bills got paid late, and that letters started arriving, informing them of rent arrears. Luckily, Rachel, James's sister, was working, and was happy to help out, but she would be going to university later in the year, and then things would become even more difficult.

On the television was a rolling news channel, and James and Alice sat there watching for several minutes while it showed footage of a politician being interviewed.

"He reminds me of Dad," James said.

"Oh?"

"Yeah. They're both full of bullshit."

James smiled as he said it, knowing that his mum would have told him off for his language if his comment hadn't been so true – not that Alice Marsh had much room to talk when it came to bad language.

James's parents had been divorced for just under three years, although they had been separated for a couple of years prior to that. James could never remember them happy together, although, as they had two kids during their marriage, he guessed they must have been happy at some point. His dad had not been violent towards his mum, but it had never been beyond the bounds of possibility, and James knew that his dad had a couple of affairs, the last of which was the reason his mum had asked for – no, demanded – a divorce. James was quite proud of her for saying enough was enough.

Since then, James had seen his dad just twice, the second time being just under a year ago. James had approached his dad, saying he wanted to see him. His mum was fine with that. He was at the age where he was curious to see what his dad was really like, and whether he was really the ogre that his mother (and his own memories) made him out to be. He had to make up his own mind. His dad had brought his current girlfriend to that get together, and James realised that the unreliability of the maintenance payments was not due to lack of money, but because he spent so much on *her*. This had become blatantly obvious by the number of expensive gifts he had bought for her while they were out – and none for his own son, it should be added.

James had made up his mind there and then that he didn't ever want to see him again.

"Have you heard from him?" James asked his mum.

"Just drink your tea while it's hot. It's meant to be chilly outside this morning."

"You're changing the subject, Mum. So you've got no work and he's not paying maintenance."

"He never has done. He's not going to start now."

"Then he should be made to. The system is fu... Screwed," James said, correcting himself.

"You should become a politician and fix it."

"I'd never keep my trap shut around all those lying creeps. I don't think politics is my calling."

"You *have* a calling?"

Alice Marsh sometimes wondered if her son was sixteen or sixty.

"Yep. School," James said, stuffing the last of his toast in to his mouth and washing it down with the rest of his tea.

"You'll get indigestion, eating that quickly," his mum said, watching him.

Better than a beating, James thought.

"Why do you always go in so early?"

"I'm meeting someone at the end of the road. We're going to walk in together and then do some work in the library. We've got some homework to do in pairs for biology, so it will be easier to do it there."

He was surprised at how much of a fluent liar he had become. He didn't even feel guilty about it anymore. It was just part of life. Part of his survival.

14

"Is it a friend?" his mum asked.

"Yes, Mum. I do have some," he lied again.

"I sometimes wonder. You never have anyone over anymore."

"You don't like kids."

"I don't mind them if they're your friends. And they're hardly kids anymore. Is it a girl?"

"No, Mum. Don't get your hopes up. You're not going to marry me off just because I'm doing work with someone. Now, I've got to be going or I'll be late."

"OK. See you tonight."

James bent down and kissed his mother goodbye before going into the hallway and putting on his coat and shoes.

"Bye!" he shouted into the lounge as he went out of the front door. He looked at his watch and hurried down the road.

There was no friend waiting for James at the end of the street; there was never going to be. He wondered how his mother could be so gullible when he made different excuses day after day as to why he was leaving for school early. Surely she knew that he was trying to avoid people rather than meet them? He felt that one day she would follow him, find out the truth, and then confront him – but it was worth the risk. He had learned over the last few months that, if he went to school early, he was less likely to run into Jason Mitchell and his friends on the way, and that, in turn, meant less chance of getting covered in yet more bruises. The last batch had occurred on the way home from school a couple of weeks earlier. His timing hadn't been so good on that occasion, and he was still paying for that, but he could never prepare for every eventuality. And bruises were only a part of what he had to worry about. Sometimes there were none, and the ordeal was just as painful.

James would have enjoyed school a lot more if there were no other kids there. He was bright and enjoyed his lessons in the main, probably more so than most. But over the last year or so, school had become more of a place of torment and torture than learning – and it was getting worse rather than better. In fact, it was fair to say that the whole situation was getting out of control. James knew it, but had no idea what he could do to stop it.

It wasn't as if the school was unaware of the bullying that went on there, although they referred to it as "discipline" problems rather than "bullying." Officially, there was not a bullying problem at the school. That is what they told parents, the local newspapers, and even the teachers. Most parents didn't know any different, most local newspapers couldn't care less, and most teachers just went along with the lie – most of the ones that cared had left and now taught elsewhere.

No, the official line was that the problem was "discipline," and the school's answer to that was to clamp down on such minor things as slight discrepancies in school uniforms. If the headteacher saw a pupil wearing trousers that were the wrong shade of grey, then he or she would get punished with a detention or maybe taken out of class altogether. Teachers had been told to clamp down on toilet breaks during lessons. Pupils couldn't wear jewellery. Certain types of haircuts were not allowed. Any form of facial hair for the older boys was a no-no. Parents had been sent letters, telling them of how such infractions of the dress and behaviour codes were no longer going to be tolerated. At the same time, they were also encouraged not to give their children sugary drinks and to make sure they went to bed at a sensible time. Alice Marsh had received her letter, declared it "a load of bollocks," torn it up, and put it in the bin. The letter had been put on social media and was reported in the local press.

Some parents (and pupils) said the school was overstepping the mark, and that its duty was to provide an education for the kids and not parenting. Slowly, though, the furore had died down. The school continued implementing its new rules, which never made any difference to either discipline or bullying. It was doubtful that anyone ever thought they would.

James's mum had asked him more than once just what kinds of discipline problems there had been at the school, and she wasn't the only parent to be concerned. Many feared the worst – drugs, mostly, or perhaps kids taking knives into school. James did his best to reassure her, telling her it wasn't that bad really. He told her what might be best called the "edited highlights." He told her that some teachers had been hit by things being thrown in class. He even told her that one of their cars had its tyres slashed. But he thought it best not to tell her about one of his classmates who was caught wanking in a French lesson.

He wished he'd had the guts to tell her everything there and then. He didn't even have any friends to confide in. Not anymore. More than once he had tried to pluck up the courage to tell his mum everything, but he had no idea as to what she would do or the ramifications her action would have. He imagined her ending up at Jason Mitchell's house and a fight erupting between her and his parents. He knew she would do anything to protect him, but he wasn't convinced that whatever she chose to do would actually help.

James continued to walk down the street and glanced at his watch – the only jewellery that any pupils could wear at Smithdale Academy. 8.07. Good. His timing was perfect. He aimed to arrive by 8.15, just as the school gates were being opened. That way, he knew he could get to the safety of the school library without being set upon, and then stay there until registration half an hour later.

As he turned the corner, James could see the school ahead of him. He felt no more accepted or safe in those large brick buildings than he had nearly five years earlier on his first day there. Now, at sixteen, he knew that he only had to get through one last term and then he could be free of the place forever if he could find a job or do his A-Levels at college.

And he couldn't wait.

2

Jason Mitchell did *not* spend his time before school watching silent films. He had other things to do. He awoke to a straightforward alarm on his iPhone. He would have liked his ringtone and alarms to be cool rather than bog-standard, but he knew that trying too hard to be cool in that way came with its pitfalls and, before you knew it, cool wasn't cool any longer and you looked like a dick instead.

He had no plans of getting to school early like James had done, and yet was awake by half past six. While he would have liked to have snuggled down in the duvet and gone back to sleep, it wasn't his style, and he had work to do. He got out of bed, pulled on a pair of shorts, and headed downstairs.

His parents were away on a business trip and he had the house to himself. It wasn't anything unusual; they had been leaving him overnight in the house since he was fourteen. He liked it, and he was quite capable of looking after himself. With his parents out of the house as often as they were, he didn't have much choice but to learn to fend for himself, but his parents compensated him with cold, hard cash each time they went away, and Jason liked having the money, although he could always get some from them whenever he wanted. They were happy to give it to him if he stayed out of their way and didn't do anything to get himself into trouble. Jason didn't always keep to his end of the bargain – he often did things that could get him into trouble, but he just made sure he didn't get caught.

Jason used the money for two things – to buy clothes so that he looked good and got attention, and, more importantly, to make more money. His friends (or followers, depending on whether you liked Jason or not) knew that he could keep them supplied in anything they wanted, or, in some cases, needed. Jason dealt in all manner of things, even if he never partook in such vices himself. The good-looking, clean-cut boy next door who could charm anyone he wanted was living proof that looks could be deceiving.

Looks were important to Jason and, perhaps, with good reason. His parents might have run their own successful business and expected him to follow in their footsteps, but Jason was not what you might call business-minded. Not in the way they wanted, anyway. He had his own business of sorts, of course, which needed its own set of skills, but he was never going to be a businessman beyond that, and he didn't want to be. He had tried to tell his parents that over the last few months, but they did their best to ignore him, or at least try to persuade him that he would "come around" to their way of thinking. But there was a huge difference between what his parents wanted for him and what he wanted for himself.

Jason wanted to go to art college. It was something he had kept entirely to himself until relatively recently, when he had shared his aspiration with his parents, finally showing them the dozens of drawings and sketches that he had worked on over the years. They had smiled and tried to feign interest, but then told him that what he needed was to go to university. Art college was not on the cards. His friends knew nothing of Jason's hobby or ambitions. His drawings and everything associated with them were safely hidden out of sight whenever one of his friends came up to his room.

He went through to the kitchen, opened the fridge door, and gulped down half a pint of milk straight from the bottle. Then he picked up a set of keys from the worktop and went outside, unlocking the garage door to reveal the gym equipment that was the reason why he had got up at 6.30 in the first place. His dad had bought it on a whim, perhaps in a sudden realisation that he was now middle-aged, his clothes were getting tighter, and he drank too much red wine at business dinners and should be looking after himself more. Like most things in the Mitchell household, the equipment was top of the range, but Jason's dad had tired of it after a couple of weeks, and it ended up being Jason who made use of it, heading out to the garage first thing most mornings. It was the only thing he worked hard at other than his drawing. And it had paid off.

None of the other boys in his year at school had a body like he did, and he got the desired attention from the girls and, in a few cases, the boys. At first, the boys bothered him, but now he revelled in it. He liked very much being the centre of attention, and his ego was swollen by the fact that he was wanted by people who could never have him. And yet, despite everything, despite the time he put in to working out, despite his good looks, despite his family's money, the best girlfriend he could manage was Claire Bramwell. He watched himself in the mirror as he worked out, his bare torso getting increasingly covered in sweat, and wondered how someone like him ended up with someone like her.

Claire had somehow attached herself to Jason nearly a year earlier, and, with his best friend joined at the hip to his own girlfriend, Jason felt that he was left out – and that he had to compete. He couldn't let Luke be the only one with the gorgeous girlfriend. And yet, it never really worked out. Jason knew that Claire was no match for Jane, Luke's other half. Jane was sexy, mischievous, clever, witty. Claire was a limpet. Once Jason had started going out with her, there was no getting rid of her. He had tried hard enough. He had tried ignoring her, and she had just turned up at the house. He had tried being mean to her, and all she did was plead for him not to be. He had tried pressuring her into sex and, while she hadn't given in to that pressure, she had made him feel so guilty that he had never tried again.

Meanwhile, Luke and Jane were at it like rabbits. At first Jason thought they were just saying that as a boast, but then, when he went to Luke's house one night, he caught them at it. They had left the bedroom curtains open and, with Luke's bedroom being on the ground floor, Jason could see right in as he walked up towards the front door. Instead of turning away, he had kept quiet and watched for as long as he dared. It had turned him on, but, at the same time, it started eating away at him that his best mate was having sex on a (very) regular basis, and yet he, Jason Mitchell, hadn't had it once.

And now, as each day passed, he came to resent Claire more and more. He would split up with her, of course, but the truth was he didn't have the guts. He wanted *her* to split up with *him*. Much easier. But his patience was running out.

After nearly an hour on the gym equipment, Jason locked up the garage and went inside for a shower. He put thoughts of Claire out of his mind and tried to concentrate on the day ahead. After all, he had plans - and they involved James Marsh.

CHAPTER TWO

The problem that James had with Mondays was the games lesson at the end of the day. He was happy to sit through the maths, the food prep and nutrition, and the biology – not that he liked, or was very good at, biology – but games and P.E. filled him with dread. They provided two times a week when everyone was unsupervised, and in changing rooms too. He knew the possibilities of what could happen there as he'd seen others suffer over the years, and he knew it was only a matter of time until it was his turn. It hadn't been that long ago that he had walked into the changing rooms only to find one of the younger kids from the previous lesson hanging from one of the coat hooks by his boxer shorts. James was the only one who had helped get him down, to a chorus of disapproval from some of his classmates. He had no idea why people had to be such jerks.

It wasn't just the fear of what Jason Mitchell and his friends might do to him in the changing rooms, it was the atmosphere of the place itself. There was that unmistakable smell: a mix of body odour and cheap deodorant. And he hated the ordeal of having to get changed in front of everybody else. He knew that his body didn't look any better or worse than other people's (except Jason's, and nobody else had a body like his), but that didn't stop him from feeling vulnerable and exposed, even without any threat of being bullied while he was there. He always tried to strip out of his school uniform and get into his games kit one item at a time and as quickly as possible before making his way to the gym where he did his best to look invisible until one of the teachers turned up.

And then there was the fact that he always seemed to be the only boy in his whole year group who didn't like games and P.E. lessons. He was useless at most sports anyway, but it wasn't just that. Team sports were meant to bring out the best in people but, from what he saw each week, it only brought out the worst. People were meant to work together, but instead it was just an excuse to blame anyone who screwed up. James didn't dislike things like athletics or badminton or tennis as much. He was awful at those too, but they were individual events, and so nobody cared if he was crap at them beyond occasionally taking the piss.

He'd got held up talking over something he didn't understand with his biology teacher, and so arrived in the changing rooms only a few minutes before the lesson started. He liked it that way. Most of the boys had already got changed and gone through to the gym.

James put on his games kit as quickly as he could, and then left, catching a quick glance of himself in a mirror as he did so and thought what an idiot he looked in shorts.

He made his way to the end of the gym benches and sat down as far away from everybody else as he could. He watched some of the others playing around on the equipment which had been left out by the previous class – not that they were meant to. They were told every week not to use anything unless teachers were present. Jason scooted up one of the climbing ropes in a way that James could only dream of. In fact, James had never made it more than a few inches off the ground. Not only did he not have the strength to pull himself up, he didn't have the co-ordination either. A couple of Jason's mates started shaking the bottom of the rope once he had reached the top, jokingly trying to make him fall. James felt a pang of guilt when he hoped that they might shake it too hard and Jason might hit the ground and break a leg. Anything to stop him coming to school for a few weeks. It might have only been a couple of months until James finished his compulsory schooling, but having one of those without Jason would be bliss.

Jason slid down the rope unharmed as news filtered through that the games teachers were on their way. Within seconds, the whole class was sitting on the benches, and the only sign that they had been doing anything else was the swaying of the climbing ropes that the teachers didn't seem to notice as they walked in.

Football. It was after the Easter holidays and they

were still playing football. James couldn't believe it. Still, he thought, at least it wasn't rugby. Things could always be worse. But there were so many things that he hated about football, like the humiliation of always being the last one to be picked for a team. Not that he blamed whoever the team captains might be – he wouldn't pick himself for a team either. But that was hardly the point. There were no other lessons where the less able were so obviously outed and embarrassed in front of their peers. And then there was the standing around in the cold, waiting for that rare occasion when one of his teammates might send the ball towards him, and hoping against hope that he might be able to pass it to one of his own side. However, his football skills were less than great and, more often than not, he didn't manage it, and then the insults and name-calling would start, sometimes accompanied by being deliberately pushed or tripped up for the rest of the match. It was then safer for him to wait outside the changing rooms after the game until everybody else had left, fearing what might be awaiting him if he went in and changed with the others. At the very least, he would be mocked by a handful for his mistake, and, at worst, his disgruntled teammates would make sure that he didn't forget his error in a hurry.

James sometimes wondered if games teachers were naïve, stupid or just downright evil. What other explanation could there be for someone like Jason being chosen as team captain week after week? James found it hard to believe that any staff at the school who came into contact with Jason on a regular basis were completely unaware of his behaviour, or that of his friends. And yet, here he was again, standing in front of the rest of his classmates, being given a position of power, and taking turns with Luke, the other team captain, to pick off the boys one by one. And James knew that it was inevitable that he would end up on Jason's team.

After the humiliation of team-picking was over, the boys walked out on to the playing field for the game. As he had done in the gym, James stayed a little detached from the rest of the group. He felt safer that way, although not everybody hated him or picked on him, but those that didn't generally avoided being seen talking to him if they could, just in case they were thought to be one of his friends. Some of them might not have been James's enemy, but that didn't mean they were his friend either. After all, they had their own self-preservation to think about. It resulted in something of a lonely existence for James, but at least he knew where he stood and who he could trust: no-one but himself and one or two of the teachers. A friend had turned on him before in order to cover his own back, and to save himself from the wrath of Jason, and James had no intention of experiencing that again.

Once out on the field, James was given his position to play in, and it was no surprise, although he never quite understood the logic of putting useless players in defence. Perhaps it was just to somehow get them out of the way for the majority of play, but surely the team captains could see that if you put your worst players near the goal, then the other team were more likely to get past them and score? Over the years, James had become aware that common sense did not necessarily go hand in hand with the sporting prowess of the team captains. The same thing happened almost every lesson, and this one was no different. The only surprising thing on this occasion was that it took nearly twenty minutes for Luke to barge past him, nearly knocking him over in the process, and kick the ball into the net. It had been inevitable. James steeled himself for the worst, and within seconds Jason had run up to him, grabbed hold of him roughly by the shirt and whispered in his ear:

"Mess up again, dickhead, and you're dead!"

He pushed him hard, and James stumbled to the ground. James waited until Jason had walked away before he got up. There was no sign of concern or interest in what was going on from the games teacher. Perhaps he hadn't seen, although James doubted that. More likely he didn't care, or perhaps had just given up trying to stop such things from happening. Or maybe he just thought it was done in jest. Smithdale Academy didn't have a bullying problem, after all.

As James walked back to his position, it started to rain, and he hoped that it would become heavy enough for the game to be called off, and perhaps the lesson could end early. It had happened before, but not often enough. But the rain didn't get any heavier. Instead, it just became a persistent, but light, drizzle that had little effect other than to make James colder than he already was and to make the pitch muddier in the places where the grass had become worn. Now, Jason and his friends started to take great pleasure in tripping him up each time they came close to him. They seemed to invest far more energy in getting James covered in mud than in the game itself. Again, the teacher didn't notice. The hour dragged on and, by the time of the final whistle, he was freezing cold and covered in mud. So much for this being the spring term, it was more like the middle of winter.

The boys slowly started to walk off the field, making their way back to the changing rooms to get showered and changed back into school uniform. James generally tried to avoid having a shower, and normally after playing football he hadn't been energetic enough to work up into a sweat anyway. This time, though, there was not much chance of getting out of it. If he put his uniform back on covered in mud, his mum would kill him. There was nothing for it but to wait around until most of the others had left. He kicked off his boots before entering the school building, hanging back in the corridor so that he could see the comings and goings of the changing rooms. Normally, Jason and his friends were some of the first ones to leave – especially with the lesson being the last one of the day. Often, they didn't even bother getting changed at all and walked home in their games kit. That wasn't really an option on this occasion given that they had got dirty, and James knew that once they got in the showers they normally took their time getting out. The situation did, after all, give

Jason a chance to show off – and, of course, take the piss out of those unfortunates in the showers with them.

Fifteen minutes went by, and James began to wonder if he had somehow missed them leaving after all. Mr. Green, James's English teacher, came down the corridor and walked up to him.

"What are you doing out here, James?" he said. "You'll be late home."

"It doesn't matter," James replied.

James and Mr. Green got on well, with the teacher being one of the few who made it clear that he knew exactly what went on in the school, and he did whatever he could to look after those pupils who had a rough time. He knew that James was one of them.

"Who are you trying to avoid?" he asked.

"No-one."

"Do you want me to go in there and see if No-one has left yet?"

James smiled.

"No," he said. "I'll be fine."

"They might have gone out of the other door."

"Maybe."

James knew that Mr. Green was probably right, and that Jason could have left by the outside door at the far end of the changing rooms, but he wasn't totally convinced. There was still a very real possibility that they were loitering in there. Waiting for him. And yet he also knew that he couldn't wait outside all day. Eventually, another teacher would come along and move him on, especially given that he was covered in mud.

He smiled again at Mr. Green and then opened the door to the changing rooms and walked in. He shut the door behind him, and stood in front of it, not yet daring to venture any further forward. He was as quiet as he could be, straining to hear any sound that might suggest that there was someone hiding in there, ready to pounce on him.

He walked forward a few steps, and, to James's surprise, he could see that his school bag was still where he left it, as was his jacket. Perhaps today wasn't going to be his unlucky day after all. Many times he had returned to the changing rooms after a games or P.E. lesson to find that his clothes and belongings had been hidden somewhere, or strewn over the floor, and he would have to spend the next quarter of an hour trying to find them, and not always succeeding. No-one ever came over to help him. There was a time when they had, but that had all changed now. He could rely on no-one.

Finally convinced that he was alone, James walked over to where he had left his things. Breathing a sigh of relief, he sat down on the bench in order to compose himself. The mud on his legs had now started to dry, and he idly picked at it for a minute or two. He was tempted to walk home in his games kit. He could always have a shower as soon as he got there. There seemed little point in having one at the school. After all, while he hated the changing rooms when they were full of other boys, the idea of showering there on his own when they were empty was enough to give him the creeps. The quicker he got out of there, the better.

He stuffed his trousers into the bag, and then started looking around for his school shirt. He was certain that he had left it hanging on the clothes peg, but it wasn't there now. He peered into his bag, wondering if he had slipped it in there earlier, but he knew deep down that he hadn't. He started looking around the changing rooms to see if he could see it, assuming some of the other kids had tossed it on the floor somewhere, or perhaps hidden it up, but there was no sign. He began to wonder how he was going to explain the absence of his shirt to his mum. Money was tight enough without shirts randomly going missing. He thought he could perhaps tell her that it had got dirty somehow and that he had put it into the linen basket. Perhaps she would then forget and wouldn't notice that it wasn't there. He hated lying to her, but sometimes it was a necessity.

"You looking for this?"

James turned around and saw Jason and three of his friends strolling out of the shower area where they had been hiding. Jason was holding the missing shirt up in the air. James could feel his stomach turn over. He didn't know what to do. He was tempted to just grab what he could of his belongings and make a run for it, but he had too much pride to do that. Instead, he found himself taking a step towards them.

"Give it back, Jason," James said, his arm outstretched, ready to grab hold of the shirt.

Jason pulled it back away from him.

"All you've got to do is ask for it," he said.

James sighed. Perhaps if all they wanted to do was play stupid games then things might not be as bad as he feared.

"Can I have my shirt back?" he said.

"*Please*."

"Please."

"No."

Jason laughed and threw the shirt to one of his friends, Neil Moore. "Badger," they called him, although no-one really knew why. James had known Badger for five years, and in all that time had only managed to come up with one suggestion as to how his nickname came about. Someone told him once that they had heard that he'd had a lock of white hair when he was a toddler, and the nickname had come from that. If so, it seemed a little harsh for a boy's own parents to give their son such a nickname. While Badger saw Jason as a friend, it was clear to everyone else that Jason saw *him* as a joke, and frequently pranked him or went out of his way to make him look a fool. And yet, through everything, Badger remained loyal.

Badger threw the shirt to Luke. Second in command, Luke had been friends with Jason for years, but more recently there had been a trace of tension between the two of them, although neither ever mentioned it. Luke believed it was partly because Jason was jealous of his girlfriend, Jane. That, in part, was true, but both boys knew there was more to it than that. There comes a time when some friendships come to the end of their natural life, especially during the gradual move from boyhood into adulthood. That was happening with Jason and Luke, and Jason was beginning to feel threatened by that. He was worried that his friend wanted to take over the group, but he couldn't have been further from the truth: Luke didn't want to take over the group, he wanted to break away from it.

Luke grabbed the shirt and passed it on to the imaginatively-named John Smith, or "Smithy" to his friends. There was less mystery as to how he came about his nickname. Smithy was one of those people that Jason knew he could rely on. Badger, at best, provided brawn to the group. Luke was a threat. But Smithy was the staunch supporter. Mr. Dependable. He was never going to let Jason down through sheer stupidity as Badger might, or turn against him because he grew tired or acquired a conscience as Luke eventually would.

And then there was Paul Baker - James's only real chance of this ordeal coming to an end prematurely. James still couldn't believe that Paul had sunk low enough to allow himself to be controlled and used by Jason in order to avoid the kind of attention that James received from him. There was a time when things had been very different – when James and Paul had been friends. That was a long time ago now, and, while James missed Paul's company and friendship, he very much doubted that he would ever be able to forgive him for what he had done.

The balled-up shirt was tossed from one of the group to the other. James was in the middle, sometimes trying to grab it out of someone's hands, and other times attempting to pluck it out of the air as it flew over his head. He knew that he was unlikely to succeed, and even if he did, Jason would just grab the shirt back again. On one occasion, James managed to grab the shirt but, as he did so, Jason kicked him in the back of the knees. James's legs buckled, and he fell to the floor. The other boys closed in around him.

"You were looking at me during the game, weren't you?" Jason said.

"No," James replied, quietly, trying to stand up as he did so, but pushed back firmly to his knees by Jason.

"Don't lie to me, *gay boy.*"

"I'm not lying."

The others laughed. It was their job.

"Don't deny it. We all saw you. *Queer.* You just want a piece of this, don't you?"

He moved further forward, gyrating his crotch in front of James. James suddenly regretted not asking Mr. Green to check the changing rooms were clear for him. This was new territory. He was used to a beating, or name-calling, or being pushed about, but he really didn't like where this was going.

"Is that what you want?" Jason asked again, the fabric of his shorts pressing against James's face.

Jason laughed as he walked away. He went over to James's school bag and picked it up.

"What have we got in here?" he asked.

He peered in, and then started pulling out the contents and throwing them across the room. James cringed as he saw textbooks and school work getting ruined as he did so. At one point, Jason pulled out a book and ripped it in two, letting it fall at his feet. Finally, he pulled out the biscuit tin that contained the contents of James's cooking from earlier in the day. He prised open the lid and looked inside, and then made his way back over to James.

"Looks good," he said. "What is it? A *fairy* cake?"

Smithy, Badger and Luke laughed on cue.

Jason put his hand into the tin and broke off a large chunk of the Victoria sandwich cake, and started stuffing it into his mouth. He nodded as he ate, speaking with his mouth full.

"It's actually quite good," he said, half-eaten pieces of cake spewing from his lips. "Want some, James? Of course, you do. You know you're nice and hungry!"

He spat the half-eaten remains of the cake into his hand, and then bent down and rubbed it into James's face and hair. James did his best not to gag.

Jason wiped his hands on James's shirt.

"Now look at you," he said. "You've got yourself all messy. And how many times have I told you before? When you get muddy in games lessons, you must take a shower, just like everybody else."

Suddenly, James realised that this was going to be much worse than anything he had imagined. A beating was one thing, but something told him that Jason had actually *planned* this. He wasn't making it up as he went along.

James's first instinct was to make a run for it and to get out of the changing rooms as fast as he could. If that meant leaving his stuff behind, then so be it. But as soon as he stood up and tried to make a move, he was held still by Badger and Smithy. The henchmen. It was five against one. Four against one if you discounted Paul in the vain hope that he might feel some pity for his former friend and take a back seat. James was never going to get away, and he knew it. As much as he hated the idea, the only thing he could do was let it happen, and hope that it would be over quickly.

Even as he told himself just to go with it, he started lashing out as best as he could with his fists and feet as Jason and the others started pulling his clothes off. His shirt was pulled up, only to get stuck when they tried to get it over his head. James started to panic now that he couldn't see what was happening, and started yelling at the top of his voice. The shirt wasn't moving anywhere, and so Jason ripped it in order to get it off. Something else James was going to have to try and explain to his mum. Luke worked at pulling James's socks off, tossing them across the room once they were removed, with one landing on the window sill, and the other behind the radiator. There it would stay, as James never found it when he put his stuff back in his bag after the ordeal was over. James continued to kick and yell as Jason leaned forward and pulled his shorts down, quickly followed by his boxers. Badger seemed to find this hilarious, although James couldn't understand what he was saying

– not that this was anything unusual.

Jason was clearly keen to get whatever he had planned over and done with. Perhaps he was now worried about getting caught. James soon found himself being carried, naked, through the changing rooms towards the showers. He heard the water being turned on, and he guessed that it wasn't going to be set to hot.

As they reached the showers, James saw Jason standing a few feet away, holding his mobile phone in front of him.

"The girls are just going to love this," he said, smiling. "Oh, and don't worry. Some of the boys, too, I'm sure."

"Don't you fucking dare!" James yelled at him.

"You'll be an internet sensation, mate. Mr. Green will watch it on repeat."

He laughed as the boys threw him into the showers, with James landing on the hard, tiled floor. By the time he stood up, he saw that the exit was blocked by the others. He ran at them despite the fact that there was no chance of getting past them. But what else was he to do? He could hardly just stand there, with the water attacking his back like a barrage of ice-cold nails. At first, he tried to hide his privates, so that Jason wouldn't get him completely naked on camera. But, in the end, he gave up and just screamed each time he tried to push past them, partly in the hope that somebody outside might hear him, although he doubted very much that would happen. If nothing else, at least they had been hit a few times with his flailing arms. Not Jason, though, of course. He was standing too far away for that. But James knew it was too late, now. The damage was done. Jason had the whole thing on his phone. Before long, it would be online, or sent to people's phones. He would be the laughing stock of the school.

Eventually, James gave up trying to escape, and went to the far corner of the shower area, sitting down in a space where he thought he was going to be hit by the water less. Soon after, the water was turned off. The game was no longer fun once he had stopped trying to escape. He sat still on the cold wet floor as he heard Jason and his friends walk off, laughing as they did so, with Jason again repeating that the footage was going to be an "internet sensation." Finally, the door of the changing rooms banged shut.

James was finally alone. He just wished that was going to be the end of it, but he knew that, in reality, it was just the beginning. He wondered how long it would take for that footage to go online. Or perhaps Jason would use it as blackmail, threatening him with its release if he failed to do certain things for him. James guessed that those things were unlikely to be legal. James's only hope was that Jason would realise that the footage could be traced back to him. He wasn't sure that even that would bother him.

James knew he had to get out of the showers, but the energy evaded him. He wondered just how many of his books and clothes had been ruined when Jason had thrown them across the room. And how long was it going to take to even find everything?

After a minute or so, he heard the sound of the door to the changing rooms opening and closing. His heart sank. His first thought was that Jason had come back for more, but for some reason he dismissed this idea. Jason would be long gone by now, probably failing to contain his excitement as to what he had on his mobile phone. It could be a caretaker, but he'd never seen one in the changing rooms at this time of day before.

James heard footsteps coming towards the showers, and he looked over when they stopped. It was Paul Baker.

"Hi," Paul said.

James didn't feel any fear at the sight of Paul. Paul was never going to start anything by himself. In fact, he knew why Paul was there.

Guilt.

"Piss off," James said, quietly.

Paul moved away and returned holding James's towel in his hand. He walked over to him and draped it gently around his shoulders.

"Come on. You need to get out of here," he said. "You'll freeze to death."

James didn't move. He didn't know what to do. He felt so many different things. Pain, because this person used to be his friend, his closest friend. Anger, because he had dared to show his face after what had happened.

"You need to get dry," Paul said. "Do you want me to get your stuff together?"

"Get out of here," James said. "I don't want to see you. Ever."

The two boys stared at each other for a couple of seconds before Paul bent down and put his hand on James's shoulder. James cringed.

"I'm sorry," Paul said.

And then he left.

CHAPTER THREE

1

Paul Baker wondered if he would ever forgive himself. He knew that James was never likely to forgive him. When everything had started, when he had first said "yes" to Jason, he had never guessed where things would end up.

He knew what Jason had planned for the video he had taken on his mobile phone, and he knew just how humiliated James was going to be. He wasn't even sure why he had gone back into the changing rooms to speak to him after it was over, but he felt he had to do *something* – and now he couldn't get the image of James out of his head, sitting there cold, wet, and naked in the showers. And, most of all, alone. And it was *his* fault.

Paul felt alone, too. He had got himself trapped in a situation where he was at the beck and call of a group of people he both feared and detested. It had seemed like the most sensible thing to do back when he made the decision to turn his back on his friend and join them instead, but he knew now it was the most stupid thing he had ever done in his life.

He was now *owned* by them. He had to do what they said – well, what Jason said anyway, and sometimes that wasn't realistic. Jason wanted to meet him later that night, but, as soon as he got home from school, Paul realised that was going to be almost impossible. The house was nothing short of a tip, not that this surprised him or was anything remotely unusual. His dad made a mess, and it was his job to clear it up. That was the way it worked.

As soon as he opened the front door, he was hit by an almost overpowering smell of strong aftershave. He slung his school bag down in the alcove under the stairs, and kicked off his shoes without bothering to untie them. He looked into the lounge and the kitchen to make sure his dad wasn't home, and then went upstairs to try and find the source of the smell. He opened the door of the bathroom and saw a broken aftershave bottle on the floor, which his dad had dropped (or more likely, thrown) and left for Paul to clear up. He had cleaned up worse.

He went downstairs and collected a dustpan and brush to gather up the broken glass, and a cloth to clean the floor with. The smell was going to linger no matter how well he cleaned up, but he opened all of the windows that he could in the hope that it might at least make the odour a little less strong. At least there was no sign yet of his dad – about the only good thing that had happened so far that day – although he now wondered what state he would be in when he returned home. If he was throwing aftershave bottles across the room when he went out, how drunk or bad tempered was he going to be when he got back?

When he had finished clearing up the glass, and getting rid of the smell as best he could, he went into his bedroom and changed out of his school uniform and put on a pair of jeans and a T-shirt. He had already showered at school after the games lesson – something he hated doing, but he had little choice. Jason did it, so he had to do it, too.

He went back downstairs and took his games kit out of his school bag and put it into the washing machine, along with some things from the laundry basket. He looked around the kitchen and his heart sank. The place was a mess. The pedal bin was overflowing, and some things had fallen onto the floor beside it, including some half-empty tins, with the contents spilling out onto the floor. Washing up was piled high in the sink. It always was. Every day was the same, and Paul could see no end in sight.

He opened the fridge door and found it nearly empty except for some ham that was out of date, and a lump of cheese that betrayed the first signs of going mouldy. He took the milk carton from inside the fridge door and unscrewed the cap. The smell that came from the milk as he poured it down the sink was enough to make him retch.

Paul knew that it would take at least an hour or so

to get the kitchen looking respectable, and that was without cleaning up and vacuuming the rest of the house. Things had never been this out of control when his mother had been around more often. There had been times when his home hadn't look like one of those houses on the TV series where the cleaners were called in to fumigate it.

He was tempted to simply put his coat back on and go out somewhere, without bothering to clean up at all. That was what he *wanted* to do. Forget everything. The problem was that he knew that, when he got back home, he could end up covered in more bruises than James if his dad still happened to be awake. The same would be true if he didn't do the cleaning perfectly, although that wasn't made easy by how long some of the crockery had been left for. He was assuming that the plates and mugs had been left in his mum and dad's bedroom, as he'd washed up everything else the night before. He was never allowed in their bedroom, even to clean up. His stomach turned as he peered inside a couple of the mugs, only to see something growing in them from the coffee dregs.

Over the next hour or so, he got the house as clean as he could, before going upstairs to his bedroom to start on his homework. But he found it hard to concentrate. What had happened in the changing rooms kept preying on his mind, and he kept checking his phone nervously in case Jason had sent a text message telling him the video footage was online. He hoped Jason had changed his mind about uploading it, but knew that things were never that easy. He had to decide what to do about meeting Jason later that evening. He doubted he would be able to get away anyway. But the main thing was that he wanted to stand up to Jason.

He had to do it sometime.

2

Andrew Green put the folder of marking on the back seat of his car, and started the drive home.

As he pulled out of the school gates, he found his mind returning to James Marsh, and hoping that he had not, after all, had any problems when he had finally gone into the changing rooms. He had been tempted at one point to return there just to check on him, but teachers walking into school changing rooms was a no-no these days, even when accompanied by the best of intentions. However, he knew James from his English class and worried about him. It was clear that he was being bullied by Jason Mitchell and his friends. It wasn't as if they even tried to hide it, with not-so-veiled threats being made in the classroom on occasion. But his hands were tied, other than reprimanding Jason for his comments. Andrew had determined to have a chat with James about what was going on at some point. It was, after all, affecting his grades, and with only a few weeks to his G.C.S.E. exams, that was something that the boy didn't need. He clearly had enough problems already.

He wondered how long it had been going on for. Quite a while, he assumed, but it had only been over the last month or so that he had noticed a change in James. He had got quieter in class. Not only was he not taking part in discussions as much, or volunteering answers to questions, he was also becoming more withdrawn in general. It was harder to strike up a conversation with him outside of class. He even seemed to smile less. And then there was the fact that he was always seen on his own. He used to be good friends with Paul Baker, and the two had been inseparable, but that friendship had clearly come to an end some months earlier, although Andrew didn't know why. The signs were definitely all there that James was being bullied, and Andrew saw it as his duty to do something about it, even if the school itself tried its hardest to prevent that from happening.

The school was a mess. Discipline was appalling – something not helped by a significant number of the best teachers leaving after trying to cope with the regime imposed by the new headteacher, who had been in place for three years. Bullying was rife, although, of course, no-one could even suggest at a staff meeting that it existed at all. And the only thing that the powers that be had come up with to change all of that were new rules about toilet breaks and stricter application of the school uniform. As if that would do any good. And Andrew refused to impose any of the stricter rules in his class. He had even wondered whether he would look for a new job at the end of the school year, but he saw that as giving up on the pupils like James Marsh who needed him. He wasn't going to desert a sinking ship.

The problem was that work was Andrew Green's life. He had no partner, no kids, no family living nearby. What else was he meant to do with his time but take extra care over marking work or preparing lessons? Or worrying about kids like James Marsh. Andrew knew, though, that something was going to have to change. He drank too many bottles of wine, smoked too much (and not just cigarettes), ate badly, went to bed too late every night after scouring the internet, and his bedsit wasn't much bigger than the dorm room he had occupied on campus during his university days. But he wasn't twenty anymore. He wasn't looking after himself, and life was slipping by.

The traffic was horrendous. It always seemed to be worse when it was raining. Stopping at traffic lights, he lit a cigarette and opened the window to let the smoke out. One good thing with not having kids was that at least he could still smoke in his own car. He had tried giving up numerous times, but always fell back in the habit within a few weeks. It was hardly surprising given the stress of work. That was his excuse, anyway.

If all else failed, blame the school.

He would blame them, too, for the fact that he would stop at the off-licence on the way home. He would try cutting back on the wine tomorrow.

3

Jason Mitchell was rather proud of himself. His plan had worked brilliantly, and James had fallen for it just as he hoped he would. Now, everyone was going to be able to see just what he was capable of.

He sat at the computer, editing the video footage that was on his phone. It had come out even better than he had anticipated. He smiled as he replayed the final version, where he had taken the best and funniest sections of the video and pieced them together, adding comic music for extra effect, and to make James look even more stupid. He had obscured faces to hide the identity of himself, Smithy, Badger, and Luke, and the music hid their voices. Only James was recognisable now. And Paul. Not that Paul had actually done much, but it was enough to implicate him. It was a masterstroke, in fact. He would tell Paul that he hadn't left him in the footage on purpose – and he would probably fall for it, too. The next thing to do was to upload it online. He would have to blur out some sections of the footage, or it would be taken down quickly, but the effect would be the same. Besides, he could just start sending the uncensored version out on his phone, and it would get passed around quickly enough.

Claire Bramwell sat beside him while he worked.

"Jason Mitchell, I think you're a bastard," she said, only half-jokingly.

"If you think that, you shouldn't be sitting here,

Claire."

"What are you saying that for? Sometimes I think you want me to break up with you."

Jason smiled to himself. Perhaps she was getting the message, finally. Claire watched him for another minute or two.

"How would you like it if someone posted a video of *you* naked on YouTube?" she said.

"Wouldn't bother me," Jason replied.

"It might do if you'd been stuck in a cold shower for five minutes beforehand," Claire quipped.

Jason glared at her. His girlfriend finally came out with something witty, and it was an attack on him. Typical. She knew the rules by now. Never talk back to him. It was asking for trouble. It wasn't something that was difficult to remember.

"It's just a bit cruel, that's all," Claire added, trying to dig herself out the hole she had created.

"Cruel? This is nothing compared to what could have happened. Admit it, it's a comedy classic. He'll live. Although he might wish he hadn't."

"What about Paul?"

"What about him?"

"He could get in trouble if you leave him in the video."

"That's the idea, Claire."

"Do you think he deserves that? He's done everything you've told him to for the last six months."

"And you think that helps him? He's an idiot. Only an idiot would have done what he's done. Only an idiot would have fallen for it. Now he's going to have nothing, and it's all of his own making."

Claire knew better than to argue. To do so would cause Jason to get angry, and she didn't want that. She had the feeling that things weren't as good between them as they had been. She half expected Jason to break up with her at any time, although she wasn't sure what she might have done wrong. She didn't want to do anything to make Jason do it. Even so, she didn't approve of what he had done with James and Paul over the last year. She had always known what he did to people and, although it made her feel a bit uncomfortable, at least he never asked her to join in or get involved (although, unknown to her, the only reason was that he didn't trust her to do what he said without cocking it up). Claire thought that breaking up the friendship between James and Paul had been taking things to a whole new level, and one that was remarkably cruel. She knew her boyfriend was cruel, but she didn't want to lose him. She didn't have much else.

Jason switched the laptop off and put his mobile phone in his pocket.

"All done," he said. "Uploaded online, and sent to all my contacts. Now the fun really begins."

Claire smiled, as if what he had done was something she approved of.

Jason stretched, and Claire watched as his T-shirt rode up to reveal a glimpse of his tanned, firm, slightly-hairy stomach. She belonged to him, one of the most good-looking boys at school, one of the most feared, too. *That* is what she liked about Jason Mitchell – that she was part of the in-crowd. She belonged to him; he was the one who called all the shots, but she liked it that way. She did whatever he said – except for one thing, and she had no plans for that to change anytime soon. Jason pulled off his T-shirt and went to the bed and lied down. He patted the bed, smiled that winning, butter-wouldn't-melt smile, and she went and lay down beside him, resting her head on her boyfriend's chest.

4

It took James at least another half an hour to get out of the showers and to get his things together so that he could start the walk home. His things had been scattered around the changing rooms, and he still hadn't found one of his socks. In the end, he gave up looking for it. The damage to his clothes and, most of all, his school books was as bad as he feared. He was still figuring out how he was going to explain that to his mum or to some of the teachers. The shirt he had worn for the games lesson was badly ripped from when Jason was trying to get it off him. James would try and blame it on a rough tackle during football, and hope that his mum believed him.

It was when he was about halfway home that he received a text message. He pulled his mobile phone out of his pocket and read the words "just a sneak preview" attached to a screengrab from the video footage that Jason had shot less than an hour earlier. The picture showed James in the showers, running towards Jason's friends, who were preventing him from getting out. It realised James's worst fears. Everyone was going to see him naked, soaking wet, cold, and humiliated. Another text message followed a minute later. "More to follow soon, Big Boy."

James had got beyond the stage of crying. There was nothing he could do about what happened next. He wondered how Jason had got hold of his mobile number, but then realised that he must have got it off Paul. James knew that, by the end of the evening, the video would be uploaded on Facebook or YouTube and that, by the next morning, half the school would have seen it. He didn't know how he was going to face them after what they had seen.

James got home over an hour later than normal. He knew he would be questioned as to where he had been. He hesitated at the end of the garden path, took a deep breath, and went in to the house.

"Where have you been?" his mum shouted through from the lounge as soon as he walked in the door. "I was worried about you."

James took off his coat and kicked off his shoes.

"Sorry, Mum. Think I'm going to be sick!" he replied, running up the stairs to his bedroom and shutting the door behind him. It wasn't a complete lie.

He had brought his school bag upstairs with him,

hoping he could work out what to do about all of the damaged books, but, in the end, he just put it down on the floor and flopped down on the bed. He lay face down and didn't move. Suddenly, he felt totally overwhelmed by everything that had happened during the last hour or so. He felt both exhausted and panicky at the same time. He tried to do the breathing exercises that his GP had shown him for when he got stressed, but it was hard to concentrate on them with his mind racing so much.

In the back of his mind was the worry of what Jason was creating from the video footage, and, when he managed to push those thoughts aside, he found himself repeatedly going over what had just happened, trying to work out if there was something he could have done differently. He knew deep down that there wasn't, but it didn't seem to help matters. He kept having imaginary confrontations with Jason, in which he told him what he thought of him. He even thought of how he would overpower Jason physically. But James knew that these were things that would never happen in real life. Again, he tried to push the thoughts aside. He had homework to do for the next day, but had no idea how he was going to concentrate on it considering the state he was in. He turned over so that he was lying on his back, and closed his eyes and tried the deep breathing exercises again.

He had lost track of the time, maybe even drifted off to sleep, when a knock on the bedroom door stirred him. He ignored it, but the door opened anyway, and his sister walked into the room, gently pushing the door to behind her.

"Are you awake?" she asked quietly.

James didn't move or open his eyes, pretending to be asleep, although he knew that Rachel was unlikely to be fooled.

"I know you're not asleep," she said. "There's no need to pretend you are."

James opened his eyes. Rachel walked slowly over to the bed and sat down beside him, putting her hand on her brother's shoulder.

"Are you alright, James?"

"I'm fine, Rachel. I'm just tired. Let me sleep."

James felt bad as soon as he had said it; he didn't mean to sound so bad-tempered. His sister had meant well, but there was nothing that she could do to help. There was nothing that *anyone* could do to help. Rachel sighed, and then got up and walked over to the bedroom door, and then she stopped and turned back to James.

"Mum's really worried about you, you know? We're both worried about you. You might think you're good at hiding whatever's going on with you, but you're not. It's not like you not to eat your food. Normally you want to eat ours as well. And Mum's not stupid. She knows there's a reason why you keep going to school early. And she knows it has nothing to do with meeting a friend to get some work done."

"I'm just tired."

"Do you want something to eat?"

James turned over and buried his face in the pillow.

"I'm not hungry," he said.

"Something's up. What is it?"

"I'm OK."

Rachel leaned against the bedroom door.

"No, you're not. We want to help you, but we can't do anything unless you tell us what's wrong."

Finally, James rolled over on the bed so that he was facing his sister. The pair didn't look much alike, what with her blonde hair and his brown. She clearly got her looks and small build from her mother, whereas his gangly frame came from his father. He was some eight inches taller than his sister, despite being three years younger, and his feet hung over the end of the bed. Rachel saw that he had started to cry. Her brother looked lost, bewildered even. She walked back over to the bed and sat down.

"What's going on, James?" she asked.

"I can't tell you."

"You don't need to keep anything from me," Rachel said. "I won't even tell Mum if you don't want me to. Is it school? The other kids again? The work? Mum's beginning to think that you're taking something!"

"Mum thinks I'm a drug addict. Great."

"To be fair, I don't think she's too up on the effects of drugs."

"Perhaps they're what I need!"

"She's never seen you like this before, though, Jim."

"I'm sorry."

"You haven't got anything to be sorry about.

James looked at his sister, and forced a smile. It was

nice to have someone there for him, even if he had no intention of telling her everything that was going on. He sat up on the bed and hugged her tightly.

He sobbed.

Rachel had never seen him so upset, but just let him cry, knowing that it would be good for him to let out whatever was pent up inside. After the tears had subsided, she handed him a tissue and waited while he wiped away the tears and blew his nose. Then she held him, and did her best to calm her brother down. It took longer than she anticipated.

"Is it school, Jim?" she asked, eventually. "You told me when there were problems there before. Why don't you tell me now? I only want to help."

James nodded silently. He knew that he needed help, or at least someone to talk to. Things couldn't go on as they were. He couldn't cope any longer. But the problem was that he didn't want to tell anyone about what had been happening to him. It wasn't just that he was being bullied, it was what they actually *did* to him. It had gone beyond bullying. It was becoming sick and twisted. How could he explain that to someone? It would be nearly as humiliating to tell Rachel that he had been accused of being gay, stripped naked, and thrown into the showers (as well as being filmed) as it was to have gone through it.

"I can't tell you anything about what's going on, Rachel. I just can't."

"Why not? Has someone threatened you?"

"No, nothing like that. I just can't talk about it."

"Are you being bullied?"

James nodded.

"Yes. But promise me you won't tell Mum, OK? I can't cope with her going up the school and making it worse. It will sort itself out, just like it did last time."

"OK. I won't tell her anything if you don't want me to, you know that. But this can't keep going on, Jim. Something's got to give eventually. Is there *anything* I can do to help?"

James got up off the bed and went to his school bag, and pulled out the ripped football shirt.

"What am I meant to do with this? Mum's going to go nuts when she sees it."

Rachel took it from him.

"What the hell happened to it?"

"It got ripped. Rough tackle."

"Yeah, right. Of course, it was. OK. I'll get you a new one tomorrow. Mum will never know."

"Thanks."

Rachel walked over to the bedroom door.

"Why don't you come down and have something to eat? It would do you good."

James shook his head.

"OK, well get some rest, then. You know where I am if you want anything."

James thanked her, and then got his laptop and started playing the film that he had begun watching that morning. Rachel walked down the stairs to the living room, where her mum was waiting eagerly for news. Rachel smiled, knowing that her brother had decided to pull himself out of his misery by escaping into his film.

Alice Marsh bombarded Rachel with questions when she got downstairs, but Rachel just said that James was feeling a bit under the weather, and that it was nothing to worry about. It was probably the fact that the upcoming exams were taking their toll on him. The last thing she would do was tell the truth and betray his trust.

James had finished the film and lay back down on the bed when he heard the notification tone on his mobile. Nervously, he picked the phone up and read the message.

"All uploaded for you, stud," it said. "Check my Facebook."

CHAPTER FOUR

1

By the time James awoke the next morning, it seemed that the whole world had seen the footage that Jason had posted online. There were dozens of text messages waiting for him on his phone – all from people not in his contact list that had, presumably, got his number from Jason. The comments ranged from piss-taking to downright abusive. It was what James had expected.

Online was even worse. There were well over a hundred messages split between his own Facebook wall and the comments beneath the video on Jason's. A few on his own wall were sympathetic, saying how sorry they were for what he was going through. Others, particularly those beneath the video, were a mix of insulting, humiliating, and even threatening. One told him that he was a "worthless piece of shit" and it would be better for everyone if he just hanged himself. James didn't even recognise most of the people who had commented, and he couldn't stop thinking how and why members of Jason's own family hadn't made him remove the video. Surely they had seen it? James had reported the video when it had first been uploaded, but it had yet to be taken down. By the time he went to bed that night, the video had finally gone, along with the comments underneath it, but the damage had been done by then – and no doubt some people had even downloaded it onto their computers, although James tried not to think about why they would want it.

When he saw all those comments, James felt almost numb. He had no idea what he should do about it, and he also wondered if Rachel had seen what was going on. She may well have noticed what had been written on his own wall – and then the secret would be out. He wouldn't be able to hide things any more. Perhaps that would ultimately be a good thing. The decision would at least be taken out of his hands. But there were other things bothering him in the short term. How was he going to face the kids at school? How many of them had seen what was posted? Most of his classmates, he guessed. And some of them would have had it sent directly to their phones, without any blurring out of the offending parts of the image that had been done in an attempt to keep it online for as long as possible.

By the time he had finished looking on his phone at the damage that had been done overnight, he realised that he was running late. He got out of bed and pulled on his discarded clothes from the night before. There was no time for a shower. He'd have one when he got home. But deep down, he knew that hurrying now would make little difference. He was going to bump into Jason on the way to school whether he liked it or not, although he had started to wonder if that might be a good thing. Get it over and done with, and then get on with the rest of the day. If only things could be that simple.

Panic set in from the outset. The toast he tried to have for breakfast kept getting stuck in his throat, which seemed to get drier by the second. He had to wash each piece down with mouthfuls of tea, but still had to struggle to stop himself from gagging on the food he really didn't want. His mum asked him if he was feeling better, and James said yes, but that he was running late, and left the house as quickly as possible to avoid further questioning. That was something he really could do without.

As he started his walk to school, he started to sweat as he always did when he got nervous. He could feel his shirt clinging to his back. He knew Jason and his friends would be waiting for him at the school gates, and that there was no other way to get in without climbing over the fence, and that wasn't an option. James already had enough torn clothes without adding to the number.

He told himself to breathe deeply as he got closer to the school. Because of the hill, he still wasn't able to see the school gates and what was in store for him. He didn't know if that made things better or worse. He should never have spent all of that time looking at the responses to the video online. It certainly hadn't helped him in any way, except that now he had a good idea of the kind of abuse he was going to receive from random strangers while he was at school.

He thought about running away. Of skiving off. He had never skipped school in his life, and yet on this one day he was *really* tempted. The nearest he had got before was pretending to be more ill than he actually was when he had a cold or a headache, meaning his mum would call up the school and inform them that he was too ill to attend that day. But that wasn't the same as taking the day off without her permission. And that had only been on days when he had lessons such as games or swimming – the thought of which had probably made him feel ill in the first place.

He wondered if anyone would notice if he wasn't there. Mr. Green probably would. How about the other kids? They would certainly know he was missing. They were probably already at school, waiting to laugh at him after seeing the video that Jason had recorded and distributed. Was there anyone who hadn't seen it? And what would his mum say if he suddenly turned up back at home again? She would make him tell her everything. He couldn't face it. Not today. He could just spend the day wandering around the park. It wasn't as if the weather was bad. No, that would be the chicken's way out, and no matter what the other kids thought about him, he was no chicken.

He knew that the school would come into view shortly, and he would get the first glimpse of what the day would have in store for him, although he had a pretty good idea anyway.

James stopped walking. There they were, just fifty metres or so ahead of him. Jason was leaning against the school gate, as if he thought he was a James Dean impersonator. He was smoking, probably a cigarette, but it could have been a joint. James couldn't tell from this far away, but Jason would be brazened enough to smoke a joint directly outside the school. Claire had her arm around his waist, not that James could work out what she saw in him. How could she fall for someone who did the things that Jason did? James hated to think how he treated her. The rest of the posse was there too, no doubt agreeing with everything their leader said. Laughing slightly too much at his jokes.

He took another deep breath and started the short walk towards the inevitable.

2

Jason just couldn't wait to find out if James would turn up for school. He and Claire had been standing at the school gates since eight o'clock so that they would be sure not to miss him if he *did* come to school. Jason was well aware of James's habit of getting to school early in order to avoid him, and so, when he didn't turn up at his normal time, he assumed that he was skiving for the day. He couldn't blame him for that. After all, who in their right mind would go to school the day after a video was posted online of them naked? Either way, the events of the previous day had been one of Jason's greatest successes. The comments on the internet uploads of the video had taken off in a way he could never have expected, and now he was about to win a bet with Luke that James wouldn't show. As the minutes ticked away to the start of school, his win appeared to be in the bag. There was no chance of him losing the twenty pounds he had stolen from his father's wallet the night before.

The only downside to the whole affair was that Claire had insisted in tagging along to his vigil at the school gates. He didn't want her there; he was still recovering from having to put up with her for most of the previous evening. The tensions only eased at the school gates when Luke and Jane arrived, although even they annoyed Jason. What he really wanted was peace and quiet or, at least, the chance to terrify the hell out of Paul after he didn't meet him as requested the night before. By the time Paul arrived at the school gates, though, he seemed to have an attitude that Jason had not seen before and did not approve of.

"You left my face in the video, Jason," he said when he arrived. He seemed genuinely angry and wasn't afraid to show it.

"I thought you'd want everyone to know about what you did," Jason replied, sarcastically.

"Where's your face then, Jason? I don't see you in the video."

"I was just employing some modesty, mate. It's not all about me, is it?"

Jason might have been acting as cocky as always, but he was unnerved. Oddly, though, it also excited him. He had begun to get bored with Paul, but now there was just a slight chance that there was still some challenge in keeping him in check.

"Where were you last night?" he asked him.

"I had stuff to do," Paul replied, again seemingly without any fear.

"I waited for you."

"I texted you and told you I wasn't coming. It's not my fault if you didn't read it. Or ignored it."

Again, this wasn't like Paul, and Jason knew it. But Jason didn't know that Paul had laid awake for most of the night, working again and again through what was going on in his life, and deciding that he had to make some changes. What had happened in the changing rooms the day before had troubled him, but the video that appeared online which didn't disguise him as it had the others, had angered him. It had made him realise more than ever that he was being used, that he was viewed as a joke. Perhaps he had known that all along, but something had to change, and he had made up his mind to start by standing up to Jason whenever he could. Or, more accurately, whenever he had the balls to.

Paul's sudden change in attitude just added to the list of things that were pissing off Jason that morning. He was beginning to get more and more annoyed by the presence of Luke and Jane. They hadn't done anything in particular, but they were a constant reminder of everything that was wrong in Jason's relationship with Claire. Luke and Jane seemed to be just as happy as they had been when they had first got together nearly a year before, and there was no doubt in Jason's mind that their relationship was far more physical than his own. This was something that he was constantly reminded of by their seemingly endless snogging, even at 8.30 in the morning. They had been at it since they had arrived at the school gates, and now Jason had seen enough.

"Will you two just stop that for two minutes?" Jason snapped at them. "It's driving me nuts!"

"Bloody hell, you're not exactly Mr. Happy this morning, are you?" Jane replied.

"I'm fed up with seeing you two snogging."

"But we lurrrve each other," Jane said. "Besides, I'm sure you and Claire have a good time now and then."

"That's what you think," Jason said, and shot a look at Claire, who quickly removed her arm from his waist.

"You get what you want," she said, defensively.

"Yeah, a wank when you've gone home," he shot back, realising too late that he was giving the game away that he and Claire were not having sex.

Claire semi-playfully slapped Jason on the arm, but he just glared at her. That was twice in a day that she had gone against him, and this time it was even in public.

"Don't you ever do that again," he whispered to her.

Claire might have endured more of Jason's wrath if it wasn't for the fact that he caught sight of James walking towards the school.

"Well, well," he said. "It seems that our little friend from yesterday is coming to school after all."

Luke looked down the road.

"Ha!" he said. "I told you he would. He's got balls, you've got to give him that."

"Yeah. And everyone's seen them," Jason replied.

"It seems like I won the bet, after all. Twenty quid is mine, I believe!"

"I'll pay you later."

"Yeah, fat chance of that, Jase. I'll have it now if you don't mind.

Jason turned on him.

"You'll have it when I say."

Too many people were trying their luck with him. First Claire. Then Paul. Now Luke. None of them could be trusted. He realised more than ever that the only people he could trust were Smithy and Badger. And Badger was next to useless. He was as thick as shit, but at least he was reliable.

As James reached them, Jason walked out in front of him and blocked his path.

"Well, good morning," he said. "And how are you today? You didn't catch a chill, then?"

"Get out of my way, Jason," James said.

"Aww, come on. You could at least say hello. It's very unsociable of you not to. In fact, I thought you might be thanking me."

"Thanking you? For what?"

"Getting you all of that fan mail overnight. You're

going to have the girls chasing after you all day, aren't you? Oh, wait, it's not the girls who you're after, is it? How silly of me. Perhaps Paul will want to be your friend again now he can see what he's missing – or has he seen it before?" Paul looked away, sheepishly. "Don't worry, you'll have people queuing up outside your house for a night of passion with the school stud. I don't stand a chance anymore!"

James pushed past Jason and walked into the school grounds. Jason began to wonder if he was seriously losing his touch. How did he get past so easily?

"That's it!" he shouted after James. "Run along inside. Your new fans will be waiting for you!"

James started running towards the school building, still hearing the laughter behind him.

3

Andrew Green's head hurt. As was so often the case, the planned glass of wine the night before had turned into nearly a bottle. The marking he was going to do never got done. Instead, he had fallen asleep in his armchair, and only woken up, complete with headache, as dawn was breaking. He had gone for a shower to try to wake (and sober) himself up for work, but, as his first class of the day started, the truth was that he was still suffering from a hangover. And his mind was elsewhere.

Part of the reason for his drinking was the pressures

of the job, and that had only got worse as more and more good teachers left the profession and, in particular, his school. He looked at the class of sixteen-year-olds in front of him and his heart sank. Here he was, trying to get them through their G.C.S.E.s, and half of them struggled with basic grammar and reading. That wasn't the way it used to be, but he didn't blame the kids. It was the way they were brought up now. How many parents actually sat down with their young kids and read to them in the way that his parents had read to him? It was much easier to sit them down in front of the television, so they could stare mindlessly at endless re-runs of *Peppa Pig* and *In the Night Garden*. Then there was the fact that half the kids had their breakfasts at school because the parents were too busy getting ready for work to make it for them. What kind of upbringing was that? What was more worrying to Andrew was that at least three of four of the teenagers in front of him were from families reliant on foodbanks. Welcome to 21st Century Britain. But there was also something nagging in Andrew's brain that he was brought up very differently, with parents who read to him, and a stay-at-home mother, but yet here he was living in a bedsit as he approached middle age, and something approaching a drinking problem. A fat lot of good a decent upbringing had done *him*.

He wished he felt differently about the clever kids, but he didn't. They might be more able academically, but it didn't mean that they worked any harder or cared any more about their work. Most of them didn't give a shit about Shakespeare or poetry and, as one of his pupils had said to him when he was moaning about the lazy mistakes in her spelling, what did it matter if she spelled words right or wrong when her laptop would correct all the mistakes for her? Sometimes he wondered what the point of it all was. But his mother had recently reminded him that he hadn't cared about Shakespeare or poetry at sixteen either. Perhaps she was right. He couldn't remember.

Deep down, Andrew knew that he was just being self-pitying because he felt crap. He liked his job, no matter how much he moaned about it, and how much he hated what had become of Smithdale Academy. But he liked his job better when he wasn't suffering from a hangover. He couldn't blame the kids for *that*. He could blame The Head, perhaps, but not the kids. And, even today, when he would much rather be curled up under a duvet, drinking tea and taking too many paracetamol, he was determined to push the motley crew in front of him as hard as he could. Deep down, despite everything, he liked them.

They had just finished watching the film of *Romeo and Juliet*. He had shown them the more traditional Zeffirelli version over the last few lessons, despite the fact that his head of department warned him that the kids wouldn't enjoy or take to it.

"It's too long and too dull, for them, Andrew," she had said. "They need something more suited to their attention span."

However, he had no intention of showing them

some half-baked version that was nothing like the real thing. Some of these kids might not be the brightest, but he didn't have plans to patronise them. He would push them as much as he could to be the best that they could be. That was his job, and he had no plans in taking the easy way out. If he had wanted the easy way out, he would have changed professions by now. And he had been tempted.

Andrew perched himself on the corner of his desk at the front of the class, took a deep breath and tried his best to promote some form of reasonably intelligent discussion on the play they had been studying.

"So," he said, "now that we've finished studying and watching Romeo and Juliet, would someone like to tell me what they enjoyed most about studying the play?"

A bunch of uninterested faces stared at him. He knew that some of them would probably want to contribute to the lesson, but would be too scared of being teased for being a swat if they did so, and he knew all too well who the main culprits would be.

"No-one?" he said. "Come on. *Somebody* must have found something they liked about it. Jane. How about you? What did you enjoy most about studying the play?"

His hopes were riding on Jane. Even though she hung around with Jason, he knew that she had brains if only she cared or, more correctly, dared, to use them. He knew he could have gone straight to James, who would, no doubt, have had something to say, but given what he now knew about the events of the day before, he thought it would be best to allow him some anonymity for the lesson, just in case it gave others in the class reason to pick on him.

"Seeing Romeo's bare bum in the film, Sir," came the reply from Jane.

The class started to laugh.

"I'm sure that the Bard would have been happy to know that you at least remember something about his work, Jane."

Join in the fun, he thought. *Keep 'em on your side. You've got nothing to lose – except a headache.*

"It was a much nicer arse than Luke's, Sir," Jane went on.

Give them an inch and they'll take a yard, Andrew thought.

"Another deep and meaningful comment, Jane. Well, as close as we're likely to get, anyway. Okay, enough about your boyfriend's posterior, if you don't mind."

"It's not as nice as James's," somebody said. Andrew couldn't catch who it was, but the whole glass giggled. Except James.

"That's enough," he said. "For the next couple of weeks we're going to look briefly at some of Shakespeare's other plays. Today we're going to look at another tragedy. Can anyone tell me the name of some tragedies, other than Romeo and Juliet?"

"Luke's arse, Sir!"

"That's enough, Jane." He was more forceful this time. It was time to get back in charge. "Anyone else?"

"Macbeth, Sir."

Andrew was surprised to see that it was Badger who had contributed to the lesson. He hadn't raised his hand before speaking, but that wasn't something he was going to complain about. Some form of utterance was better than nothing, and a correct utterance from Badger was something to behold.

Paul Baker put his hand up.

"Yes, Paul?"

"Hamlet."

"Good." Andrew noticed the stare that Jason gave Paul as he spoke. He didn't envy Paul when he got out of the classroom. "Anyone else?"

James raised his hand tentatively. Andrew's heart sank. He wasn't doing himself any favours. Perhaps he didn't care.

"Yes, James?"

"King Lear, Sir."

"Good, James. And that's the play we are going to look at today."

Andrew took a pile of dog-eared copies of the play from his desk and started passing them around the class to the sound of moans and complaints at the idea of more Shakespeare.

Jason Mitchell leaned over towards James.

"What's going to happen to you later is going to be a fucking tragedy, Marsh!" he whispered loudly.

Unknown to Jason, Andrew had been standing behind him. He had to stop himself from swiping Jason around the head with one of the books. But enough was enough. He wasn't willing to stand for that kind of behaviour or language, although the language bothered him less. He slammed his hand down on Jason's desk and leaned in towards him.

"Any more of that language, or any more threats, Jason, and you'll be going to see the Head."

Jason tilted back on the two rear legs of his chair, his hands behind his head and a smirk on his face. Andrew started wishing that the chair would topple over. Sadly, it didn't.

"I don't think that's likely, *Sir*," the boy said.

"And why is that?"

Jason leaned in towards his teacher, close enough to invade his personal space.

"My Dad knows the Head, *Sir*. You know that. You wouldn't want to get on the wrong side of him, now would you?"

Andrew moved away, taken aback by what he had just heard.

"Are you threatening me, Mitchell?"

Jason sat back in the chair, an innocent look on his face.

"Wouldn't dream of it, Sir."

"I'm glad to hear it."

Relieved that the little confrontation was over, Andrew walked back to his desk and sat down once more. He didn't like being threatened and, for the first time in his teaching career, he was actually unnerved by an event in his classroom. Jason Mitchell had basically told him to back off. *Or what?* What was he going to do if he didn't? But Andrew knew he would have to do something, he couldn't allow threats of physical violence towards other pupils, or himself. But, for now, he had to forget about the incident and carry on with the lesson.

"Now, back to Shakespeare," he said, as he returned to the front of the class. "King Lear is one of Shakespeare's most harrowing plays, not least because of the level of violence it contains. In one scene a character is literally blinded."

"Is that because he wanks too much, Sir?"

Jason again. Andrew looked directly at him. His patience was wearing thin.

"If that particular myth was true, Jason," he said, "I'm sure we'd see you wearing glasses and reading from a large print edition of the text book at our next lesson. Isn't that right?"

The class laughed, and Andrew took great pleasure in seeing Jason Mitchell's face turn bright red. He smiled at his own wit, but realised that he had now made an enemy that he could do without. Jason Mitchell clearly wasn't accustomed to being humiliated in front of his friends. He started to laugh along with the rest of the class, pretending he was OK with the joke, but his pride had been wounded, and he clearly wasn't happy.

To Andrew's relief, the remainder of the lesson went without incident, apart from Jason glaring at him at every opportunity. As the bell rang to signal the end of the class, he informed them of their homework (which he very much doubted most of them would do) and sent them on their way.

He knew he had no choice but to ask James Marsh to stay behind. He wasn't really sure how he was going to approach things. He knew that James had been having problems with Jason and his friends, but a boy had come to him this morning and shown him a video that had been sent to him on his mobile phone. The boy seemed as upset by the footage as Andrew which, at least, showed that not all of the kids these days were heartless. If Andrew was being honest with himself, what he had seen on the video was probably making him feel more ill than the after effects of the wine the night before. He hadn't been able to get it out of his mind throughout the lesson. The threats that Jason had just made towards both James and himself had only compounded the problem. And Andrew was well aware thanks to the sniggering at the beginning of class when James had walked into the classroom that virtually everyone had seen the footage.

James packed his things away slowly and looked worried as he approached the front desk and the final members of the class went out of the door. Andrew told him to take a seat and smiled to try to put him at ease. It didn't seem to help.

"Sorry for holding you back for a couple of minutes, James, but I just need to have a chat with you."

"That's OK."

"How's it going? You alright?

"Sure."

"How about the other kids? Everything alright?"

James shuffled nervously in his seat.

"Yeah, everything's cool," he said.

Andrew knew that everything wasn't "cool", but, somehow, he had to try to make James admit it himself. This wasn't going to be easy.

"James. Look. I know what's going on between you and Jason."

"I don't know what you mean."

"There's no use pretending everything's fine when it isn't. I saw how worried you were about going in the changing rooms after your lesson yesterday – and now I know why." What was the easy way to say it? "I've seen the evidence," he said, eventually.

James stared at him. Andrew could see the tears welling up in the boy's eyes. He felt awful for him.

"Someone came to me this morning before school," he went on. "He showed me some video on his mobile phone that had been sent to him last night. It showed you in the..."

"I know." James didn't need it spelled out for him.

"You're aware of this, then?"

James nodded.

"Yes," he said. "It's everywhere. Well, it was, anyway. It might have been taken down now. But it was on Facebook and YouTube. Maybe some other places, too."

"You don't have to put up with this. *Nobody* should have to put up with this."

"It's Ok."

"No, it is *not* OK. This is serious, James, and it's

affecting your grades. It's potentially a police matter, even."

"It's not affecting my work. The work's just getting harder."

"That's not what you really think, is it?" James solemnly shook his head. "Do your family know what's going on?"

"No. My sister has an idea, but she doesn't know everything."

"You should probably tell them."

"I can't tell them." He wiped a tear from his cheek. "You saw the video. You saw what they did. How could I explain that to my mum? All hell would break loose. She'd take me out of school."

"I wouldn't blame her if she did." He leaned back in his chair. "OK. What if I see what I can do about it? I'll go to The Head and talk to him about what's going on. He'll probably want to talk to you, but I'm sure Jason will be dealt with once he finds out what he's been doing. Either way, I can talk to Jason. I can tell him about someone coming to me with the footage. Let's face it, he knows you wouldn't do it yourself, considering what's in it. Are you alright with me doing that?"

James nodded solemnly, although he knew that this could make things worse. If Jason thought he had gone to a teacher, he would probably kill him. But James also knew that he was at breaking point. He couldn't cope with anymore.

"Good," Andrew said. "I'll try to see him this

afternoon, otherwise it will be tomorrow. Hopefully, it will bring this to an end. In the meantime, if anything happens you come and see me, OK? You know where I am."

James nodded again.

"OK."

"The school counsellor is there for you too. What you say to her would be confidential. You know that."

"I'll be fine."

"You'd better be running along, then, or you'll miss your entire break."

James forced a smile and walked over to the door. He grabbed hold of the handle and then turned to Mr. Green.

"Thank you," he said, and walked out of the room.

Andrew Green sat perfectly still for a couple of seconds, trying to understand what James was going through. The boy was right, of course. How could he tell his parents about what had happened to him the day before? He couldn't imagine being humiliated like that. He opened the small cupboard door under his desk and pulled out his flask of coffee and put it down on his desk. He really wasn't in the mood for the hustle and bustle of the staff room right now. He wasn't feeling sociable. He didn't want to listen to the moans and groans of his colleagues. He just wanted a quiet coffee in peace.

As he poured it into the flask's plastic cup, he wondered how he would have coped with the sorts of things James was going through. He couldn't imagine. But when he was James' age, twenty years ago, there were no mobile phones or internet. Perhaps that wasn't such a bad thing.

4

James left the classroom not knowing whether he should feel moved by his teacher's concern for him, or embarrassed that someone had shown him the video footage. He had watched it himself on his own phone. He looked so stupid and helpless. And naked. That was probably the worst thing. And his attempts to escape from the shower had made him look even more foolish. And now, not only had the other kids at the school seen it, but his favourite teacher had too. He hoped that Mr. Green wouldn't show it to others as he tried, most likely in vain, to stop it from happening again. He wondered who it was who had shown his teacher the video. He guessed whoever it was had done it for the best reasons, but James wished they hadn't, nonetheless. He just wanted the footage erased, not just from people's phones and the internet, but from his own mind. He wanted to forget about the whole thing, but he knew this was just the start, and not the end.

James knew that, if he didn't hurry up, he would be late for his next lesson. Break was now nearly over, so he cut around the back of the school building in order to save time. As he walked (marched, almost – he didn't have the energy to run, given everything that had happened), he couldn't get out of his head the events of the last 24 hours. He had thought that, perhaps, the last few weeks of school would be easier for him, but it looked as if things were actually getting worse. And Mr. Green was right, the bullying was affecting his grades, and that was something he didn't want to happen. But it was so difficult to concentrate on school work when you were frightened all the time of what might be just around the corner. He sometimes wondered what Jason got out of it, and how far he would go, but he knew he had to put these kinds of thoughts out of his mind. It was something that he didn't want to think about.

Things weren't about to get any easier. If he hadn't been so preoccupied, he might have caught sight of Jason peering around the end of the school building, waiting for him. But he was so wrapped up in his own thoughts that he didn't notice Smithy's foot stuck out in front of him as he reached the corner of the building. James tripped on the foot and slammed into the concrete, face first. Jason, Smithy, Badger, Luke and Paul emerged from their hiding place and strolled over to where he lay.

"Sorry about that," Jason said as he reached them. "Smithy has such big feet, don't you think?"

James turned over and picked himself up off the ground. Apart from the palms of his hands being grazed, he seemed to have come out of the fall relatively unscathed. He started to back away, but Jason and his friends gathered around him. He was tempted to make a bolt for it, but he knew that they were quicker than he was, and they would run him down before he could reach the relative safety of his next lesson's classroom. Even if he did make it there, he knew he would only be delaying the inevitable. He couldn't believe that this was happening again. Hadn't Jason got enough pleasure out of what had happened the day before?

"So, what did old Greeny want with you, then? You enjoyed sucking up to him in the lesson, didn't you? Or were you sucking him *off?* After all, we've heard the rumours about him too, you know?"

His friends sniggered as Jason grabbed hold of James by the front of his shirt and pushed him up against the wall, the rough bricks digging into his back.

"Sadly for you, a lot of people are pissing me off today, and so I've got to take it out on someone, right? Now, you remember that guy in the play? The one who got his eyes poked out?" Jason was so close to James that he could feel his saliva splattering his face as he talked. "That's what we're going to do to you, Marsh."

Things had got to the stage where James could no longer tell when Jason was serious about his intentions and when he was not. Up until recently, such a far-fetched scenario would have just been a wind-up, but now it seemed that anything was possible.

Slowly, Jason removed the glasses from James' face.

"Stamp on them, Jase!"

Jason turned to face Badger.

"Sometimes you are so thick, you know that? Don't you think somebody might notice if his glasses landed up smashed? Stupid prick." He turned back to James. "We could always say you broke them when you fell, though, couldn't we?" James looked away. "Perhaps not, eh?"

Jason passed the glasses to Luke and then turned to face James again. He spread wide the ring and middle fingers of his hand and moved them slowly towards his eyes. James started to squirm and tried to get away, but he knew deep down that he would never manage it. Jason's fingers were now touching his eyes and James instinctively shut them as hard as he could, but the pressure of the fingers on them became heavier. Amid the shouts of encouragement from the other boys, Paul cried out.

"You're hurting him!"

Jason turned his head, but kept the pressure on James's eyes.

"Who asked you? You've pushed your luck already this morning. Now, don't put me off, or there could be a nasty accident."

He pressed even harder with his fingers. James thought his eyeballs would squash or burst if he pushed any harder.

Then, suddenly, it was over. Smithy whispered, "Quick, someone's coming," and, within an instant, the pressure on his eyes was gone. He slowly opened them, and Jason was now a little way away, laughing at him with his friends. James felt himself slide down the wall, the bricks scratching his back as he did so, until he was sitting, hunched up, on the ground.

"Look at the little queer boy cry," Jason said as they walked off.

The teacher who had inadvertently saved him glanced at James as he went past, but didn't stop to ask him if he was OK. James was glad. He would have just burst into tears. He watched Jason and the others as they disappeared into the distance.

When the register was called at the school that afternoon, James wasn't there to answer his name. Those who knew what had happened over the last couple of days were not surprised. Following the incident with Jason, James had run out of the school gates. He knew that it was giving up in a way, but he didn't see what else he could do. He had had enough, and could only take so much.

The rest of his day was a long and lonely one. He walked to the park situated nearly a mile away from the school, buying himself a portion of chips for his lunch on the way; not that he was hungry. He meandered aimlessly around the park a couple of times before coming to rest on a bench overlooking the children's play area. When school finished for the day, the area would be teeming with young children, especially at this time of year. But now, the only people other than him were two teenage boys, probably a couple of years older than he was. They were sitting on the swings, and moved slowly back and forth just chatting to each other, smoking and munching on packets of crisps. James couldn't make out what they were saying and they barely even acknowledged that he was there, which was just the way he liked it. He was in no mood to be sociable.

He took out the copy of *King Lear* that Mr Green had given out during the English lesson. He tried his best to concentrate on the section that he was meant to read for homework, but the words didn't make sense to him. Not now. His mind was too muddled.

Mr. Green had been right; his schoolwork had been going downhill. It was bound to happen. English was his favourite subject, but he was even struggling with that now.

He wished he had stayed at school instead of bunking off. Now he had to kill another couple of hours before he could go home; a couple of hours in which he would dwell on what was happening to him, making him more depressed and scared than he already was. And he was already more scared than he ever thought possible.

5

Paul's day had not turned out as planned. He certainly had not woken up that morning with the intention of standing up to Jason as he had outside the school gates while they waited to see if James would arrive. And he knew it was frowned upon to answer questions in class, and yet his hand had gone up somewhat without thinking when Mr. Green had asked about other Shakespeare plays. And then he had shouted at Jason to stop when he was bullying James after the English lesson. He thought he was really going to hurt him. Paul had learned to cope with most things, but he wasn't willing to keep quiet while Jason messed around with James's eyes.

Paul had paid the price for butting in. He now had a couple of bruises on his arm and a sore stomach from where he had been punched afterwards. The lesson had supposed to be that he should not argue with Jason, or show him up in public, but Paul had begun to question that. After all, what was Jason going to do that he had not done already? He had been beaten, humiliated, dominated and forced to abandon, not to mention bully, the one person in the world that he had cared about. Jason had no more cards to play, and Paul was beginning to realise that. Paul could do what he wanted now, and Jason could do nothing about it, except more of the same. If Paul had survived things once, he could do it again. His life had been run by his father and Jason. It was time for Paul to take control.

Jason's posse had begun to disintegrate. Smithy and Badger were as loyal as ever - Jason's reliable "yes men," despite the fact that he tried to humiliate Badger as much as he did James. Elsewhere, though, things were changing. Claire had spoken to Paul on a number of occasions about how scared she was of Jason, but would never dream of leaving him. "He's all I have," she would say. She had said that he kept trying to make her have sex with him, but that she always refused. Jason was, she had said, ashamed that he was a virgin, although he had no idea that she was aware that he was. But she wasn't willing to do something just to satisfy his ego.

Paul could see that Luke and Jane were no longer loyal either. Outwardly, they still joined in with whatever Jason got up to, but secretly (or not so secretly) they were trying to find a way out without getting hurt. They had encouraged Paul to do the same before he no longer had the chance, because Jason had got him involved in something that could really land him in trouble, and not just at the school. Despite everything, Luke and Jane were good people, and, slowly but surely, they were trying to work out how to distance themselves from Jason.

Now, it was up to Paul to do the same. As soon as he saw that James was missing from class, he realised that the time had come for him to take action. It was time for Paul to finally do what he knew was right.

CHAPTER FIVE

1

For the second day in a row, James Marsh did not eat his evening meal. As with the previous day, he had come home and gone straight up to his room to lie down, saying that he was feeling unwell. His mother had gone up to talk to him ten or fifteen minutes later, but he had pretended that he was asleep. When Rachel had come home, she had knocked on his bedroom door and asked if he wanted something to eat. He mumbled that he didn't, and she had gone back downstairs again, uncertain whether it was best to talk to him again as she had the previous night or to simply give him time.

After a minute or two, James heard Rachel and his mum talking in the kitchen, and assumed that he was the topic of conversation. He wasn't wrong. He hoped that there hadn't been a call from the school asking where he had been during afternoon lessons. However, considering how many kids at the school were missing from lessons, especially those due to leave a few weeks later, he realised it was unlikely that his absence would be chased up.

After a couple of hours, James was beginning to feel hungry after all, and was debating whether to go downstairs to find something to eat, but he doubted he would be able to cope with the worried questioning he would get from his mother without turning into a blubbering wreck. While he was thinking about this, the doorbell rang. James heard Rachel move down the hallway to open the front door. She started talking to whoever it was, but James couldn't make out what was being said or who the other voice belonged to.

Rachel had opened the door to a rather sheepish looking Paul Baker. She was somewhat surprised when she saw him standing there.

"Paul. Wow. Long time, no see," she said.

"I know. I'm sorry." Rachel had no idea what he was sorry for. "Is James in?" he asked.

Rachel looked behind her, checking that her brother hadn't come down the stairs in order to hear the conversation. She didn't want James to hear what she was going to say, so she stepped outside and pulled the door to behind her.

"He's home, Paul," she said quietly. "But I don't think he's well. He's up in his room. I don't know what's up with him. Do *you* know, Paul?"

Rachel wasn't sure why she should think Paul would know what was troubling James, but it was just an inkling that she had that Paul's sudden reappearance after more than half a year was not a coincidence.

"I don't know," he said, uneasily, shifting his weight

nervously from one leg to another. "I didn't really see much of him at school today," he added, looking down at the ground.

Rachel realised that there was something (probably a lot) that Paul wasn't telling her. She knew that he and James had been really close friends for years – since they were little – and that Paul used to come around and see him often. He even used to stay over some nights when things were bad at his own house. He had become part of the family. And then that had suddenly stopped, and Rachel had assumed that there had been an argument of some kind between them. It wasn't as if they had grown apart, as friends often do eventually, because it had happened too quickly. The break was too severe, too sudden, for that. Now, Rachel got the impression that things were more complicated than just an argument. She realised that Paul might hold the key as to what had been bothering her brother, and why he had been acting so strangely. Perhaps that was why he was here – but to make things better or to make them worse?

"Look, come in, Paul," Rachel said, opening the front door again. "Let's go up to his room and see if he wants to see you. But don't be offended if he tells you to go away. You know what he can be like at the best of times, and he's really not feeling up to much at the moment."

She smiled, and Paul forced a smile back before stepping into the entrance hall. He nearly turned around and ran back off down the street, to the relative safety of his own home. This was going to be much more difficult that he could have possibly imagined.

Rachel offered to take his jacket, but he refused. He wanted the chance to get out of there as quickly as possible if things went wrong. They walked quietly and solemnly upstairs. Rachel knocked on James's bedroom door. There was no answer from inside, but she had not expected one. She opened the door and peered in. James was lying down on the bed hugging his pillow as if it were a teddy bear. Music was playing quietly through his computer speakers. He looked lost.

"There's someone here to see you, James," she said.

"Who is it?" he replied, almost whispering.

He slowly got off the bed and Rachel ushered Paul in quickly from the hallway, so that James didn't have time to stop him from entering. Rachel backed out of the room, leaving the two boys staring at each other. For a few seconds, she put her ear to the door to try and hear what was going on, but she heard nothing. Either they weren't speaking, or they were talking so quietly that she couldn't hear them. She desperately wanted to keep standing outside the door to try to hear what was going on, so that she might get to the bottom of everything, but she knew that wouldn't be fair on the boys. She wouldn't want someone listening in to *her* conversations. Paul had already looked scared to death when she had answered the front door, but she didn't want to jeopardise any chance there was of him and James making up. She liked Paul, and knew that her brother must miss him. After all, they had been friends nearly all their lives.

Rachel walked down the stairs. Her mother was eagerly waiting for her in order to find out who James's visitor was. Rachel told her, and suggested that they should leave the two of them alone to see if the visit sorted out any of James's problems. She sincerely hoped that it would, as she was extremely worried about her brother. They had their moments when they argued, and periods when they even seemed to dislike each other, but they were few and far between. They genuinely cared for each other a great deal, and Rachel was beginning to get upset at the thought of James being hurt.

2

James and Paul stared at each other for a few moments, perhaps each as surprised as the other that they were there in this position. It was Paul who broke the silence.

"Hi, James," he said.

James continued to stare at him, half scared of why Paul was there, and not quite believing that he had dared to show his face at the house after everything that had happened.

"What do you want?" he said eventually. "You know what? I don't care. I just want you to go."

He walked across the room and opened the bedroom door, standing there and waiting for Paul to leave. Paul was half tempted to take the chance to leave, but he was determined to see this through.

"I didn't know if I'd back out of coming," he said.

James let the door shut and then leaned against it.

"What are you expecting? A medal?"

"I don't want anything."

"Then why are you here?"

The problem was that Paul didn't really know. Something had changed. He knew things couldn't carry on as they had been. He couldn't bear that any longer. Somehow, he needed to sort things out, even though he knew that wasn't going to be easy – and not just from the point of view of how to explain things to James. He had sneaked out of the house without even cooking his dad's evening meal, something that he might pay for later – and if Jason had found out that he had seen James, then all hell would break loose, although at least that would break Jason's hold over him one way or the other. Whatever happened as a result, though, this was worth it. Eventually he would have to stand up to his dad and to Jason. It might as well be now. He had a job to go to in a few weeks, and things had to change.

"I didn't come here to be nasty," he said.

"A bit late for that, don't you think?"

Paul's words had come out all wrong. He had sounded like a child trying to cover for himself when he had done something that he knew was wrong. James's reply was truthful, if blunt. Perhaps it *was* too late, after all, to put everything right again.

"I suppose Jason sent you here, did he?" James went on. "What does he want now? Hasn't he done enough this week?"

"Jason didn't send me," Paul said. "He doesn't even know I'm here. He *mustn't* know I'm here!"

"Why? Because you could end up like me? Perhaps you should have thought about what that might be like before."

"I'm telling you the truth," Paul said.

"And I'm meant to believe that? How am I meant to believe anything you ever tell me? Do you realise what you've done?"

"I was scared!"

"I was scared too! At least we could have been scared together.

Paul didn't know what to say. James was right, of course. Paul should have stuck by him. It would have made things easier for the pair of them.

"You weren't at school this afternoon," he said, quietly.

"And you're surprised?"

"Not really. Where did you go?"

"What? You want me to tell you so you can tell Jason and he can come and find me next time? You must think I'm stupid."

"I wouldn't tell the others. Honest."

James sighed and sat down on the edge of the bed. He felt tired. Drained. But Paul thought he saw, just for a second, James relaxing for the first time since he had arrived.

"I just went to the park, that's all," James said. "I couldn't come back here because Mum would know I was skiving off. And Rachel. And then they'd want to know why. Rachel's started to put things together as it is. But they mustn't know anything. Look, I don't know why you're here, or what you want, but I just want you to leave, Paul. I can't be doing with this."

Paul turned and moved towards the bedroom door. He had, at least, tried. But he was beginning to think that it was pointless. And he didn't blame James. He would feel the same way if it was him. He would say what he came to say and then just leave. He put his hand on the door handle and then turned back towards James.

"I came here to say sorry. That's all."

James started to laugh.

"Now you're really taking the piss," he said.

"I'm not. I mean it." He walked over to the bed where James was sitting. "I am so sorry for what they do to you."

James moved away from Paul, almost as if he couldn't bear to be close to him.

"*They?* You're there too, Paul. Are you forgetting that?"

"No."

"Then what do you want?"

"I just want to sort things out," Paul blurted. "I want to make everything right. I want things to go back to how they were."

"That's not going to happen. Now just go."

James opened the bedroom door again, and then went over to Paul and pushed him towards it. He pushed him again, this time out into the hallway. The two boys stared at each other.

"Is everything all right up there?" Rachel called up.

"Fine," James replied. "Paul was just getting ready to leave!"

"I don't have any choice," Paul whispered to James. "I'm protecting myself. That's why I join in. You know that. I'm a coward. A stupid, shitty coward. I admit it. And I'm sorry. But who was it that went back into the changing rooms yesterday to make sure you were OK when the others had left? They'd have killed me if they found out. We used to be friends, James."

"That was last summer, Paul. A lot has happened since then."

An uneasy silence fell between them again.

"I need someone to talk to, Jim."

"Then find someone else," James replied, shutting the bedroom door in Paul's face. He leant back against it, relieved to get Paul out of the room.

Paul knew that he should have expected this reaction and couldn't blame James for being suspicious and angry. Or for hating him. But he hadn't come this far to give up now. He knocked gently on the bedroom door.

"Look, I know I had no right to come here," he said quietly. "But I still like you, you know?

And there it was. The first mention of what had started the whole thing off. Paul hadn't really intended to bring it into the conversation, but now he had nothing to lose. And now there was no turning back.

3

Right from the start, the school summer holidays had somehow seemed different to previous ones, partly because James and Paul had spent almost every day together. Sometimes they had wandered around the shops in town, while other times they had headed to the park, with no purpose other than to hang around and pass some time. Once or twice, they went swimming – something neither of them enjoyed at school, but without the threat from other pupils who would often take the piss out of them either in the changing rooms or because of their lack of ability, it became far more fun. Neither of them were good swimmers, and both looked awkward in the water as they struggled from one side of the pool to the other, but outside of school that didn't matter as nobody was watching. They had gone down to the coast once or twice, too, and spent time on the beach – but most days had been too cold to get much enjoyment out of that, and most of the time they ended up with goosepimples rather than a suntan.

The highlight of the summer had been a trip to London on their own for the first time. James's Mum had been wary of letting them go and, unknown to James, was wary of the cost too, but in the end, she let her credit card take care of that. Just this once. They promised to stay in contact while they were gone, and stuck to their word, and spent their time wandering down Oxford Street and queuing up to get into Madame Tussaud's. They arrived back home just before midnight, and were promptly chastised for not getting an earlier train.

Other times, normally when it was wet (which, that summer, had been often) they stayed at James's house and played computer games or cards, or just watched TV. James's Mum and sister had both been at work on most days, and so they'd had the house to themselves, which suited them just fine. James was used to cooking his own lunch, and liked doing it, and so being at home alone wasn't a problem.

The time had flown by – for James, because there was never any tension when he was around Paul, and for Paul because he had been able to escape from his own home for much of the time, often sleeping at James's house in a sleeping bag on the bedroom floor. Staying with James so much had allowed him to realise for perhaps the first time how abnormal his own home life was. Other than the fact that he had to cook his own meals, Paul's dad didn't seem to notice he had gone, and Paul's mum was rarely at the house at all anyway. Paul knew that she was sleeping with another man, and his dad knew it too, but he no longer seemed to care as long as he still got his dinner on the plate when he came home.

The friendship between James and Paul slowly started to change over those six weeks. Though neither of them acknowledged it openly, their friendship had started to develop into something different, something more than just friends. Perhaps it had been because they had their guard down more often as they hadn't been *around other kids or their parents for most of the time. And perhaps part of it was to do with the fact they were sleeping in the same bedroom for some of the time, slowly but surely making them less self-conscious around each other as such an arrangement was bound to do.*

But sometimes the change in the dynamic of their relationship had been spurred on by more conscious decisions. About halfway through the holiday, there was a game of truth or dare (mostly truth) that had come about through nothing more than sheer boredom due to the wet weather and the realisation that watching Judge Rinder every afternoon eventually lost its appeal. They thought that playing such a game was daring in itself, and they started probing away at the other one, trying to find out what secrets they could, despite the fact that they had known each other for so long that there wasn't much to find out. It was, on the face of it, a pointless fact-finding mission.

"Who do you find most attractive at school?" James asked Paul when it was his turn.

"You can't ask me that," Paul predictably replied.

"I can ask what I want. Go on, who is it?"

Paul dithered, trying to come up with a name that at least sounded relatively believable.

"Jenny Wright," he said, eventually.

"Really?"

"Yeah. Why not?"

"She's two years older than us."

"I like a girl with experience," Paul said, sending

them both into fits of giggles at how ridiculous that sounded coming from one of them, considering neither of them had any experience with the opposite sex whatsoever.

They stuck to truths because both of them seemed to find it more embarrassing coming up with dares for the other one than actually doing them.

"We're shit at this," Paul said, eventually, when James chose "dare" and Paul couldn't think of anything that seemed worthwhile.

"I reckon you'd come up with some good dares if Jenny Wright was here!" James replied, resulting in another few minutes of giggles, and the game coming to a premature conclusion.

Despite the awkwardness of it, the half-hearted game had paved the way for more. With the house to themselves during the day, it was inevitable that they would return to the idea as they continued to get bored due to the persistent rain that prevented going out from being a pleasurable experience. The second attempt resulted in various stupid bets that seemed to be little more than an exercise in testing the water as to what was deemed to be acceptable and what might be going too far. In the end, it was a rash boast made by James about a week later about his ability at a particular computer game that resulted in him red-faced and naked, with carefully-placed cupped hands over his private parts, which, rather typically, had decided to take on a life of their own at just the wrong moment. Neither James nor Paul really thought that the other would make them go through with the forfeit if they lost, but, after James lost the game rather spectacularly, Paul called his bluff and told him to "get on with it" while pretending to not really be interested. Neither of them spoke for a few seconds once the task was completed, until James declared that "Mum will be home in a minute," and hurriedly started to get dressed.

Things seemed a bit awkward between them for the rest of the evening. Somehow, the events of the afternoon had crossed a line that they hadn't crossed before, and neither of them really knew what to make of it, despite the fact they had seen each other naked often enough in the swimming pool changing rooms at school. They didn't speak about it and, if they had, they would have both said it was just a bit of fun, just some silliness on an otherwise dull afternoon. Nothing to make a big deal about. But James's mum noticed that something was up, and asked them at dinner if everything was OK, and made sure they hadn't had a row. They pretended everything was fine, but convinced no-one, including themselves.

After they had eaten, they decided to go up to James's room and watch a movie on his laptop. They both got comfy on the bed and started the seemingly endless task of finding something that looked appealing on Netflix. After about twenty minutes, they found something that they both agreed on and set the film running. Neither of them could concentrate on it, but they sat there in silence, pretending to be engrossed. And then, after half an hour or so, Paul took a deep breath.

"James?" he said quietly.

James turned to face him, and Paul kissed him quickly on the lips.

"Sorry," he said. "I just had to. Sorry." He got up off the bed and started getting his things together while James watched.

"Where are you going?" he said.

"Home," came the reply. "I'm sorry. I just had to," he repeated.

James got from the bed and walked over to him.

"It was about time, right?" he said, and kissed Paul back.

This time, it didn't last for just a second like the first time. Neither of them had kissed anyone before, other than family, or an aunt who wasn't really an aunt. They really didn't know how to; it wasn't something they taught you how to do at school. But they pretended they knew what they were doing.

It was clumsy. And awkward. And confusing. And scary.

"Wow," James said afterwards. "I can't believe we just did that. What were we thinking?"

"Do you want me to go?"

"No. Of course not."

"I've been wanting to do that all summer," Paul said.

"Me, too."

"And then, when you got naked..."

"I've got to get my own back on you for that."

"I hope so," Paul said, and grinned.

There was a lot more kissing over the next few days, but, a week later, the school holidays were over, and they had to spend seven hours a day at school pretending that nothing had changed. They even had a sense of paranoia that something they did or said might give the game away that they were now, effectively, boyfriends. Not that either of them had used that word to describe their relationship. Perhaps doing so would be too scary for them both – not just a kind of verification of what their own friendship had now become, but a never-go-back term that confirmed they were gay. While what they were remain unnamed, it seemed safer, less threatening, less intimidating, and less permanent just in case one of them changed their minds – in case it was just a "phase," although both of them were pretty sure that it wasn't.

After having such a relaxing summer mostly with just themselves for company, being around the other kids all day at school seemed somehow stifling, almost claustrophobic, and the weekend didn't help matters entirely as James's mum and sister were at home – and Paul's parents were rarely out of the house.

On the first Saturday afternoon after the return to school, James and Paul went to the cinema. It was a last-minute decision, and one they both ultimately regretted. They had arrived late and gone in just as the trailers were ending, and they sat down at the end of an empty row. The film was a horror film that wasn't particularly good, but they hadn't gone just for the film; they thought it would be a place where they could relax without anyone watching them. James felt brave enough to move his hand on top of Paul's about thirty minutes into the film, and there it stayed for the remaining hour. Just as the credits were about to roll, Paul quickly kissed James on the cheek.

"You can't do that in here," James whispered to him, louder than he intended.

"No-one can see, it's dark."

"Not that dark."

As the lights came up, they sat there, waiting for the other people to leave before they got their own things together and made their way down the stairs to the exit, with the plan that they would perhaps head to McDonald's to get something to eat before heading home. But that didn't happen. When they went out into the foyer, Jason and Badger were waiting for them.

"Well, well, if it isn't the two little love birds," Jason said. "Holding hands all the way through the film. So sweet! Next time you do that, you might want to check who is sitting behind you. And the kiss at the end – so touching. But then 'touching' is probably what you've been doing a lot of during the summer, isn't it?" He pushed Paul up against the wall. "So, Paul, why don't you tell me exactly what's going on here?"

4

It was something that James had been trying to get out of his head ever since that day. He wanted to forget about what happened when they came out of the cinema, and he wanted to forget what had happened that summer. The more he remembered those few genuinely happy weeks of his life, the more it hurt that they were gone. And James knew that they were never coming back. That was their one chance at happiness, and they had blown it. *Paul* had blown it.

"Can't you let me in?" Paul said from the other side of the bedroom door.

"No," James said quietly.

"*Please*. Look, I feel such a bastard for telling them that it was all your idea when they caught us. That you had come onto me. I know I shouldn't have done that. I should have told them the truth and just dealt with whatever happened afterwards. But I panicked. And it's too late now. I have tried to stop them doing stuff to you, but they won't. The only reason I still go around with them is because I don't want to be in your position. I'm a coward. I know that. But I'm trying to stand up to them. I'm trying to get away from them. I promise."

James wished Paul would just shut up and go away. It would make things a whole lot easier. He knew that Paul had a rough home life. Deep down, he knew that he had betrayed him because he just couldn't cope with anything else. But that didn't stop it hurting every time he saw Paul with Jason. Or when Paul was there when

Jason was bullying him.

"I don't know whether I came here thinking that you might understand," Paul went on. "There's no reason why you should. I know that. And I don't want your sympathy because I don't deserve it."

"No, you don't," James replied.

He took a deep breath and opened the bedroom door.

"What do you want, Paul?" he said.

Paul tried to force a smile.

"To be honest, I don't really know."

James walked back over to the bed and sat down. After everything that had happened over the last two days, he felt exhausted. It was almost as if his legs could no longer carry him. Paul followed him into the room.

"Look, I should never have come here. This is all a mistake. Pretend I didn't come. I've got myself into this mess, and I don't know how to get out of it. And I want you back. I want our friendship back. That's all. I miss you."

James held up his hands.

"Will you just stop talking for ten seconds?" he said, louder than he intended.

He just needed some space. The events of the last two days had got to him. He was still getting comments from people about the video, even though it had now been removed online. People still had it on their phones, though, and James had turned his off so that he couldn't see what people were saying to him or about him. And now, Paul turning up out of the blue had really thrown him. He wasn't sure how he could cope with anything else.

James didn't know how he felt about Paul's arrival, and supposed apology. Part of him felt sorry for Paul, despite everything that he had done. James liked to think that he would never have made the same decision to betray a friend in order to save himself, but his home life wasn't the same as Paul's and, to a certain degree, he understood why Paul had done what he had. James knew that Paul got no pleasure out of being around Jason, and he knew how uncomfortable he looked when Jason was bullying him. Deep down, he knew that Jason was to blame for everything, not Paul. But that still didn't make things any easier.

James stood up.

"Come here," he said to Paul, finally.

Paul walked over to him, and they stood facing each other for a long couple of seconds before they instinctively moved towards each other to hug. It was, James hoped, the turning point in getting his friend back.

"I'm sorry for telling you to piss off yesterday," James said. "But you have no idea what it's been like, Paul."

"It's OK. I probably would have done the same. Look, I've got to go. I've got to finish getting things ready at home before Dad gets back. If he isn't back already. Nothing's changed there, either."

A few minutes later, James walked Paul down the stairs to the front door. They said their goodbyes, and Paul walked down the pathway. He turned and took a couple of steps back towards James.

"I want us to be friends again," he said.

"Me too, Paul. But at the moment you're still one of them. I don't know how long it will take to change that. I need to learn to trust you again. Things aren't going to change overnight."

"Sure."

"How about you coming over again tomorrow night? Just for an hour or so. So we can talk properly. "

"I can't. It's Jason's birthday party. I don't want to go, obviously, but if I don't, he'll think something is up. I don't want him to be suspicious."

"OK."

"I'm free at the weekend, though. Mum and Dad are going away to see my aunt. They're not back until Monday. You could come over. I could get us something to eat. We'd have the place to ourselves."

James wasn't sure.

"I'll think about it and let you know, OK?"

Paul nodded. James waved as Paul walked down the road, then he came in and shut the door. His mum and Rachel came out of the lounge as he was going back up the stairs.

"Everything all right, Jim?"

"Everything's going to be fine, Mum. Is there are food left from tea?"

She smiled.

"I'll put it in the micro."

"Cool. I'll be down in a minute."

James ran up the stairs and into his bedroom. He

turned on his mobile phone and then sent a short text to Paul telling him that he would come over on Saturday afternoon.

CHAPTER SIX

1

Despite his love of alcoholic beverages, Andrew Green was not what you would call fond of pubs, clubs and bars. Especially "gay-friendly" ones. The dislike of the latter had begun when he first plucked up the courage to enter one when he was a teenager, not that anyone had done anything in particular on that occasion to make him nervous or uneasy. He hadn't known any other gay men at the time, and so had gone alone.

Things were different back then.

Andrew seemed to say this more and more the older he got, but it was true. Other guys his age hadn't been out when he was young, and the internet hadn't yet developed into the space where teenagers could explore their sexuality or speak to others like themselves. Not that the internet was always a good thing, as Andrew had been reminded earlier in the day when he saw the footage of James from the day before.

Gay bars, thankfully, didn't have the same intimidation factor that they had when he was young, but that first experience had stayed with him throughout adulthood.

Despite this, on the way home from work that night, he felt he had to stop off *somewhere* for a drink. He knew that if he went in the off-licence he would buy a bottle of wine and drink the lot during the course of the evening - or, more likely, before nine o'clock – and he had no interest in feeling crap at work again due to drinking too much. The hangover he had experienced earlier in the day had been enough. So, the pub seemed the most sensible option. At least he could only have one drink as he was driving. And the Queen's Head was closest to the flat.

He had stayed on at the school after lessons had finished in order to do the marking that he should have done the night before, and to get some paperwork done. He found it easier to concentrate there without the distractions of the telephone, internet and television – all of which were adept at pulling him away from anything that he was *supposed* to be doing. As the previous night had shown, alcohol was also a very good distraction. His bed was, too. Many an evening, it would lure him in for a quick doze after he had eaten, and then the next thing he knew it was two o'clock in the morning – not that he normally had much reason to stay awake other than to work.

Despite his best intentions, he still wasn't able to totally concentrate on the paperwork he should have been doing after school. The events of earlier in the day kept on replaying in his head – that awful video that one of his form had shown him on his mobile phone, of James Marsh being bullied in the changing rooms the day before. Then there were the threats that the boy had received in class from Jason Mitchell, and the chat that he himself had with James which was hardly what he might call a resounding success. Andrew hated to think just how long James had been suffering like this, but was determined to do something to bring about an end to it. He wondered how many other kids were in the same position without anybody knowing. The thought frightened him. Sitting back and watching from the sidelines wasn't an option. He had to *do* something, no matter how many obstacles might be put in his way.

From the outside, the Queen's Head looked like an ordinary pub, with the exception of the rainbow flag hanging above the door, and inside were the familiar pool tables and fruit machines. There was even a small area out the back where you could sit and relax during the summer months if you didn't mind being bitten by the hundreds of gnats that seemed to hover there every evening. However, it was a gay pub through and through. The music that filtered through the speakers was a mix of cheesy pop tunes, with an occasional Streisand or Judy Garland track thrown in for good measure, depending on who had been at the jukebox. In the toilets there were machines that dispensed every shape, flavour and size of condom in existence. Ironically, the machine next to it also gave customers the chance to buy paracetamol. One night a week, there was so-called entertainment, hosted by Luscious Lou, a drag queen who invariably belted one or two predictable camp classics in each performance, whether it be *Maybe This Time* or *I Will Survive*. Friday was karaoke night, and served to prove that the songs of S Club 7 & and Steps were far from dead. However, while the Queen's Head might have been a place that, musically, allowed 40-something gay men to relive the days of their youth in the 1990s, it also had a laid-back, relaxed and friendly atmosphere which even an unsociable curmudgeon like Andrew could appreciate and be grateful for.

Although a couple of smiles greeted him as he walked into the main area of the Queen's Head, it wasn't because Andrew was a regular there. Far from it. He had come here once on a date with a guy he had talked to on Grindr for several weeks, which had gone disastrously wrong and he hadn't come back since. That was the night when he realised that using ten-year-old pictures of yourself and knocking more than a few years off your age was normal behaviour on such websites. Most people had probably known that for years, but Andrew only occasionally felt the urge to meet other men in the vain hope that his double bed might not be used by just one person for ever, as well as to give his mum at least some hope that she might get to go to a gay wedding eventually. Now, he wondered what he was doing at the Queen's Head, especially on his own. No-one went to a gay pub alone. He of all people should know that. He should have just gone to the off-licence so he could drink as much as he wanted by himself. He self-consciously walked up to the bar and waited nervously to be served.

He had obviously come at a busy time. There was just one bartender, but he was working his way from one customer to the next with proficient ease. At least he was nice to look at, Andrew thought, being about twenty-two years old and wearing a well-fitting shirt with the first three buttons undone, revealing a toned, tanned chest that the teacher couldn't help but admire. There was a tear in his jeans on his backside that revealed a flash of red boxer shorts each time he bent over which, Andrew was pleased to note, was quite often. Perhaps he *should* come here more often after all. He needed cheering up, what with the state the school was in.

"You can look all you like, Mr. Green, but he's taken, I'm afraid."

He turned and saw a young man of about twenty-five smiling at him. He was wearing a dark suit and had obviously called into the pub on his way home from work, just like Andrew. His tie had been loosened around his neck, and his suit jacket was unbuttoned.

"Sorry, do I know you?" Andrew said.

"You probably don't remember me. I was in your class for G.C.S.E. English about nine years ago."

Andrew looked closer at the man, but still didn't know who he was. He couldn't imagine that one of his past pupils had grown up to look like this.

"I'm sorry, I don't…" he said.

"Jonathan. Jonathan Lewis."

Andrew smiled.

"No way! I remember you! Good to see you again, Jonathan." They shook hands. "I'm sorry I didn't recognise you."

"It's Ok, you can't remember all the people who pass through your classroom."

"I try my best, nonetheless."

"Well, I've changed quite a bit."

"Yes, that's an understatement." Andrew realised that wasn't the best thing to say under the circumstances, but the skinny kid with braces had turned into something really quite different. "So, what are you doing now?" he said, trying to move the conversation beyond his ex-pupil's good looks.

"I'm doing Ok. Writing. I'm a journalist."

He sat down on the bar stool beside Andrew while he waited for the bartender.

"That's great. You always did have a good imagination."

Jonathan smiled.

"It's a local paper, not the *Daily Mail*! Can I get you a drink?"

"That would be nice. Thank you. G & T please."

The bartender approached them, smiled and winked.

"What can I get you boys?" he asked.

"I get called a boy in here?" Andrew said to Jonathan.

"The place of dreams!"

Jonathan ordered from the bartender and then turned back to Andrew.

"So, are you still teaching?" he said.

"Yeah. Same place, same classroom. Different kids."

"That's good. The kids need someone like you. Someone who gives a shit about his pupils."

"Wash your mouth out, young man! Such language!"

He smiled and winked at Jonathan. He remembered him to have been a slightly geeky kid, an impression helped along by his looks. But those had changed in the years since he had left school. The glasses were gone, no doubt replaced by contact lenses, or maybe even laser treatment. Who knew, these days? The teeth had been straightened out, the hair somewhat more controlled. He had filled out, too and, Andrew suspected, spent a fair amount of time down at the gym, like so many young guys these days. Andrew didn't have the willpower to keep up a regime at a gym and there was no-one in his life to show the results of his work-outs to anyway. But there was still time. He was only in his early forties, after all, but that was still fifteen years older than the ex-pupil that was standing beside him.

"Hey, I'm serious," Jonathan said. "You were one of the best teachers I had."

"That's very kind. Thank you."

Andrew was not used to getting compliments, and not good at taking them. He wondered what he might have done that had made Jonathan like him so much. He was tempted to ask.

"So, are you a regular here?" Jonathan asked, before Andrew had the chance to pursue the subject.

"No, not here on any other pub, to be honest with you. But especially not here. I generally just drink at home." *Alone, like a sad middle-aged loser*, he could have added, but just stopped himself before he did. "It just happened to be the most convenient on the way home from school." He hesitated a moment. "I guess it gives a new viewpoint on your old teacher seeing him in a place like this."

"Doesn't really make any difference to me, but then it wouldn't, would it? Or I wouldn't be here myself. Most of us knew anyway."

Andrew was shocked.

"That I was gay? Really? How?"

"I don't know. We just did. Word gets around. Kids don't miss much."

That was all Andrew needed. Did that mean that the kids in his class knew he was gay? He certainly hoped not, although why it should matter he wasn't quite sure, but for some reason it worried him that someone like Jason would know the truth. Did that mean that all the kids talked about him behind his back? He didn't like the sound of that.

"So, late night at school?" Jonathan asked.

"I stayed behind. Had marking and paperwork to do. It's all paperwork these days. You know how it is. It's easier to do it there than when I get home. Less distractions. And I had something on my mind, too."

"Everything OK, I hope?"

"Yeah, just a pupil having some problems. The same old issues at school. Sometimes it's difficult to leave these things at work, you know?"

"Yeah, I know what you mean. You want to talk about it?"

"No. But thank you. It's all confidential anyway, of course."

"No worries." Jonathan stood up. "Well, I've got some friends waiting over there, so I should be getting back to them. Or you're welcome to join us?"

"No, thanks all the same. This is just a quick stop on the way home."

"I understand."

Jonathan opened his wallet and pulled out a business card and handed it to Andrew.

"Call me sometime," he said, "if you think you might like to go for a drink. It's your teaching that got me this job, so I'd like to say thanks."

"That's sweet of you, Jonathan. I'm not sure my teaching had anything to do with it, but I might take you up on the offer anyway. And thanks for the drink."

"Not a problem. See you around I hope."

He smiled, and Jonathan walked across the pub to the table of friends that were waiting for him. Andrew turned the business card over in his hands a couple of times and then pulled out his own wallet and slipped it inside. Then he picked up his drink, downed it in one, and walked out of the door and back to his car.

Jonathan watched his old teacher leave. He was surprised to find that the schoolboy crush he had nearly a decade earlier hadn't gone away. He hoped he would receive that phone call about a drink.

2

"What do you mean, I can't come?"

Jason Mitchell sat up on the bed and looked at his girlfriend. He was beginning to despise her more and more by the minute. He had hoped that, by telling her she couldn't come to his birthday celebrations the next night, she might just get the hint that things were coming to an end between them. It didn't look as if his plan had worked. She seemed more confused than hurt or angry, and her arms were still wrapped around his bare chest. It was the fact that she clung to him like a limpet, that she *needed* him so much that annoyed him more than anything else about her. And now she had reacted to his plan by whining like a spoilt kid.

More and more, he wanted his own space, and didn't always want Claire tagging along behind him like some over-affectionate pet dog. It wasn't even as if he wished that his girlfriend was someone else, he now wished he didn't have one at all. He'd much rather have time to himself so he could concentrate on his drawings and sketches. He still had plans to come up with something so good that even his parents couldn't deny that he had talent and would allow him to go to art college. That wasn't going to happen while Claire was around.

"I mean you're not invited," he said.

"You're kidding."

Jason removed her arms from his chest, and moved so that he was sitting on the edge of the bed. He didn't look at her as he spoke.

"Do I look like I'm kidding?"

Claire knelt behind him on the bed and put her hands on his shoulders. He tried to shrug them off.

"But I don't get it."

"Well, best you try. No women at my birthday party. I just want a quiet night in with the guys."

He wasn't telling the truth, and he wondered if Claire knew it. The hope was that she wouldn't find out – or maybe it would be better if she *did* find out. That way she might want to break up with *him*, although it was more likely she'd just whine or cry and ask for an explanation. Or keep saying she was sorry when she hadn't done anything wrong.

"It's nothing for you to get in a mood about, Claire."

"I am not getting in a mood!"

"Really?"

He stood up and pulled on a pair of jeans over his boxer shorts.

"Really. It would just be nice for you to want to spend your birthday with me. I *am* your girlfriend!"

"Are you?"

She missed the comment entirely. Jason had hoped it might have led them on to the subject of sex. Another way he might be able to get rid of her.

"Most guys go out for a meal or something with their girlfriend on their birthdays. Or go to the cinema," Claire said.

"I'm not most guys, Claire."

"Luke and Jane do."

"I'm not Luke – and you're most certainly not Jane!"

Claire stood up, trying to get more of her boyfriend's attention, putting her arms around his waist.

"Sometimes you seem to think more of the guys than you do about me," she said

Her comment only made Jason more annoyed.

"Don't be so bloody stupid," he said. "We've been through this before!"

"Then why can't I be there? Have you got other women coming?"

Jason walked over to Claire and pushed her forcefully down on to the bed. He towered over her. How should he answer that? Perhaps he should just say yes and try to piss her off.

"No," he said. "My birthday is not going to turn into some orgy. I haven't got any women coming, more's the pity. Satisfied?"

He marched across the room and picked up a can of deodorant. Claire looked up at him as he sprayed himself, the sweet smell wafting across the room towards her. She knew he was lying, and said quietly:

"Luke is bringing Jane."

"Who said?"

"He did."

Luke was meant to keep that quiet. Surely he knew that? What the hell was he doing mentioning it to Claire? Perhaps he had done it on purpose. Nothing would surprise Jason. He would have to sort him out in the morning. Perhaps Luke was becoming as thick as Badger. Or perhaps he just wanted to stir things up. Luke wasn't the same as he used to be, and Jason wanted to get to the bottom of it. But there were other things to be sorted out first. Too many things were going on at once, and he was struggling to stay in control.

The problem with trying to dump Claire was that Jason felt she was so pathetic that he ended up feeling sorry for her. Not for long, but just long enough to stop him truly upsetting her.

"Look, Jane is different," he said, quietly.

"How?"

"It just is.

"Bollocks. There's something going on, isn't there? Admit it."

Jason turned and looked at her. He had finally lost his patience.

"You really want to know?" he said. Claire slowly nodded. "Ok. I'm bored. Of you."

"What do you mean?"

Claire put her arm around Jason's shoulder. Jason pulled it off.

"What do I mean? I mean that we've been going out for months and I'm still waiting. That's what I mean. You seem to have not got it into your thick head that wanking me off is the same as a shag. Couples have sex, Claire. We don't."

Claire was quiet for a few moments.

"Does it mean that much to you?"

"Yes, it does. It means that you trust me."

"Of course I trust you."

Jason smiled.

"Then prove it."

His annoyance with her wasn't just about sex. But he knew she had no plans to change her mind on the subject. He hoped that this would be the one thing that would drive her away from him. The one thing that she wouldn't back down on.

They stared at each other for a few seconds, with Jason willing Claire to just get up and leave and not come back.

"OK, then, if that's what you want," she said, and started to undo her blouse.

Ten minutes later, Jason Mitchell and Claire Bramwell had sex for the first time.

When Claire's parents asked her how she had come to tear the top she was wearing, she told them she had fallen off her bike and been thrown into some bushes. She explained that was how she also got the bruises on her arms. Given what had really happened, she wished she *had* been thrown from her bike. It would have been preferable.

Her parents couldn't see the bruises elsewhere, and they would never know how much Jason had hurt her both physically and emotionally that night when she had lost her virginity. A night, incidentally, when a scared Jason also lost his.

CHAPTER SEVEN

1

Andrew Green was relieved not to have to cover during his free period. He sat at his desk in his empty classroom, with a pile of essays in front of him to mark. But he had barely looked at them. Instead, he had taken Jonathan Lewis's business card out of his wallet and was absent-mindedly turning it over and over with his fingers.

The encounter the night before had thrown him a little. Of course, he had seen some ex-pupils from time to time, when he was shopping or, perhaps, out for a meal – not that he went for a meal out very often. Some of them said hello and asked how he was, while others ignored him, and there were even those who simply took the piss. But Jonathan seemed different from all the rest. Perhaps it was because it was the first time that a pupil, past or present, had told him that they were aware that he was gay, or had admitted that they were gay themselves. Or perhaps it was because he had seemed genuinely pleased to see him. Or maybe it was because he had grown from a gawky teenager into a handsome young man *and* bought him a drink. It wasn't very often *that* happened. In fact, Andrew was racking his brains trying to remember if it had *ever* happened before.

And what had Jonathan meant when he had asked him to call him so that they could go out for a drink? Did he mean, literally, a drink? Or a *drink*? A date. Andrew decided that his imagination was working overtime. The guy was much younger than he was. That sort of thing didn't happen. Not to him. And should he go along with it anyway, with him being an ex-pupil? Surely it wouldn't be wrong after all this time?

There were other things on his mind, too. Jonathan had told Andrew that he had been one of the best teachers at the school and, somehow, it alerted him to the fact that he might not have been living up to that description lately. He had been going through the motions. If that. He had been arriving at school with a bleary head, or worse, from either no sleep or too much drink. Or both.

And there was something else too. James Marsh. If he really was the teacher that Jonathan made out he was, then he would be able to do something for this kid. He would be able to fight for him – and others like him. If James Marsh was being bullied in this way because he was gay, then others were, too. It was his job to help them. He had spent much of the previous evening searching the web for reports and studies on homophobic bullying in British schools. Then he had tried to read everything he could about possible ways to combat it. And some of the ideas seemed to work – according to the reports, at least. Andrew thought they might be worth a shot. Hell, anything was worth a try. It would be difficult to make things worse than they already were

He was so caught up in his own thoughts that he didn't hear the headteacher tapping at the classroom door the first time. It was only when he knocked again and opened the door that Andrew was brought back to the real world.

"Mr Green?" The Head asked. "Are you Ok?"

"Yes, yes, sorry Headmaster. I was miles away. Daydreaming, I'm afraid. I didn't hear you knock."

He felt a fool. Why did that kind of thing always happen to him when someone important was sure to find out?

"We all do it from time to time." The Head offered a fake smile. "I understand you were looking for me earlier?"

He came into the room, letting the door slam behind him.

"Yes, I came by your office but you were in a meeting, I think."

"I seem to always be in meetings."

Meetings were a way of getting out of real work, according to Andrew – but he wasn't about to say as much to The Head. The Head looked around the classroom, almost as if he had never seen one before.

Andrew wondered how many times he actually entered them to teach. The Head walked over to some posters about Shakespeare on the walls.

"I was going to see if you were back when I'd finished this marking," Andrew said, determined to get this out of the way as soon as possible.

The Head turned to face him.

"Yes, my secretary told me. But I have to shoot out for another meeting this afternoon at County Hall, and so thought I'd come and find you instead. What can I do for you?"

Resign. That was the answer that Andrew had wanted to give. The two men had never got on. Personality clashes were always to be expected from time to time in any job, but this always seemed like more. The Head almost seemed to have a vendetta.

Their last big bust-up had been over a drama production that Andrew had directed at the school. The Head had come in to watch one of the dress rehearsals of *The Resistible Rise Of Arturo Ui* in the week leading up to the show, and had claimed that the play was unsuitable for a school production, being too "political." "We don't want to upset anyone, do we now?" he had said. Andrew pointed out that people would be more upset if the play was cancelled considering how much money had been spent on it. Finally, The Head backed down, although he insisted on some last-minute revisions to both script and on-stage action. Andrew thought that there was a certain irony in a Brecht play having to be censored, although this was something that would have gone over the headmaster's head. He knew that, if The Head had taken as much interest in drama and music as he did in the school sports teams, he would have discovered that he found the play unsuitable a lot earlier. Andrew's requests to direct further productions had been turned down. They were now deemed too costly.

The Head seemed to resent him, while Andrew thought that the man was an arrogant dick who cared far more about his own image than about the pupils in his care.

"I'd like to talk to you about one of my pupils."

"And who is that?"

The Head faked another smile and perched himself on the corner of the desk at which Andrew was sitting. He would have much preferred not to have had the man's ample backside at such close quarters but thought it might be obvious if he asked him to sit on a chair instead.

"His name is James Marsh. He's being bullied by a group of other kids. The usual suspects, I'm afraid."

The Headmaster grimaced.

"I wish you wouldn't use that word, Mr. Green. I have told you before that we have no bullying problem in this school."

"I know what you like to tell the public…"

"I don't think you understand."

"I'm not seeing things, Sir."

"I am not saying that you are." He sighed again and looked at his watch. "What I am saying is that this lad,

Marsh, or whatever his name is, is simply having problems relating to his fellow classmates."

"No. He is being *bullied*. He was videoed on a mobile phone being stripped naked, thrown into the cold showers in the changing rooms and made to stay in there for nearly five minutes."

"Innocent tomfoolery, I'm sure, Mr. Green," he said.

"Would you call it that if it happened to you?" Andrew asked, secretly hoping that there would be an uprising one staff meeting and such an incident would take place – although seeing the man naked wasn't high on Andrew's agenda. The Head ignored his question.

"Bullying does not exist here," he said. "I think it's good that *overtly caring* people like yourself are in the teaching profession. However, it is essential that you realise that teaching and education is now a business."

He got up off the desk and moved over to a window and opened it wide. He turned back towards Andrew and wiped the perspiration from his face.

"In order to get the best pupils," he went on, "we have to be seen in the best possible light. If there is a whiff in our catchment area that there is bullying here then we lose pupils. Losing good pupils means losing good money. Losing good money means losing good teachers who I would rather like to keep at this school. Do I make myself clear?"

"Perfectly." Andrew got up from his desk and shut the window that had just been opened. "In order to keep good money, you want to prevent good teachers from doing good work. I entered this profession to teach kids, not to be a politician."

"The aims and objectives of all jobs change from time to time, don't they?"

"Ok. So what would you suggest that I do in this case?"

"Close your eyes. It will go away. It always does."

"I don't think you understand the severity of the situation."

"I understand the severity completely, Mr. Green. However, perhaps you had better devote some of your energy into finding out what James Marsh is doing in order to aggravate his fellow pupils."

"He's the victim, not the cause!"

The Headmaster walked to the classroom door and opened it. He clearly didn't have time for such trivial matters as student welfare. He turned back to Andrew.

"I'm afraid I have to get on," he said. "Perhaps you'd like to keep me informed of the situation and we'll see how things progress."

Andrew looked at him, dumbfounded.

"Is that it?"

"Yes, Mr Green. That's it."

"I'm afraid it's not," Andrew stammered as the Head was about to walk out of the door.

"I'm sorry?"

"That's not the end of it," Andrew said, his voice shaking. "There has to be some changes. This kid is being bullied because he's gay. That shouldn't be happening. We need to make the school safer for him and other pupils like him."

"Do we now? Do you have a specific interest in this?"

"You know I do. If you don't want the public knowing we have a bullying problem, then you need to do something to eradicate it. There are things a school can do that reports suggest have helped."

"And what do you suggest – as you seem to be the expert?"

"There is something I've seen online, called a gay-straight alliance. It's a club of sorts. It's not going to be a perfect solution, but if it helps…"

"You know full well that the budget for clubs of any sort have been cut."

"This cannot continue," Andrew said. "I won't let it. This is the welfare of our kids. Kids I care about. If you won't let me do something with your blessing, then I will do something without it."

"You should make sure you have another job lined up if you do," The Head said.

Andrew watched him go out of the door.

"It's not going to help the image of the school when James Marsh sues us," Andrew shouted after him.

"I shall pretend I didn't hear that, Mr Green," he shouted from the corridor, and walked away.

Andrew stood up and kicked at a chair as he walked back to his desk. What was he meant to do? Was he really meant to sit back and watch the poor boy suffer? He now had no alternative but to talk to Jason Mitchell himself, and that was something he wasn't looking forward to. But there was something else he could do – something he had thought about doing since the previous evening when the James Marsh situation had really got under his skin. He wasn't sure that he had the guts to go through with it – but he had already surprised himself in his conversation with The Head. Suddenly he had a purpose.

He sat back down in his chair and took his mobile phone from his jacket pocket and keyed in the number on the business card that Jonathan Lewis had handed him. If he was going to do this, then he needed to start looking out for himself a little too. What harm could a drink with an ex-student do? He pressed the "call" key on the phone and waited for an answer at the other end. Jonathan politely told him in a recorded message that he was currently unable to take the call. Andrew left a message, saying that he would like the drink if it was still on offer.

He sat at his desk for the next ten minutes until his next class started filing in. He watched them as they took their seats and got out their books. When the bell sounded to signal the beginning of class, Andrew stood up.

He was visibly shaking, and some of the class noticed. Eventually, they were silent.

"Everyone, just put down your books for a moment," he said. "We'll start the lesson in a moment. But first, there's something I want…There's something I want to talk to you about.

2

James was relieved that Jason wasn't at school. He wasn't surprised at his absence, as he knew it was his birthday and that he was having a party at his house that night. The day at school passed quietly and without incident, with Jason's friends not even acknowledging that James was there, and that was something he did not mind a bit. The respite was more than welcome. He just wished that school was like this every day. He had forgotten that it could actually be enjoyable.

He even managed to get a couple of minutes alone with Paul, something that he hadn't done at school in more than six months – not that he had wanted to since Paul had sold his soul to Jason. They had arranged to meet behind the cricket pavilion during lunch break. It was quiet and secluded behind the pavilion and nobody seemed to go there. They had hung out there in the past, too, when they had wanted some peace and quiet, and to get away from the other kids during breaks. Paul was a few minutes late, and James was worried for a while that he wasn't going to turn up, but eventually he saw Paul running towards him and waving.

"Sorry I'm late. I bumped into Badger. He wanted to find out what time I was getting to the party tonight. I thought he was never going to stop talking."

"You're really going then?" James asked.

Paul leaned back against the wall and sighed.

"I don't have an option. I don't want to go. God knows what's going to go on there tonight. It's going to be horrible. I wonder what Jason's house is like."

"You've never been?"

"Nope."

"Couldn't you say you were ill?"

"No. I'd never hear the last of it."

"Well, perhaps it won't matter if you're really trying to get away from him."

"Nah. It'll be easier if I just go through with it. Get it over and done with. It will stop him suspecting anything for a while."

The boys sat down on the grass. They were completely shaded from the sun by both the trees and the pavilion, and the still-chilly spring breeze penetrated their school shirts with surprising ease.

"Thanks for the email," Paul said. "I didn't think you'd make your mind up so quickly about the weekend."

"It was a spur of the moment thing. I figured that I had nothing to lose. It doesn't mean what has happened is forgotten, though. It's just that I want to see if we can sort this whole thing out. And perhaps we can sort Jason out between us. Let's face it, you must know quite a bit about what he's up to and what he wants after spending so much time with him."

"I guess. I'm not sure he *wants* anything. He's just, well, *Jason*."

"But at least you have some knowledge of what he gets up to. You could use that against him."

The boys sat in silence for a few seconds, the school suddenly seeming miles away from where they were sitting.

"What do you want to do when I come over, then?" James asked.

"I don't know. You could come for tea. We could watch a DVD or something?   Just play it by ear and see what happens."

"Sure. Sounds good to me."

"Cool."

Paul stood up and brushed the grass off the backside of his trousers.

"I've got to be going," he said. "Lunch finishes in five minutes, and we can't be seen going back together."

"Yeah, I know. That's fine. Good luck for tonight, Paul."

"Thanks, I need it." He started to run back across the school playing field. "See you Saturday!" he called back.

James smiled, despite the constant worry that this was all some elaborate hoax and that he wasn't doing the right thing. There was still that chance that things could work out. He had nothing to lose. Things could hardly get any worse.

He started to walk back toward the main school building, and heard the bell signalling the end of lunch break in the distance.

3

Earlier in the day, Jason had told Luke about the events of the night before. He had left out some important details, such as the fact that it was the first time for him as well as for Claire, and that it wasn't a pleasurable experience for either of them. He also omitted that he'd had no idea of what he was doing, that he panicked when he started losing his hard-on, and took it out on Claire.

He was boasting about his conquest, and trying to show that he had some authority and still got his own way whenever he wanted. The rest was unimportant. Luke didn't know whether to tell Jane, but thought she might want to know in case Claire approached her, and so told her what Jason had said as they made their way from one classroom to the next.

"Claire's not going to be there tonight," he said.

"Why not? It's his birthday."

"Jason doesn't want her there apparently. He told her last night."

"That was nice of him."

"You're telling me. To be honest, I don't think Claire had a good night. Just thought I'd warn you in case she seems a bit off today."

"What do you mean?"

"They slept together last night."

Jane stopped dead in her tracks.

"Luke that's not funny. You know how Claire is about that. She'd never have let him…"

Luke walked over to her and put his hands on her shoulders.

"I wouldn't lie to you, babe. That's what he told me this morning." Jane stared at him. Luke had never seen her quite so angry. "I think he probably used some gentle persuasion," he said. "That's not what he said, but she wouldn't have done it otherwise, would she?"

"He's such a bastard."

"I know."

Luke leaned against the wall, looking down at the ground. Jane walked over to him and kissed his cheek.

"What's up, babe?" she said.

Luke looked her in the eyes. She thought he was going to cry.

"We're as bad as he is, aren't we?" Luke said. "I mean, we go around with him. We say yes to everything. We jump when he tells us to. I want out, Jane. I *so* want out. We're leaving school in a few weeks. If we stick around with him we're going to land up in trouble, I can see it coming a mile off."

He was right, of course. Jane knew that, once school was out of the way, beating kids up would not be high on Jason's agenda. Before long it would be theft, drug dealing and possibly worse. Jason was already involved in some of that already, but at least he didn't ask anyone else to get their hands dirty…yet. Jane didn't want to be a part of that any more than Luke did. But neither she nor Luke had any immediate ideas on how to break away from him. But that would have to wait. Now, Jane wanted to make sure that Claire was OK, and she waited for her to come out of her final class of the day.

They walked home together like they often did, and Jane told Claire what Luke had said earlier.

"I can't believe Jason told everyone," Claire said, with tears forming in her eyes. "He said I wouldn't be just another shag. He said that I could trust him."

Jane put her arm around her friend, not quite knowing what to say.

"You *can't* trust him. You know that. What on earth made you do it?"

"I don't know. He said that he was bored of me. That we would have to break up."

"Would that have been so bad? Me and Luke would be quite happy to get out of his way. You should be too. He's a bastard, Claire. You deserve better than him."

"I know."

They walked the rest of the way home in silence. As they reached Claire's house, Jane said:

"I'm sorry for what happened, Claire. I really am."

"It's OK. I asked for it, I guess. As you said, I know him well enough now."

"That doesn't mean that he should pressure you into sex."

The two girls hugged and Claire finally broke down and began to sob.

"It was horrible," she said. "He hurt me. I mean he *really* hurt me."

She broke away and sat on the low wall at the foot of her front garden. Jane sat down beside her, and put her arm around her.

"What do you mean, Claire?" she asked.

Claire wiped her eyes and blew her nose with a tissue that Jane handed to her.

"He was so rough. I've got bruises everywhere," she said finally. "I don't remember what he did. He must have slapped me, I guess. It started off all right. He was being really gentle with me, and asking me if I was OK. Then suddenly he seemed to lose it. Perhaps I wasn't doing it right. I don't know. He ripped my top. I had to tell my parents that I fell off my bike coming back. I couldn't tell them what really happened. Dad would have gone there and killed him."

She wiped more tears from her eyes.

"I never thought it would hurt so much. I wasn't expecting it to hurt. It's meant to be nice, right? That's how it started off. I thought it would be good. I thought it would bring us together, that we would be close like you and Luke. But now I'm just scared of him. I'm scared he'll want to do it again, Jane. What am I going to do?"

CHAPTER EIGHT

1

Paul could hear the *thump*, *thump*, *thump* of the music coming out of Jason's house from a hundred metres away. The sound filled him with dread and he felt his stomach churn. He had known from the start that the party was hardly going to be a sedate affair if Jason had anything to do with it, but he could hear people shouting and yelling from the house as he got closer, making him wonder what he was letting himself in for. He felt sorry for the neighbours.

He hesitantly walked up the garden path and rang the doorbell. When no-one answered, he was tempted just to leave, to walk away and say that he couldn't make himself heard. But he knew that no-one would believe him even if he *was* telling the truth, or at least they would make out that they didn't believe him, and it would only make things worse. Still, he wouldn't take much persuasion to leave, and perhaps spend the evening with James instead.

He rang the doorbell again and, when no-one came to the door, he slowly turned the handle and stepped into the hallway of Jason Mitchell's house. It took a few seconds to take in what he saw. To Paul, it was like entering a different world. Much bigger than it looked from the outside, it dwarfed his two-bedroom terraced council house. What's more, he could see even from where he stood in the hallway that it was tastefully and simply decorated, with modern artwork hanging on the walls. Whether they were prints or originals, he couldn't tell for sure, but he guessed the latter. Jason had always boasted that his family was rich, and now Paul finally believed him, making him hate him even more.

The music was coming from the lounge, although it made the whole house vibrate, and Paul walked slowly into the room, stopping just inside the doorway. He was surprised to see that there were only a dozen or so people there, most of whom he knew from school. He thought there would be far more. Perhaps Jason wasn't as popular as people assumed he was. Paul thought that the music was ridiculously loud, especially as no-one was dancing – or perhaps dancing was seen as uncool. He wasn't upset if it was; he hated it and was useless at it. Instead, people were just sitting around, chatting and laughing. Luke and Jane were on the sofa, snogging away in their own little world. Smithy and Jason were both on armchairs, drinking lager from a can, with Badger perching on the arm of Smithy's chair, looking as much of an interloper as Paul felt.

Jason looked across, saw Paul, and stood up. He grinned and walked over to him and, to Paul's surprise, gave him a big hug.

"Our final guest has arrived!" he shouted above the music, to cheers from a couple of the others, who already seemed well on their way to being drunk.

Jason, Smithy and Badger seemed to do their best to make him feel at home, but Paul felt that they were playing with him. Something wasn't quite right, but he couldn't work out what it was, or what was in store for him. He felt completely alone and vulnerable, and he knew it was going to be a long night.

2

Andrew Green had already been sitting at the bar in the Queen's Head for twenty minutes when the screen on his mobile phone lit up to indicate that he had a message. It made the tone to announce this also, but the music was so loud, and the patrons so noisy, that he would not have heard it anyway. He had the phone in his hand as he was expecting a message. He was expecting Jonathan to cancel their meeting for drinks that he had finally been able to arrange earlier in the day. Andrew had still not got his head around the fact that his ex-pupil might want to meet him. That type of thing didn't happen to the Andrew Greens of this world. He was bound to back out, or perhaps "work" would be a convenient excuse to postpone.

Andrew truly thought that he had never been so nervous in his life. He didn't really know why. It wasn't as if this was a date, was it? It was just drinks and a friendly chat. At least, that was what Andrew was telling himself. In truth, he wasn't really sure. Jonathan hadn't really been that explicit.

He read the text message with a mix of relief and fear. Relief because Jonathan hadn't actually bailed on him, and fear because he was still having to go through with the date, drinks, or whatever the hell it was. And Andrew wasn't good in these situations. His hands trembled, his stomach made noises that were nearly as loud as the music in the pub, and, in the twenty minutes he had been waiting, he had felt the urge to pee three times. It was just like being fifteen again and going on a date for the very first time. The problem was that, despite his years, this *was* Andrew's very first date. The last time he had been in the Queen's Head for a date, he was the only one who showed. According to the text, Jonathan had got held up at work but was now on his way and would be there in ten minutes.

Andrew got up from his bar stool and made his way for the fourth time to the toilets. The lone cubicle was in use and so he waited just inside the main door. A couple of the urinals were free, but he knew with his current attack of nerves that he wouldn't be able to use one with someone standing beside him. He had problems using urinals at the best of times. He heard the toilet flush and the door to the cubicle opened and a young guy of about twenty emerged and smiled at him. Andrew smiled back and squeezed himself into the small space, locking the door behind him.

When he came out of the cubicle, Andrew went over to the sinks, turned on the taps and washed his hands. Then he fumbled in his jacket pocket and pulled out a blister strip of tablets and popped one out of the packaging. He had already taken one of the tablets that the doctor had given him for when he got stressed or had a panic attack, but he figured another one wouldn't kill him on this occasion. He put the tablet in his mouth and bent down to get a mouthful of water out of the tap. After getting the tablet successfully lodged in his throat because of the strange angle he was drinking the water, he made his way back to the bar area, fishing out a small bottle of hand sanitiser from his jacket pocket and using it as he walked. Jonathan was waiting for him. Seeing Andrew, he moved over and gave him a hug.

"I was beginning to think you'd given up and gone home."

"No, just nipped to the loo."

"Cool. Sorry I'm so late. I got stuck at work, had to get a story done before I left off and it just wasn't happening. Here now, though. Thanks for waiting."

"Not a problem."

"What can I get you?"

"No, you paid last time. My turn tonight."

The barman from the night before had dispensed with the shirt altogether on this occasion, revealing his smooth, toned chest in all its glory.

"Now you know the attraction of frequenting gay bars," Jonathan whispered in Andrew's ear.

With drinks ordered, they went and sat down at a small table at the back of the pub. Jonathan took off his suit jacket and hung it over the back of the chair. Andrew winced as a new song began playing that seemed even louder than the last one.

"It's bloody noisy in here tonight," he said.

"I know. It always is on a Wednesday," Jonathan said, taking a sip of his drink. "It's gay night at one of the clubs in the city, so people come here to get pissed first before going there. The drinks are cheaper here. And don't worry, I'm not suggesting that we go clubbing. Unless you're desperate to dance the night away."

Andrew grimaced.

"It's funny, but I'm not."

"Surprising that." Jonathan smiled. Andrew realised, rather guiltily, that it was a smile he could grow to live very much. "Work better today?"

Was work better today? Andrew nearly laughed. A row with The Head, and then perhaps the most stupid decision he had ever made.

"Not really," he said. "To be honest, I'm thinking seriously about giving in my notice and giving up teaching. Perhaps it's time for a change. Been doing it ten years now. Things aren't what they were."

Jonathan looked genuinely shocked.

"You can't do that," he said.

"I'm beginning to think that I don't have a choice. I'm having quite a few run-ins with 'The Head.' That's how most of us refer to him. He's one of those money-orientated dickheads who don't seem to give a shit about the kids."

"It seems to be the way things are going these days, though. School is a business, and the cuts are hardly helping. I don't know what Smithdale is like, but we ran a story a few months ago about a school that was asking parents to chip in towards pens, pencils and paper. It's nuts. Education doesn't matter anymore. It's all about saving the bucks."

Andrew nodded and took a sip of his drink.

"That's about it," he said. "I wouldn't mind so much, but there's a kid having some problems and I'm being warned off doing something about it. He's getting bullied by some lads in his year. It's not a nice situation. From what I can gather they're accusing him of being gay, beating him up and filming it on their phones…"

"Happy slapping. There was quite a bit about it in the media last year from what I remember. So, is he?"

"Gay? I don't know for sure. I don't think it matters. Either way, he won't report what is going on because he's too embarrassed about it. The Head has said that, in order to keep the schools' reputation and therefore keep getting the best kids and so the biggest budget, we don't have a bullying problem."

"That's ludicrous."

"Tell me about it. There was less of a problem in your day, Jonathan. And I'm sure you knew it was going on even then."

"Sure. We all knew people who were being bullied."

"I spent most of last night looking up possible ways to help this kid – and others like him. There must be others like him. He's not the only kid at Smithdale being bullied because he's gay – or because others think he's gay. I blame that on you, by the way. You were the one who had gone on about me being a wonderful teacher. I realised I hadn't been so wonderful lately, and so set out to help him. I said to The Head that I wanted to start a gay-straight alliance at the school. It's something I read about. It would be a start, you know?" Jonathan nodded. "But he wouldn't hear of it."

As Jonathan took a mouthful of his beer, Andrew gazed around the bar. He felt old. He even thought that perhaps Jonathan felt old. Most of the people couldn't have been older than twenty-one. He envied them. He wasn't even out by that point. At that age, he'd only just plucked up the courage to buy a copy of the Gay Times over the counter in a newsagent and, even now, he felt as if he was being scrutinised whenever he did so. All those wasted years.

"So, what are you going to do?" Jonathan asked.

"I came out to my class today."

Jonathan sat back in his chair.

"Wow," he said,

"Well, you said the kids knew anyway, even in your day. And I was angry and frustrated. I needed to let them know that I was on their side if they were in

James's position."

"James? Is that the name of this bullied kid?"

Andrew nodded.

"So, what happened when you told your class you were gay?"

Andrew began choking up.

"They applauded," he said, wiping away a tear.

Jonathan put his hand on top of Andrew's and squeezed it.

"Hey," he said. "That's great, right?"

Andrew nodded.

"I guess so. One class down, another half a dozen to go. They're not all going to be like that one. But I'm not willing to stay in a job where I have to compromise my morals. Sorry, that sounds, I don't know, self-important or something. But I mean it. That's not why I went into teaching. This isn't the 1980s. I suddenly realised that there's no reason why I shouldn't be out at school. I didn't tell them exactly why I was telling them, but I think they knew. I reckon everyone at the school knows what's happening to that poor kid."

"You did a good thing," Jonathan said.

"I hope so. The Head's not going to like it when he finds out."

"You've done the hard bit. Telling him where to go is going to be easy in comparison."

"Thanks," Andrew said, and finished the rest of this drink. "You know anywhere a bit quieter we can go to?"

"Not really. Shame. I can hardly hear myself think in here."

Andrew opened his mouth to speak, and then thought better of it.

"What were you going to say?"

"Nothing."

"Go on. Don't be shy."

"I was going to say that I only live up the road if you want to go there for a coffee."

"A coffee, huh?" Jonathan said, beaming.

"Yes, and I *mean* a coffee!"

Jonathan finished the rest of his drink and they left the Queens Head and made their way to Jonathan's car. He unlocked it and they both got in and Andrew gave him instructions on how to reach his flat. As they pulled out of the pub car park, Jonathan said:

"You know, I can always do some research on this Head of yours."

"What are you suggesting?"

"I don't know. But something might come up that might be of use."

"I'm not sure what good it would do. Don't go getting either of us into trouble, Jonathan."

"There's probably nothing to find out, having said that. But there's no harm in looking. I wouldn't print anything without your say so, anyway."

"Thanks. Mind you, I guess I could use whatever you found out – if there is anything to find out – as leverage, couldn't I?"

"I might have to start charging for my services, Mr. Green."

Andrew smiled.

"I don't think you can call me Mr. Green anymore, by the way."

Jonathan looked across and laughed

"What should I call you instead? Sir?"

"*Definitely* not Sir! Cheeky bastard! Turn left here and don't say another word!"

3

Truth or dare. For some reason it wasn't exactly what Paul expected at Jason's birthday party, but everybody had been drinking (even Paul) and half a dozen or so seemed up for the game when someone made the suggestion. Paul, volunteered by Jason to play, didn't know whether to be relieved about the game or not. Although it meant that he could still fall foul of Jason, he also knew that he could just keep choosing "truth" all night and remain relatively safe. The problem was that just the thought of the game reminded him of the one he had played with James the summer before, and made him want to spend time with him even more.

He became more relaxed when Jason suggested using playing cards to decide whose turn it was. Everybody would be dealt two cards and the person with the lowest hand would be asked "truth or dare" by the person with the highest. Then the whole thing would start again. At least with a random system, Paul knew that he wouldn't be picked on relentlessly as long as the game wasn't fixed – and he couldn't see how it could be, unless Jason was a magician with the cards.

Jason, Smithy, Luke, Jane, Paul, Badger and Ellie (Badger's girlfriend of the week) sat in a circle on the floor as Jason shuffled the cards. The others sat around the room, talking to themselves or just watching. Paul didn't really know any of them, although he thought he recognised one or two of them from school. Probably think themselves too cool for Truth or Dare, Paul thought. He had tried to sit the game out himself, but Jason was having none of it.

"Just so that you know, I'm not getting my tits out, no matter what," Jane said.

"No reason why we should ask you to," said Jason, "we've all seen them before!"

Jane reached over and slapped Jason playfully on the arm.

"Cheeky bastard," she said.

Jason grinned at her, but clearly hadn't appreciated the slap, no matter how playful it had been.

"Except Paul, of course," Jason said. "Paul hasn't seen your tits. You want to see them?"

"Leave him alone, Jason," Luke said. Paul wasn't sure whether Luke was sticking up for Jane or for him. Perhaps it was both.

Paul had detected that things weren't right between Luke and Jane and Jason. He wondered what might have happened to make Jason be on edge with them. The tension was high, and Paul was savvy enough to know that wasn't a good thing. It felt like an unexploded bomb that was just waiting to go off. He watched closely as Jason dealt the cards, but didn't see any sign that they were being tampered with as they were dealt. He picked his two cards up and was pleased to see that he had a score of 14 between them. He was pretty sure that there would be someone with a lower one than that, and he wasn't wrong. Badger only had a score of 5 between his two cards, but it was his girlfriend, Ellie, who won the hand. Badger looked relieved. Jason didn't look pleased. Even at this stage, it was clear that he intended to make some trouble, and Badger being at the mercy of his girlfriend was not what he had planned.

"Beginner's luck there, Ellie," he said.

"Something like that," she said, and turned to Badger. "So, truth or dare?"

"Truth," came the reply.

"So predictable, Badger!" shouted one of the onlookers.

"Hey, if you can do better, then come and play!" Badger shouted back with a little more enthusiasm than he had intended. "So, what's the question?" he said to Ellie.

Paul watched as Ellie thought for a moment. He had never met her before – he hadn't even known that Badger *had* a girlfriend.

"How many girlfriends have you had before me?"

Jason laughed.

"I'm not sure Badger can actually count that high. He's bottom set for maths you know!"

"Sod off. So are you," Badger bit back. Jason glared

at him. He was beginning to get pissed off with people answering him back. "I haven't had that many. Not *girlfriends*. Friends who are girls, perhaps. But that's different."

"You have at least two different ones a month, Badger," said Jason.

"That's not fair. They're dates. Not girlfriends. There's a difference, you know?"

"Yeah, right."

"Three, El. I've had three girlfriends before you."

"So I'm your fourth?"

"Yeah."

"Well, that's not so bad," she said. "Could have been worse."

"Would have been, if he'd told the truth. This is called *truth* or dare, Badger. Not *lie-to-get-myself-out-of-trouble* or dare," said Jason.

"Up yours! My deal."

Badger collected up the cards, shuffled them clumsily and dealt. Paul knew he was safe again when Jane threw her cards down on the floor.

"Four. Two cards, and a sum total of four. That stinks!"

Jason laughed.

"Well, it's the game, Jane," he said. "And look at me with twenty, the highest hand of the round."

"Bollocks."

"Are we to assume it's a truth for you then, my dear?"

"Screw you! Dare!"

Jane took a mouthful from her can of lager while the boys in the room gave a cheer and gave shouts of "go girl!" Jason sat quietly, watching. He was clearly hatching up a plan, or wondering how to put the one he already had into practice. He played with the cards in his hands until everyone was quiet once again. He looked at Paul, smirked, and then turned to Jane.

"Paul looks as if he needs cheering up. I think you should give him a lap dance."

The boys again cheered, with the exception of Luke, who looked over disgustedly at Jason. He put his hand on Jane's shoulder.

"Don't do anything you don't want to, babe," he said.

"It's fine. I agreed to play. But I will get my own back before the evening is through. Looks like it's your lucky day, Paul. To be honest, you deserve something for putting up with this arsehole for the last six months anyway!"

She gestured towards Jason, who clearly wasn't amused at the insult.

Paul, who thought it was anything but his lucky day, was encouraged to sit down on a chair in the centre of the circle. He knew he was going to be more humiliated by the experience than Jane was. A couple of the lads started leerily singing "The Stripper" and Jane began to cavort in front of Paul. He wanted to look away, but knew it was in his best interests do look as if he was enjoying it. Jane undid a couple of buttons on her blouse and then moved towards him, running her finger along his cheek before moving behind him, reaching round and sliding her hand down the front of his shirt, to cheers from the others. Paul began to blush.

"Got a boner yet?" someone shouted.

He hadn't, and was thankful that the chances of one occurring were slim, despite Jane's best efforts. Paul knew that Jason had set them up together in order to humiliate him. This was Jason's chance to start getting his own back at the people who had not been as obedient as they should have been all week. Jane moved around to the front of him again and started rubbing herself up against his crotch, and pulled his head down so that it was buried in her breasts. When he sat back, she moved in towards him and whispered "I'm sorry" in his ear before kissing him full on the mouth. Then she moved away.

"That's it," she said.

The others gave her a round of applause and she bowed and sat down. She stared at Jason as Paul sheepishly went back to his place, somewhat bemused at Jane's apology. What was *that* about? Paul wondered if Luke and Jane might actually be his allies if he approached them about wanting to get away from all of this. Perhaps they wanted out as well.

Jane picked up the cards and dealt. Everybody seemed to be a bit wary when they picked up their cards this time. The animosity between Luke, Jane and Jason had made the room tense, and it was obvious that at some point in the game real sparks were going to fly. This time it was Jason who found himself with the lowest hand, and he didn't look happy about it. In fact, he looked surprised, and Paul again wondered if he was trying to tamper (albeit unsuccessfully) with the cards. Luke looked very happy about having the highest scoring hand, though, and asked him whether he wanted a truth or a dare.

"Truth."

There were shouts of "chicken" from around the room.

"You lightweight," Luke said. "You make Jane do that to poor Paul and then you chose truth."

"Poor Paul?" Jason shot back. "He loved it! Didn't you see him with his face in your girlfriend's…"

"You need to watch your mouth, Jason."

"Yeah, yeah. Stop whinging! It's my birthday. I'll do what I want. Just ask me a bloody question. Anything you like."

"Sure," Luke said. "Ok, then. Why are you such a wanker?"

The words had escaped Luke's mouth before he realised what was happening, and he immediately regretted what he had said. This could mean trouble, and he didn't want it here with a group of people on the sidelines that he neither knew or trusted.

"You need to watch your step, Luke," came the reply.

Luke didn't offer to take back what he had said.

"I asked you a question," he said.

"In answer to your question," Jason said, sarcastically, "I am a wanker for the very practical reason that I can't get a good shag from Claire!" He turned to his audience. "A man has his needs, you know? Even Paul. Practice makes perfect."

"That's odd, I heard rumours that you did shag Claire," Jane said.

"Not a rumour, Jane, but I said a *good* shag."

Luke and Jane turned to each other, and Paul realised suddenly that relations within the group were even worse than people thought. The evening was turning ugly quickly.

Jason picked up the cards and started to shuffle. Paul thought he saw him slip a couple of extra cards into the pack, but he couldn't be sure. His suspicions grew when Jason once again had the highest hand and Luke, who had just smart-mouthed him, had the lowest.

"Dare, Jason," Luke said. "I'm not chicken-shit like some people."

Jason appeared to ponder over what he should make Luke do, but Paul was becoming convinced that the whole thing was pre-planned.

"Ok," Jason said finally. "Your dare is to get naked and spend fifteen minutes in the cupboard under the stairs with whoever got the second lowest hand."

Luke rolled his eyes.

"For Christ's sake, Jason. What is it with you and naked guys? You go on about James, but I'm beginning to wonder about you."

Jason glared at him.

"I've warned you once tonight," Jason said.

Under other circumstances, some of the others

160

would probably make fun of Jason for being in a temper, but they knew their leader well enough to know when not to go there. Those not playing were now paying far more attention, and looked ready to pounce on Luke if Jason gave the nod.

"Now," Jason went on, "who got the lowest score out of the rest of you?"

It was Paul – something else which added to his feeling that Jason knew exactly who was going to lose the game and when. Luke rolled his eyes at him, and they got up and went through to the entrance hall of the house, followed by the rest of the group.

"When you're ready," Jason said.

There was something about his behaviour that told Paul that this wasn't just about having a laugh, or making him and Luke feel embarrassed, but about teaching them a lesson.

The two sixteen-year-old boys reluctantly stripped off their clothes, retaining their modesty by covering their private parts with their hands, although they had been naked around each other in the showers at school that Jason had made them take after games lessons.

The others were surprisingly quiet, not quite knowing what to make of the dare that Jason had set them or the reasoning behind it. Jason just stood and watched, stony-faced. When they were undressed, Jason walked over to the large cupboard door under the stairway and opened it. They realised that there would be barely enough room for the two of them to stand in there, due to a number of cardboard boxes on the floor and a hoover just inside the door. However, they managed to squeeze in side by side, and watched nervously as Jason closed the door and pulled the bolt across, leaving them in complete darkness, save for a small strip of light that seeped in from under the door.

The boys stood in silence for a couple of seconds, both trying to stay as far away from the other so as not to rub up against them. They could hear talking from the hallway, but neither of them could make out what was being said.

Luke broke the ice.

"Well, this is fun," he said quietly.

"Hardly," Paul replied.

"I know. I'm sorry you got stuck with this."

"It's not your fault, Luke."

Again, the boys fell into silence before Luke started to giggle.

"What are you laughing at?" Paul asked, before starting to laugh as well.

"I just suddenly realised that I'm standing here with my hands in front of me so you can't see my dick, and here we are in the dark!"

"Hey! Me, too."

Nonetheless, both Paul and Luke's hands remained where they were.

"Are you Ok, Paul?"

"Yeah. Thanks. Could be worse anyway. I could be stuck in here with Ellie."

Luke smiled.

"She's not what my mum would call 'refined', is

she?"

"Hardly. Worse still, I could be in here with Jason."

"If you had stood up to him at the cinema last year, you wouldn't be in this mess, Paul. You know that, don't you? You'd have got it in the neck from him for a couple of weeks and then he'd have got bored of it."

"Perhaps. But I can't change things now."

"Nobody was fooled when you said James had made a play for you. You just fell into his hands. Doesn't bother me whether you're gay or not. I mean I'm standing next to you with no clothes in a cupboard and I don't think you're going to make a play for me. You know what I mean? It probably doesn't matter to Jason either. I wonder about *him* sometimes. It's all just ammunition; something he can use against you. And he's milking it for all it's worth. But he's running out of steam."

Paul was beginning to see Luke in a new light. He had always been the quiet one of the gang, but Paul also thought that he was the one closest to Jason. Perhaps that wasn't the case, after all.

"You're different away from him," he said.

"Tell me about it. Things are changing. Me and Jane are going to try to break away, but not sure how we're going to do it. But he knows that I've just about had enough. His little empire is falling to bits, and he knows it. Would have happened anyway once school finished. Can't get away from him there very easily. Once it finishes, he no longer has that hold."

"Is that why he put you in here with me?"

"I think it's a test of my loyalty after I asked him why he was a wanker, and for calling him a chicken. Probably not my best moves. He's wanting me to bang on the door, begging to be let out because you've grabbed my dick. That's what he wants."

"Are you going to?"

"Not unless you grab my dick," Luke said, jokingly.

"I couldn't find it in the dark," Paul replied.

"You're in enough shit with him as it is. And the less I do what he wants, the better it will be in the long run."

Luke started to shuffle around in the cupboard.

"What the hell are you doing?" Paul asked him.

"I had a hoover attachment up my arse. It wasn't comfortable."

"I can imagine."

They stood in silence, not sure of what to say. Finally, Luke spoke.

"Paul, I shouldn't be telling you this, but you're a nice guy and you've gone through enough. You need to make a run for it when he lets us out of here."

"Why?"

"Jason's got something planned for you tonight. I honestly don't know entirely what it is. But I know something's going on."

"Like what?"

"I don't know for sure. But there's someone else here. There's a girl. He told her to wait upstairs. She might be a stripper or something. Or worse."

"Worse?"

"Use your imagination."

"He's just a perv."

"So, when he lets us out, you just get your clothes on and run out of the front door, Ok?"

"Ok. Thanks. I'll try. But what about you? He'll know you told me."

"Don't worry about me. I can deal with Jason. And perhaps a fight is the only way to get away from him. I'll take my chances."

The boys stood in silence for a few moments.

"How long have we got to go in here?" Paul asked.

"I don't know. It can't be much longer."

"I hope not."

"Oh, thanks."

"I didn't mean that. Not because I'm here with you."

"Naked."

"Yeah. Naked. It's just because I'm in a cupboard where I can't move and I'm freezing my bollocks off."

"I'm not going to warm you up."

"I'll survive."

"Shame," Paul said, adding quickly "just a joke."

"I know."

They heard the sound of people approaching the cupboard and Jason knocked on the door.

"Opening up!"

Paul and Luke tensed up as the bolt slid across and the door opened. The light hurt their eyes, but both realised in time that they couldn't shield their eyes with their hands as they had no clothes on. They braced themselves for what was to follow, with Paul trying his best not to let on that Luke had told him of Jason's plans.

"You two have fun in there? Release any pent-up energy?" Jason said, beaming.

"Sorry, Jason, nothing happened. You'll just have to continue with your fantasies later," Luke said, coming out of the cupboard and going over to his clothes, pulling on his boxer shorts and jeans.

Paul remained in the cupboard while he scoured the hallway for his clothes.

"Are you coming out of the closet – I mean cupboard – or staying there all night?" Jason said.

"I don't see my clothes," Paul said. "Where are they, Jason?"

"Ah yes. I forgot about those. I put them in my bedroom for safekeeping. It's the first door on the right at the top of the stairs."

Paul stepped into the hallway and looked across at Luke. Luke took a couple of steps towards Jason.

"Get him his clothes, Jason," he said. "It's not funny."

"No-one said it was. He's quite capable of getting them himself, Luke. Although you won't be able to walk if you keep talking to me like that."

Jason and Luke stared at each other. Paul watched them, not knowing what to do. He half expected them to lunge at each other and start fighting any second. Instead, Luke sighed and took off his jeans again and threw them to him.

"Wear mine," he said, and threw him his T-shirt

too.

"I can't take your clothes."

"Just put them on and get out of here!"

Jason ran up to Luke and punched him hard in the stomach and the two of them started fighting. Soon both of them were rolling on the floor, first one getting the upper hand, and then the other.

Paul didn't wait to see the outcome of the fight. He took Luke's clothes and ran outside, pulling on the jeans as he made his way down the footpath. He had nothing on his feet, and he winced with each step he took because of it, but knew he couldn't go back for his shoes. He hobbled down the street, pulling on Luke's T-shirt as he did so. He didn't stop to look back until he was a quarter of a mile from the house, and sure that nobody had come after him.

4

Jonathan parked the car, and the two men got out and made their way up the stairs to Andrew's flat.

"I'm sorry if the place is a bit of a mess," Andrew said. "I really wasn't intending to ask you back here."

Jonathan laughed.

"That's what *you* say," he said. "I don't believe you. I'm sure it was your plan all along to invite me back to your den of iniquity."

"If only I was that brave."

Andrew unlocked the front door and went in, with Jonathan following behind him. The bedsit was small, and Jonathan almost felt pity for Andrew. Here he was, in his early forties, in a dingy flat in which the lounge/bedroom and kitchen areas combined were probably no bigger than the classroom in which he taught. A stack of washing up was piled on the work-top nearest the sink, and papers and exercise books covered the whole surface of the coffee table. The television was just a portable and neither flat or widescreen. Jonathan wondered if it was even colour. A couple of DVDs were sitting on top of the player. One was *Chinatown* and, from what Jonathan could make out, the other was some cheap gay soft porn. A bulky, out-of-date PC sat in the corner of the room, with the monitor sitting on the floor. It was not what Jonathan was expecting, and he wondered how and why Andrew hadn't set up a decent home. He wasn't in a relationship, and didn't have kids and, while teacher's pay was not what it should be, it didn't warrant a pokey flat like this one. Somewhere, something had gone wrong. Whatever it was, he now didn't doubt that Andrew was not intending to invite him back to the flat. He would have at least tidied up in advance.

Andrew went over to the kitchen area and washed up a couple of mugs. He asked Jonathan if he wanted tea or coffee.

"Coffee, please. Black, one sugar," Jonathan replied, although he was slightly concerned as to what germs might have been growing in the mug he was going to drink from. He tried to put the idea out of his head.

Andrew turned around to face Jonathan and smiled.

"I'm glad you said that. I'm out of teabags and milk."

He went over to the sofa-bed and took the magazines and papers that littered the cushions and put them on the floor.

"Have a seat, now you can find one," he said, and went back into the kitchen and Jonathan sat down. "I did say I wasn't expecting visitors."

"And you weren't lying, I'll give you that."

"I suppose it's a bit of a shock seeing me living in a place like this, huh?" Andrew asked, as he brought the coffees through and made space for them on the coffee table.

"It's not what I expected," Jonathan said. He added quickly, "but hey, if you don't get many visitors and you're single at the moment, what does it matter?"

He hoped that was the right thing to say, but was unsure.

"I'm always single," Andrew said, and sat down at the other end of the coffee table. "How about you?"

"I've been single three months. But it's Ok. I'm enjoying the freedom, I think."

"I can imagine."

"No, not like that!"

"Sorry, I didn't mean to insinuate that you were..."

"Putting it around?"

"Yeah."

"Not really my style, to be honest."

"So, what happened, if you don't mind me asking? Had you been together long?"

"A couple of years. Just over. I thought it was all going well. We'd moved into a flat together and I thought I'd found the man of my dreams. But, as clichéd as it may sound, I came home from work one day and found him in bed with somebody else. A woman."

"Oh shit. I've heard about them."

"So, that was the end of that. I'm still pretty cut up about it to be honest, but I've just got to move on. I packed up my stuff and moved back to Mum's for couple of weeks, but now I've got myself my own place again. Things are getting back to normal."

"That's cool. I'm glad to hear it."

"How about you? How long have you been single?"

Andrew turned away and sipped at his coffee.

"I'm sorry. You obviously don't want to talk about it."

Andrew turned back to Jonathan and forced a smile. "It's Ok," he said.

But it clearly wasn't. This was an area of Andrew's life that nobody knew about. Although he sometimes felt that he would like to talk the whole thing out, to offload his issues on to somebody else, he never had. The truth of the matter was that he had never been with a man, nor with a woman. In fact, it was worse than that, he had never even kissed someone, not in the way that one kisses a boyfriend. He was, as the kids at school years earlier had drummed into him, a "loser." A real-life forty-year-old virgin who lived in one of the smallest flats known to man that he had let get into such a mess that he no longer felt inclined to even try and clean it up. Of late, he had even begun to think that it was he alone who filled up the bottle bank at the end of the road each week, such was his alcohol consumption.

He wanted to turn his life around, but it required too much effort and, as he admitted to himself all too often, he really didn't know where to start or what to do. Sometimes it was difficult just to hold down the teaching job.

He knew he should have tried to sort things out years earlier. He should have made that trip to the GP to admit he was depressed, but couldn't be bothered. Alcohol numbed everything enough for him to plod on with his life, such as it was. But, sitting beside him was someone who, for whatever reason, seemed to give a shit. Jonathan Lewis was clearly upset by how his ex-teacher was living and he had made it obvious that he was both interested and wanted to help, and Andrew knew that he would never have a better opportunity than this to tell someone else who he really was.

So, for the first time in his life, Andrew Green talked.

He told Jonathan of how his time at school had not been much different from that of James Marsh, and how the other kids seemed to know he was gay even before he did himself. He told him how he never admitted his sexuality while he was at school – kids didn't back in those days - but that he was made to feel dirty by the taunts of others and how it made him withdraw into himself and try to ignore sex and the idea of relationships as he grew up.

"The idea of that kind of thing terrifies me," he said. "That doesn't mean I don't want it, just that I don't know how to go about finding someone and, if I did find someone and things got that far, I would be so nervous I wouldn't be able to do anything anyway. The longer you wait, the worse it is, isn't it? I haven't even kissed anyone, Jonathan. Nobody even sees me with just my shirt off, never mind naked. I'd be petrified. And it's not even that I think I look like Quasimodo or something. I know I don't. It's just that…it's just that I'm used to hiding. It's safer that way. If people don't know who you are, then they can't attack you. At least at school I'm in charge of my own classroom. Well, I try to be anyway. Sorry, I'm gabbling. You don't want to hear this. That's not what you met me for."

Jonathan shuffled along the sofa towards him and put his arm around him, pulling him closer so that Andrew's head was resting on his chest.

"It's OK," he said.

Andrew didn't reply. He felt stupid for offloading his baggage on an ex-pupil, of all people. And yet he knew that, eventually, he would feel better for it, too. Jonathan tried to calm him down.

"It's not too late," he said.

5

"I can get someone to talk to you, if you'd like," the nurse said. "If you need some help."

Luke shook his head.

"I'm fine, thanks all the same."

"Yeah, you look it, Buster."

Luke forced a smile.

It was just past midnight. Luke and Jane had sat in the Accident and Emergency department at the hospital for just over two hours before they were finally called for. Luke hadn't wanted to go to the hospital, but Jane had insisted. As soon as they were a little way from Jason's house, she had taken out her mobile phone and called for a taxi to take them there. Luke had been hardly able to walk. He was doubled over with pain in his chest following the beating from Jason, and he had just learned that he had two cracked ribs. He now also had half a dozen stitches just above his right eye. The nurse had told him that things could have been much more serious had the punch landed just a centimetre lower. There could have been permanent damage to his eye.

Jason, it seemed, was out of control. Luke and Jane had talked about it as they sat waiting to be seen. It had taken three people to pull Jason away from Luke as he lay sprawled on the floor, subjected to kick after kick. Yet, despite what had happened, Luke knew that he had done the right thing by warning Paul of what Jason had in store for him. He had wanted to break away for a long while, and he knew that the time had come. He was worried that his cracked ribs were just a sign of things to come, but at least the decision had now been made. There was no going back.

"Right, you're all fixed up, young man," the nurse said. "But you've got to take it easy. No school for you until at least Monday, you hear?"

"I hear you."

"I hope you do. We don't want that pretty face of yours being damaged by some bastard and his fist, now do we? That lovely little girlfriend of yours that's waiting out there for you won't be too pleased, you know?"

Luke got up off the bed.

"Thanks for everything," he said. "You're a star. And thanks for not calling my folks."

"It's my job, honey. But take Aunty Estelle's advice and, if he decides to fight you again, you get yourself some high heels and kick him in the balls first!"

Luke smiled, although it hurt.

"Are they all like you in here?" he said.

"Oh no. I'm one of a kind! Now, get out of here and I don't want to see you back next week. Or you'll have *me* to answer to!"

Luke thanked the nurse again and walked back through to the waiting room. Jane was still sitting there, looking worried and drinking yet another cup of coffee.

"Come on, Jane. Let's go home," he said.

CHAPTER NINE

1

Rumours about the events at Jason's birthday party spread through the school quickly the next day. Neither Luke nor Jason attended school for the rest of the week, causing even the most sceptical recipients of the rumours to start believing what they were hearing, and Jane told her version of what happened to anybody who wanted to listen. There was no need for her to embellish her story, the facts were gruesome enough.

Luke was barely able to get out of bed for a couple of days, and so Jane visited him after school each day, staying with him long enough to fill him in on the day's events, to have dinner, and then snuggle up to him on the bed as they watched a movie. Claire also visited a couple of times without Jason knowing. Luke and Jane did their best to try and get her to break up with Jason, but she wouldn't hear of it, despite everything that had happened, and how Jason had treated her.

The absence of Jason at school was a blessing for James and Paul, who both felt that they could relax a little in the knowledge that the rest of the gang were unlikely to start anything without the say so of their leader. Despite this, they were unwilling to be seen with each other in case word got back to Jason. They managed to get together for a few minutes at lunch times, however, by meeting at the back of the cricket pavilion as they had done before. It was there that they made arrangements for the weekend, with James agreeing to go to Paul's house at about five o'clock for tea.

They still had to be careful about meeting, even in such a secluded place. Paul would go to the dining hall to check that Badger, Smithy and the others were busy eating their lunch before running over to the pavilion. None of Jason's gang would have anything to do with Jane, although Paul wondered whether that was because they didn't want to, or because they were too scared of what Jason might say if he found out. It was hard to tell, and none of them had talked to Paul about what had happened at the birthday party. In fact, they barely paid Paul any attention at all. The fight between Jason and Luke meant that Paul's attendance at the party was all but forgotten – including the fact that he was naked with Luke in the cupboard. Because of the awful events of the party, there was now a little hope for James and Paul that Jason's hold on his remaining friends (and enemies) might finally be cracking. With Luke gone, Jason was without the person who had been, until recently, his most trusted ally. Smithy and Badger might well be devoted to Jason, but they were hardly as level-headed as Luke.

On Saturday afternoon, James's mother began to think that her son had finally found himself a girlfriend. He had spent three times as long in the shower as he normally did and, when he finally emerged from the bathroom, not only was she shocked to see that he had styled his hair (something he *never* did) but she also realised that he smelt as if he had used an entire can of Lynx, which wasn't far from the truth. He got dressed in his best trousers instead of jeans, and put on a brilliant white shirt that he himself had ironed and that he knew he looked his best in. His mum questioned him about why he was getting dressed up, but he said he was just going out. He didn't tell her where or with whom. The less his mum knew at this point, the better.

Although the walk to Paul's house was only ten minutes, it seemed never ending to James that day. He was always nervous that he might bump into Jason on the street, but today he was more scared than ever, as he knew he would be instantly aware that something was going on if he saw James dressed up. Eventually he reached Paul's house and he approached it with trepidation, not knowing quite what to expect from the evening that was to follow. By the time he reached the front door and knocked, he was literally shaking with nerves. Paul opened the door almost immediately, and James saw that, like himself, Paul had dressed up for the occasion. The boys looked at each other for a few seconds, not knowing what to say. Paul grinned.

"You look good," Paul said, finally.

"You, too."

Paul asked James in and he stepped into the front hall and Paul closed the door behind him. For a moment, James questioned what he as doing. What if it was all a ruse after all, and Jason was hiding in the house somewhere. He knew by now that anything was possible, no matter how unlikely.

"It's a while since I've been in here," James said.

"I know. But nothing's changed. It's still a dive. I've been up and down all day, looking out of the window every time I saw someone go past in case it was you."

"I'm not late, Paul."

"No. I was just hoping you'd be early."

Paul's eagerness at least *seemed* to be genuine. James smiled and followed Paul through to the living room. He stopped in his tracks when he went through the door. Paul's house had never looked like this when he had been there before. He remembered the place as being a complete mess normally, but today it was spotless and there, in the middle of the room, was the dining table upon which were two candles and some badly arranged daffodils in a drinking glass of water.

"You've gone to so much trouble," James said. "Are you expecting someone special?"

"Not that I know of," Paul said, smiling. "Sit down at the table. I've nearly finished the meal. I'll bring it through in a second."

James took off his jacket and hung it on the back of the chair, then he sat down at the table as Paul went back through to the kitchen. James played aimlessly with the knife and fork in front of him, and looked around once more, amazed at the transformation of the room, and realising that it would have taken Paul at least a couple of hours to clean up just the lounge. He guessed that much of the rest of the house had also gone through such a transformation.

"I hope you haven't gone to too much trouble, Paul," he shouted through to the kitchen.

Paul re-emerged in the doorway, holding two portions of fish and chips, still wrapped in their paper.

"Not at all," he said.

He went over to the table and put one package down in front of James and then sat down with his own.

"I hope you don't mind having this for tea," he said. "I just wanted to make sure that the food was edible, and this was the only way I knew how. Dad eats my cooking, but he'd eat anything, no matter what it tastes like. I got them delivered."

"Believe me, it's fine. Mum's got us all on a health food kick at the moment. If I see another lettuce leaf, I'll go nuts. She thinks she's some health guru." This wasn't exactly true, but he thought it might make Paul feel better. They unwrapped the takeaway and began to eat. "But I know you're putting yourself down, Paul. I'm sure your dad likes your cooking."

"I don't know. It's hard to tell. But I get fed up with cooking for him, so I live on takeaways when Mum and

Dad are away."

"Are they back together then?"

"Not really. Mum has been staying with my uncle quite a bit. Well, she says she has anyway. She's never there when I call him. I think she's probably having an affair. Dad probably knows too. He's not stupid. But my aunt who lives down in Somerset is ill, so they've gone down there together to see her. From what I gather, they won't have another chance."

"I'm sorry."

"It's Ok. I don't know her. Don't think I've even met her. They're not back until Monday."

"All alone for the weekend, then?"

"Yeah. I don't mind." Paul paused for a second. "You're more than welcome to stay over if you want."

James stopped eating. Paul had slipped the comment into the conversation so as to not to make it sound like a big thing. But it was. James was beginning to feel more relaxed, but he still didn't want to be tricked. Rightly or wrongly, he still didn't trust Paul.

"I've already told Mum that I'll be back tonight," he said.

"You could ring her."

"We'll see. Let's just see how the evening pans out."

"OK."

"You haven't said much about the party when we met at school. Is what people are saying about it true?"

"Pretty much. Jason and Luke certainly had a fight. That was when I left. Luke had told me that Jason had something planned for me. When Jason found out, he just lunged at him. Luke had thrown me his jeans so I could escape."

"Why didn't you have your own?"

"Long story. Truth or dare."

James raised his eyebrows.

"So you finally got a taste of being naked through a game, then?"

"Yeah, right. In a cupboard. With Luke."

"Could be worse. He's cute."

"Jane said he's really badly hurt."

"I heard that, too. Have you been to see him?"

"Do you think I should?"

"Yeah. Probably. I mean, you're the reason he got hurt. He was trying to stop something bad happening to you. You should go and see him. To say thank you, if nothing else."

They finished eating their meal and then went through into the kitchen to do what little washing up there was. The kitchen, like the living room, was clean and tidy, and even smelt fresh. The last time James had been there, the washing up was piled high on the worktop and the tiled floor looked as if it hadn't seen a mop in months.

"You been having a good clean up, Paul?" James asked.

"I'm glad you noticed. I only did it because you were coming."

"I feel honoured."

"So you should be. It took me bloody hours. Now,

catch!"

Paul threw James a tea towel and the two boys began to wash and dry.

"What do you want to do tonight?" Paul asked.

"I don't know. What do you fancy?"

"I thought we could watch a DVD or something, if you'd like. I've got a couple of horror movies upstairs. Perhaps we could watch one of those?"

"Yeah, sounds good to me. I'll call my Mum in a bit and tell her I'm staying here tonight. If the offer is still open that is?"

Paul stopped washing up and hugged James.

"Of course it is," he said.

"But you've got to make sure you behave yourself!"

Paul returned to the washing up.

"I always behave myself," he said.

"I don't!"

With that, James lunged at Paul, backing him up against the room and started tickling him in the ribs. He knew Paul hated it.

"No tickling!" Paul blurted out. "No tickling!"

"Can't hear you!" came the reply.

Paul broke free and, laughing, ran away from James and ran up the stairs into his bedroom. James followed him and soon the two were standing on either side of the bed, facing each other and laughing.

"You know you're not going to get away!" James cried and climbed onto the bed, pulling Paul towards him and then climbing on top and pinning him down. As he once again started to tickle him, Paul began screaming for mercy. He kicked and slapped at James, eventually pushing him off, and the boys lay back on the bed, exhausted. They were quiet for a few seconds as they came to terms with what had just happened. They both knew that it was more than just a stupid tickling match. Something else had happened too. Nothing had changed since the summer holidays.

Paul slowly sat up, staring out in front of him. Quietly, he said:

"Why don't you hate me?"

James propped himself up with his elbows.

"Because I know why you've done stuff."

"But how can you like me after everything that's happened?"

"I don't know. I can separate the two things I guess. It's not like I didn't know you before. Or that I wasn't there when Jason came for us that day."

"I wonder what Jason would think if he could see us now?" he said.

"He'd probably get a boner!" James replied and laughed.

Paul let his gaze wander down to the prominent bulge in James's jeans.

"Looks like he's not the only one!"

James instinctively put his hands over his crotch and began to blush.

"That's not fair! You're not meant to notice things like that!"

Paul playfully tried to grab at James's hands to pull them away from his crotch. He started tickling him and the hands moved away.

"Time to get my own back," he said. "Your hands wouldn't have hid *that* when you lost the game last year!"

James swore at him, and Paul moved so that he was straddling James and then pinned his arms down on the bed. He moved in towards him and the two boys began to kiss. James broke away.

"You said you'd behave yourself," he said.

"I always behave myself."

Paul's mobile started to ring downstairs.

"You might want to get it. It might be your folks," said James.

"No, they wouldn't bother ringing. Let it ring, they'll ring back if it's urgent."

They ignored the telephone as they began to kiss once more.

2

"He's not bloody there!"

Jason Mitchell ended the call and threw his mobile phone across the room, with it landing on the armchair under the window.

He didn't know why the fact that Paul wasn't answering his phone pissed him off so much. But he knew there was more to it than just an unanswered call. It was just another sign that things had changed. He may have come out of the fight with Luke relatively unharmed from a physical point of view, but his pride had been dented when someone who he thought was his best friend had betrayed him. True, he had set up the possibility of the betrayal on purpose, just to see what Luke would do. Luke had been acting strangely lately, and he had to test him. But he had never expected him to actually befriend Paul. He was beginning to find out who his friends really were. Not that Luke had heard the last of him, of course. Jason had plans for him, although he was beginning to wonder whether he could be bothered to go through with them.

"Perhaps Paul's gone out," said Claire.

Jason looked at her. He had been trying to forget she was in the room. After they'd had sex a few nights earlier, Jason had thought she might finally walk away. No such luck.

"This is Paul. He doesn't go anywhere. He's a loser. Remember?"

"You're being irrational, Jason. He might have gone to the shop."

She was right, of course, but he did not approve of being called "irrational." He could have been anywhere, but Jason knew deep down that something was up. It was just a gut feeling. His dad always said that he should listen to his gut feelings.

He looked at his girlfriend and felt nothing but contempt. Here she was, leaning over him constantly as if to remind him that she was there. He wasn't likely to forget, he just wished that she were somewhere else.

Her top was wholly undone, revealing a rather unflattering bra that drew attention to her breasts, both of which still had the bruises he had inflicted a couple of days before. He hated to be reminded of what he had done.

He still didn't know what to make of the events of that night. He hadn't intended to be quite so rough, although he was always happy to show her who was boss. But with his boxer shorts down past his knees and Claire's underwear on the floor, he had climbed upon her and realised that he had little idea of what he was doing. He had felt his dick starting to go limp, and had begun to fear he was making a fool of himself. As he had started to sweat through sheer fear, he had hit out at her through frustration and desperation, needing to remain in charge of the situation. He had wanted to stop to say that there was something wrong, but he couldn't. He could never show that he was vulnerable; it wasn't in his nature. And all he could think of was Luke and Jane, continuously shagging like rabbits. He wasn't planning to be upstaged any longer by *them*. Not now that he had finally made progress with Claire. He was barely inside her when he came. The whole thing turned into a farce, but one that Claire would thankfully not want to talk about. He had done the deed, and that should be all that mattered, not that any of his mates thought it was his first time.

But there was something else. Something that even Claire did not know. When it was over, before Claire had even left, Jason had gone to the bathroom and thrown up. Claire didn't have a clue. He'd told her he needed to pee. The problem was that it was the act of sex itself that, for some reason, had made him want to puke. He had tried to put it out of his mind ever since – tried to convince himself that it was nothing to do with the sex, and that he had got a stomach bug or had eaten something that didn't agree with him. Deep down, though, he knew that wasn't the case. Was there something wrong with him? What guy throws up after he loses his virginity? His world seemed to be falling apart.

He had hoped that the experience would have got rid of Claire, made her run off crying to her mum and break up with him, but sadly that hadn't happened yet. He knew that he was getting to the point where he would do the breaking up himself. It was either that or he would really lose his temper with her, and he didn't want that to happen again. Even worse, she might suggest having sex again.

"There's something going on with Paul," he said. "I don't care what you say."

"Does it matter? We've got other things to do."

She was trying her best to be sexy with her pathetic attempt at a Marilyn Monroe tone of voice, but she was failing miserably. She went in closer to him and gently kissed his chest, her fingers playing with his small patch of chest hair while she toyed with his nipple with her tongue. She moved to the other nipple as her hand softly glided down his chest and over his stomach towards the waistband of his boxer shorts. She slid her hand underneath, but Jason felt nothing but revulsion. He couldn't believe she was doing this after everything that had happened. He pushed her away.

"Stop it, Claire," he said. "This isn't the time."

She glared at him.

"What do you mean?"

"I mean, *my sweet*, that I have other things on my mind. I'm not interested in your pathetic attempts at turning me on at the moment."

Claire stood up and started buttoning her blouse.

"You're a shit, Jason Mitchell. What with this, and you telling the guys about what we did the other night…"

Jason smiled, and lay back on the bed. Perhaps she would split up with him after all.

"Ah, so that's what's been bothering you, huh? Well, did you really expect me not to tell them? How long have you known me?"

"You said we should do it because you loved me."

"Look at you. You're pathetic. I don't know how I've put up with you for so long, you know that? Do you really think I love you?"

She moved towards him, pleading.

"Don't say that!"

"It was nothing more than sex, Claire. That's it. Get it?"

"Don't, Jason…"

"It took me a bloody long time to get there, but that's all it was. Do you understand? Is that plain enough for you?" He stared at her. "I think you should just go home!"

"What?"

"I said go home. I want to go out with the lads and you're hardly making me want to change my mind. You bore me."

Claire moved around the bed and put her arms on Jason's shoulders. He shrugged them off.

"I could try harder!"

"I don't think so." Jason walked across the room and picked up his mobile phone from where he had thrown it and, satisfied it was working OK, he slid it into his pocket. Claire crossed the room to face him.

"Are you seeing someone else?" she said.

Jason pushed her away and walked towards the door.

"Of course I'm not, you dumb bitch. How can I see someone else? *You're* always here. But it's time to move on."

"What do you mean?"

Jason stared at her from across the room.

"For Christ's sake, Claire. Look at you. You're pathetic. An embarrassment. You're so desperate. I can treat you like a piece of shit and you don't care. That's not attractive, it's pathetic. *You're* pathetic. You would do anything I say. Shit, if I told you to shag Badger, you would. You think I want to go out with someone like that? Do you? You disgust me."

He had said more than he had planned, but now it was time to finish the job and get it over and done with. Claire walked towards him, crying.

"Why are you being like this?" she said.

Jason walked towards her and pushed her.

"Just get out."

"I don't believe this!" Tears were streaming down her face as she tried to put her arms around him, but again he pushed her away.

"I told you to get out, Claire. It's over. Get it?"

Claire stepped away and wiped her eyes and then looked at Jason and slapped him hard in the face.

"You're a bastard, Jason!"

"You little bitch!"

Jason walked towards her, and pushed her down to the ground. She backed away from him, but he still kept coming until she found herself trapped on the floor in the corner of the room with him standing over her. She started to plead with him not to hurt her, but he just stood and watched her. He was shaking through a mixture of anger and excitement. He knew he could do anything he wanted to her at that moment, one final time before throwing her out. He could overpower her with ease, force himself on her and then chuck her out of his house and his life for good. And she would never even try to come back; there would be no fear of that. He breathed in deeply, trying to clear his head. He was aroused for the first time since they'd had sex a couple of days earlier, but then it dawned on him that it wasn't because of the thought of having sex, it was the thought of violence. The realisation horrified him. There really was something wrong with him. He took a couple of deep breaths.

"Get out, Claire," he finally said, quietly. "Get out now. Before I do something that we both regret."

Claire looked at him one last time, unable to believe he was letting her go unharmed, and then got up quickly, opened the bedroom door and ran down the stairs and out of the front door. As the door banged shut, Jason remained where he was standing, relieved that she had gone and that he hadn't hurt her, but also scared as he realised what he was really capable of for the first time, and how close he had come to seriously hurting the girl who, until a few minutes before, had been his girlfriend.

He rushed into the bathroom and threw up for the second time that week.

3

"It was Jason on the phone. He didn't leave a message," Paul said as James walked back into the bedroom.

James got back on to the bed and sat down next to Paul. They had been in the bedroom for more than an hour. It may have been more than six months since those blissful few weeks during the summer holidays, but they had managed to continue from where they had left off. They had not felt pressure to take things further than kissing and cuddling, although both knew it wasn't beyond the realms of possibility that they might do by the time James left the next day, even if neither of them admitted it.

"What do you suppose Jason wanted?" James asked.

"I don't know. I haven't heard from him since the party. He probably wants to tell me that what Luke said was a pack of lies. Or perhaps he just wanted to know if I would answer a call from him. I didn't reply to a text message he sent me the day after the party."

"He won't come around here looking for you, will he?"

"I doubt it. He's scared of my Dad."

Other than saying that his parents were at his uncle's, it was the first time that Paul had mentioned his dad since James had arrived.

"How *are* things with your Dad?" James asked.

Paul's dad had been violent towards both his wife and his son in the past. James knew that Paul didn't like to talk about it, but he was also concerned, as things at home had been getting worse during the summer holidays the year before – which was part of the reason why Paul had spent so much time with James. There were often rumours around the school about things Paul's dad had done, mostly started by a boy who lived next door, but James never knew whether to take them seriously or not – especially as he hadn't been in a position to ask Paul himself during the past few months.

"Nothing much has changed," Paul said. "When there's a bad patch, Mum goes and stays elsewhere, and I stay here."

James couldn't believe what Paul had just told him.

"She lets you stay *here,* alone with him, despite

knowing what he's like?"

"Yeah."

"Couldn't she take you with her?"

"If she's staying with another bloke, they hardly want me tagging along."

It wasn't the first time that his mum had had an affair. There had been one before Paul was born. She had only come back because she was pregnant. Paul was still unsure whether she had affairs because his dad was like he was, or whether his dad behaved like he did because she had affairs. It seemed like a vicious circle.

"I can look after myself now," Paul continued.

"Can you?"

"Mostly."

James placed his hand on Paul's shoulder.

"What about the other times, Paul?" Paul didn't answer; instead he just looked down at the bed. "What about the other times?" James repeated.

"I manage, OK? I manage with my bruises, just as you manage with yours."

He got up and walked over to the wardrobe at the far end of the bedroom. He grinned. The serious moment had passed.

"I've got something for you," he said. "A present. You're really going to like it."

James sat up on the bed, wondering what the present was. Was this where he suddenly found out that the weekend was a hoax, and that Jason himself was the surprise present?

"Should I be worried?" he said.

"No, no. This is for real. You're going to really like it. At least, I hope you will anyway. Now close your eyes."

James reluctantly closed his eyes, not really knowing what to expect. Paul bent down and reached behind the wardrobe, his hand cutting through a cobweb as he did so. He withdrew his hand and wiped it on his trousers to get rid of the cobweb, and then slid it behind the wardrobe once more. He pulled out a large roll of paper held together by a piece of ribbon with a bow on it. He placed it on his friend's lap.

"Ok, you can open them," he said.

James opened his eyes and looked down. It was quite obvious that it was a poster of some sort.

"Can I open it?"

"Yeah. Go on!" James unrolled the poster as Paul spoke. "I'm not sure if it's the kind of stuff you're into. I thought you could frame it or something."

The poster laid out before James was old. *Very* old. James guessed it was from around 1920, but he wasn't sure, and he couldn't find a date. The edges had a few scuffs and small tears, but he knew that was to be expected for something nearly a hundred years old. The poster was advertising a film starring a man called Jack Pickford. James knew a little bit about him as he had seen one of his films before, when his uncle had sent him a silent version of *Tom Sawyer*. He was the brother of Mary Pickford who, James knew, had been the "Queen of Hollywood" during the 1910s and 1920s. There had been a scandal surrounding Jack, but James couldn't remember what it was exactly. The picture in the poster looked like a still from the film, with Pickford comically fainting in the arms of someone after a car crash. The film was called *Mile-a-Minute Kendall*. James knew it was a collector's item. He looked at Paul.

"This is beautiful," he said. "But where did you get it? This is worth money; you can't afford something like this."

"I found it. In the loft. We had been hearing scratching coming from the loft and assumed it was a mouse or something. Dad kept saying he was going up there to set a trap, but never did, so I went up there a couple of weeks back when he was out of it. There was loads of stuff up there. Old papers and things. They must have been here when we moved in. They're not ours. I had a sort through and found that. I thought it might be something to do with what you were into. Do you like it?"

"I love it. It's awesome." He kissed Paul on the cheek. "But you should sell it or something, especially if it's in this kind of condition. You remember that old shop I go to on Fitzgerald Street? He'd take it off you. Or you could sell it online or something."

"It's for you. I don't want to sell it!"

"Are you sure it's not your mum and dad's? That they don't know it's up there?" James asked.

"Positive. It was just stacked up in the corner with a load of other crap, away from all our junk. Besides, there's no reason why something like that would belong to us. It's definitely from whoever lived here before –

and they moved out ten years ago."

"I'll take it to Alfred and see what he makes of it. This is really nice, thank you."

James rolled the poster back up and propped it against the wall.

"I suppose you want me to pay you for this?" he said.

"Only in kind!"

CHAPTER TEN

1

When Jonathan arrived at Andrew's flat for dinner on Saturday night, he couldn't believe the change since his last visit a couple of days earlier. He had been wary of even agreeing to eat there considering how dirty some parts of it had looked before. He really could do without a case of food poisoning, but Andrew had obviously made an effort. A huge effort. The papers that had previously littered the floor were gone, and the carpet had not just been hoovered but *cleaned*. The kitchen looked so different without the washing up piled on the worktops. Even more surprising was that the computer was now standing on a desk, which looked as if it had been put together just a few hours earlier (as it, indeed, had). The old-style television had gone, replaced by a new slim, widescreen effort which seemed just a little too big for the room in which it was housed. A small music system had also appeared and was sitting on a small chest of drawers that was also new. The androgynous voice of Chet Baker emerged from the speakers.

"You like what I've done with the place?" Andrew asked, as he cooked their stir-fry.

"It's one hell of a transformation in two days! It looks like you've spent a fortune."

"The money was sitting in the bank, and it's not doing me any good there, is it? Despite what they say, a teacher's pay can be very nice if you don't have a family to look after. And, as you may have guessed, I don't have a wife and kids – well, none that I am going to tell you about! I saw the look on your face when you first came in here the other day, and it was a bit of a wake-up call. I hadn't noticed how far I had let the flat go. And myself, come to that. I realised that something had to be done if I was going to start having 'gentleman callers.' I even started looking around to see if there was anywhere better available. I could do with somewhere bigger, really."

"Well, it goes without saying it looks much better. It looks nice, Andrew."

"Thanks. It took bloody hours to do."

"I can imagine."

"It was my own fault. I shouldn't have let it get that bad."

Jonathan walked into the kitchen area and leaned against the now grime-free worktop while he watched Andrew cook.

"Smells good," he said.

"Thanks. It will probably taste foul."

"I'm sure it won't."

"It's the first thing that's been cooked in this kitchen in months – except for the ready meals in the microwave – which has also been cleaned, I might add, in case you were wondering."

"I wasn't, but I appreciate the effort. Is there a clean duvet cover on the bed, too?" Jonathan said, smiling.

"Cheeky bugger."

"How's things at the school?"

"Oh, you know. Much the same. The kid who was bullying the boy that I was telling you about has been off for a couple of days. I haven't heard any of the teachers complaining about his truancy, unsurprisingly. Apparently, he beat up his friend at a party during the week and he landed up in A&E."

Jonathan raised his eyebrows.

"Nice. Remind me never to be *his* friend."

"I will. Although I'd disown you if you even tried! It's a shame, though. Luke is a good lad. Just got in with the wrong crowd. Perhaps the beating has given him a way out."

"Maybe."

"Hey, I need to dish this up. The one thing I haven't bought is a table. Not enough room really in this stupid little flat. We're stuck with eating it on our laps, if that's OK?"

"Sure, I don't mind. I'll open the wine, yeah?"

"Sounds good to me."

"You got a corkscrew?"

"Oh yes. I'm never without a corkscrew," Andrew said, taking one from a drawer and throwing it to Jonathan.

Andrew added the final touches to the meal while Jonathan opened the wine and poured two glasses. He sipped at it as he carried it through to the living area.

"The wine's good."

"Wine always is. Just like the food, I hope."

Andrew carried the stir-fry through into the lounge, and the two men began to eat.

"This *is* good," Paul said.

"Thanks. I thought I'd be out of practice, but it's not too bad. And thank you for coming." He picked up his glass of wine and held it up. "Cheers," he said.

"Cheers."

2

James and Paul lay naked on the bed. For a while, they said nothing.

They hadn't had sex, but the end results of their clumsy fumbling had been the same. They had stunned themselves into a kind of pleasurable embarrassment following their first sexual experience. Neither of them had done anything like that before but it hadn't come as a complete surprise that the evening had ended in that way. But now a kind of melancholy had descended. James turned onto his side and put his arm across Paul's chest, pulling him closer towards him.

"What's up?" he said.

"I'm worried about Monday," Paul replied quietly.

"About Jason?"

Paul nodded.

"It'll be OK. Everything will work out somehow. We're halfway there already."

He kissed Paul lightly on the neck and Paul turned to face him. James could see tears appearing in his eyes.

"This has been so cool," Paul said. "I just hope we get to do it again. I don't know if this is going to work. But I want it to so badly. Everything would be fine without Jason."

James tried to calm Paul's fears.

"Of course this will happen again. Look, we can sort out Jason, somehow," he said.

"Nobody stands up to him, you know that."

"Luke did."

"Yeah, and look what happened. He landed up in hospital. Jane thought Jason was going to kill him." He was quiet for a few seconds. "I think you've been really brave through this whole thing. I don't know how I would have coped if it had been me."

"It hasn't been much easier for you, Paul. You've had your dad and Jason to cope with." James ran his fingers over Paul's cheek and kissed his nose. "Do your parents go away very often at the weekend?"

"No, sadly not."

"That's a shame. I could get used to this. Not that *this* weekend's over just yet of course." Paul forced a smile. "Look, everything's going to be fine. But we've got to be strong and stick together. If we do that, everything will be fine."

"I know."

"I think everything needs to change *now*. On Monday at school, we don't pretend that this weekend never happened. We go to school *together*, united against Jason. We need to make that step, show him that things have changed. If Mr. Green can come out to his pupils, then we can do this."

3

It was a nightmare that woke James up, with the images continuing to linger in his mind and refusing to go away when he closed his eyes and tried to drift off back to sleep again.

He looked across at Paul who, surprisingly, had slept through the commotion of James screaming out in his sleep. Paul slept peacefully, and James watched his chest rise and fall with each breath that he took. He looked as if he didn't have a care in the world. James knew that nothing could be further from the truth. Not only did he have Jason to contend with, he also had his messed-up home life. Perhaps that's why he was so tired that he could sleep through the commotion. Or perhaps just having James here with him for the night meant he could relax enough to catch up on some much-needed sleep.

James tried to put the nightmare out of his mind. He kept telling himself that it was just that: a nightmare. Perhaps the bizarre events of the past seven days had simply caught up with him. It wasn't even a week since he had been videoed in the changing rooms and now, here he was, sleeping with a friend that he had thought he would never speak to again. As the contestants on TV talent shows were fond of saying, it had been a "roller-coaster ride." Part of James didn't really know what to make of it at all. There were times when he understood everything – and others when he understood nothing. He thought he had a good idea of what had made Paul side with Jason all those months ago, but he was no closer now than he was two years earlier to getting to the bottom of why Jason did what he did. What was it that made him the way he was? No-one seemed to know. Most people didn't seem to care.

James noticed that the room had got considerably brighter over the past twenty minutes or so as the sun began to rise. The birds were singing their morning chorus at a volume that James never heard on his tree-less street. There was a surprising amount of heat in the sun as it began to pour through the windows. It was a sign of the hot day that the weather forecasters had promised – a day that would have been perfect for lazing around in Paul's back garden, but James knew that he would never be forgiven by his mother if he didn't go home for Sunday lunch. She seemed somewhat shocked that he had wanted to stop at a friend's house for a night in the first place. But not as shocked as he was. She would probably be thinking that he had a girlfriend, after all. The next thing would be that he'd be sat down by his mother while she told him the facts of life. He wouldn't put it past her. However, getting Paul pregnant was one thing that he didn't have to worry about.

The sunlight began to take away the last remnants of the nightmare, and James began to relax. He looked up at the ceiling and played over in his mind the happy events of the previous day. Paul stirred in his sleep and turned over, his arm coming to rest across James's chest. Suddenly, James felt safe, his eye-lids felt heavy and he slowly drifted back to sleep until the alarm on his mobile phone woke him and Paul up a few hours later.

James became fully awake quickly, while Paul simply groaned and opened one eye as if it was the biggest task in the world.

"Good morning," he said, sleepily.

"Morning, sexy."

"You sleep OK?"

"Reasonably. You?"

"Sound-o. What's the time?"

"Ten o'clock. We need to get up. I've got to be home for lunch."

"I know, I know. I wish you could stay here though."

"Me, too. I'm sorry."

"Don't be. It's not your fault."

Paul told James to stay in bed while he went

downstairs to make breakfast. He returned ten minutes later with coffee, cereal and toast on a tray that he placed in the centre of the bed.

Paul was surprisingly subdued as they ate breakfast together, saying simply that he was quiet because he knew that James had to go back home after they had had such a good time together. James knew it was much more likely due to having to face Jason again the next day at school. It was something that neither of them was looking forward to, but it was Paul who was going to have to face the consequences of running away on the night of the party, and Jason's beating of Luke was ample proof of just how far he was willing to go when people were disloyal to him.

When they had finished eating, the boys padded along the hallway to the bathroom and stepped into the shower, the hot water blasting away any remnants of sleep that may have been lingering. They kissed and hugged under the running water, but there was none of the fun and playfulness of the previous day. James secretly wondered if there ever would be again, but tried to put it out of his mind, telling himself that he was just being silly.

As they stepped out of the shower and started to get dry, James said:

"Let's go and see Luke and Jane. We've got time before I need to be home. His house is on the way anyway."

Paul seemed less than enthusiastic.

"Really? Today?"

"Yeah. You need to thank him for what he did for you last week. Now is as good a time as any."

4

James and Paul had assumed that Luke would have been at his house, but he was instead staying at Jane's, and so James called his mum to say he would be a bit late for dinner, and the two boys walked the mile or so to Jane's house.

When they got there, a rather surprised Jane answered the door and led them up to her room. It soon became clear why Luke preferred to stay there. Jane's room was massive; a converted loft space that ran almost across the entire house. Both James and Paul could have fitted their own bedrooms in the room side by side and still have space left.

Luke was propped up on the bed, dressed in a pair of well-worn, not-very-becoming jogging bottoms. He wasn't wearing a shirt, and James and Paul wondered whether this was due to it being a hot day, habit, or because the touch of the material against his body hurt him. His chest was heavily bruised and bandaged, but he smiled as James and Paul entered the room.

"Well, well," he said. "And when did this reunion happen?" he asked.

"Over the last week," James said. "At the weekend, really."

"Well, it's good to see you two together," Luke said. "Perhaps this wasn't for nothing after all."

"You look terrible," Paul said.

"Thanks."

"I didn't mean that. I meant your bruises. They look awful."

"I'd like to say they look worse than they feel, but it wouldn't be true. They hurt like hell."

"Are you feeling any better?"

"Not a great deal, to be honest. But I'm hoping to go back to school tomorrow. I get fed up with being at home. Even with Jane to keep me company!" He winked at her. "Besides, I want to know Jason is up to."

Jane told James and Paul to sit down, and she went over to the bed and sat next to Luke, holding his hand.

"I'm sorry for what happened to you, Luke," Paul said. "I didn't want any of this to happen."

"It's OK," Luke said. "I didn't want it to happen either. But we're glad it did in a weird kind of way. We needed to get away from Jason. Now we have no excuse. The break has been made. We're really happy about that. I'm not sure we would have done it, otherwise. But what about you two? Are you...together?"

James and Paul looked at each other.

"Are we?" James asked.

Paul nodded.

"I think so."

"Good," Luke said. "And how are you going to break the news to Jason?"

"We haven't worked that bit out yet," James said.

"Then don't tell him anything. Just go to school tomorrow like you've come here today. Together. You know he'll break you down if you don't. You have got to have each other's backs."

"You can do this," Jane said. "Jason isn't as strong as he was. He's lost us. He broke up with Claire yesterday."

"Really?" James said.

"He tried to phone me yesterday, but I didn't take his call," Paul said.

"Claire said it was awful," Jane went on. "He really lost it. She seemed to think he scared himself as much as he scared her. But everything's going wrong for him. You need to make the most of it. Even Mr. Green came out at school. You know that. If you have problems, you can go to him. Just don't let Jason rule your life. We know we both have had something to do with that, and we are both really sorry but, as you are well aware, Jason is very good at getting you to do things you don't want to do."

"It's OK," James said. "Everything is going to be OK."

CHAPTER ELEVEN

1

The next morning, Paul awoke from a dream in which James was living with him. His Dad had left for good and the two boys were happy and in love.

When the alarm woke him up, Paul still expected James to be lying beside him. When he realised he wasn't there, Paul turned over and stared up at the ceiling, coming to terms with the fact that his dream was not yet a reality and that, in a matter of just an hour or so, he would have to face Jason for the first time since the party, but at least he and James had made plans to walk into school together. The united front was going to be important.

Paul eventually got out of bed and stumbled across the bedroom floor and pulled the bedroom curtains open, only to see that Jason was leaning up against the fence at the end of the garden path. Paul felt his stomach start to churn, but hoped that he was meeting somebody else there and tried to forget about him as he walked through to the bathroom and showered. Twenty minutes later, showered and dressed, Paul once again peered out of the bedroom curtains. Jason was still there. Now, he was looking up towards Paul's bedroom window. Paul tried to get out of sight as quickly as possible, hoping that he hadn't been seen already. In the end, it wouldn't matter. He knew that he was going to have to face Jason eventually, so it might as well be on the walk into school – if he made it as far as school.

Paul picked up his mobile phone and texted James, telling him that Jason was outside his house and that they would have to walk in together another day. James replied quickly, saying that they could walk in together anyway, and it would be one way to let Jason know that things had changed. As tempting as that was, Paul declined the offer. He didn't even really know why, other than to put off letting Jason know what had happened over the weekend. He told himself he would do it later. Get over seeing Jason for the first time since the party and *then* tell him later about him and James.

As Paul went downstairs and made himself some tea and toast for breakfast, he wondered what was in store for him. He was on a downer now that the weekend with James was over, and he didn't even bother switching the TV on as he ate. Instead, he gulped his breakfast down and packed his school bag as quickly as he could and went out of the front door, thinking that he might as well get things over and done with as soon as possible. Well, *some* things, at least.

Jason turned towards him as he approached the street, and pushed himself up away from the fence on which he had been perching.

"Well, well," he said. "You're alive then?"

"What do you mean?" Paul said, as he pulled the garden gate shut, trying to look as relaxed and casual as he possibly could.

"Nothing. Just saying. Not seen you around."

"You were the one not at school, Jason. Not me."

"Alright. Keep your hair on." They started walking slowly down the street. "So, are you OK?"

"Yeah. You?"

"Fine."

"Where's all the others? You normally walk in with them."

"You mean you were expecting Luke and Jane to walk in with us? Hardly likely, all things considered, don't you think?"

"I didn't mean them, Jason."

"Badger and Smithy are going in a bit later. Just told them I wanted to go on ahead, that's all. I wanted to make sure there were no hard feelings about the party the other night. I don't know what nonsense Luke was telling you in there, but there was nothing planned for you. I promise."

"Really?"

"Of course."

"How did you know that he was telling me about something you had planned, then? You didn't speak to him afterwards."

"Don't try and get cocky, Paul. This is me being nice."

"Then why did you two fight?"

"Oh, you know how it is. People are friends, and then they start going their different ways. Tensions, my friend. Just tensions. Luke is coming to a crossroads in his life. These things happen, don't they? One person wants something that the other person doesn't want."

Paul did know, all too well. He knew that he had his own crossroads to deal with right now, and he was beginning to doubt whether he would choose James over an easy life. He wanted to be with him, but knew that an easier option would be to just go along with whatever Jason wanted. But Paul wasn't sure he could do that anymore. Things had happened, and there was no way to undo them. Images from his dream flashed into his mind, and he suddenly remembered how happy he had been over the weekend.

"I came here really to make sure that you were OK. That you were alive," Jason went on.

"Of course I'm alive," Paul said, wondering what Jason was getting at. "Why wouldn't I be?"

"Nobody saw you over the weekend."

Of course, this is about the time he tried to call and didn't get an answer, Paul thought.

"I am allowed to stay indoors, you know?"

"Sure you are. I just thought you might be avoiding me. You didn't answer my calls."

Paul hesitated.

"My battery was dead. I didn't notice you'd rung

until late at night, and so I didn't call you back. I didn't want to wake you up."

Jason smiled. "Well, that obviously explains that," he said, making it clear that he didn't believe a word of what Paul had just told him.

The boys walked on in uncomfortable silence. Jason was playing a game, and Paul didn't like playing at the best of times, and it was even worse when he didn't know the rules from the outset, and what you had to do in order to win. School was still a long ten minutes walk away when the newsagents came into view. Paul had an idea.

"Go on without me," he said. "I just want to get some chocolate for break."

Jason put his hand on Paul's shoulder, and rubbed his knuckles into his shoulder.

"Oh, I can come in with you. There's no hurry, we're nice and early anyway."

Paul realised that there was no hope of him losing Jason. After Paul had gone into the shop and bought the chocolate that he didn't want, they continued on their way to school.

"Me and Claire broke up over the weekend," Jason said.

"I heard."

Jason stopped dead in his tracks.

"Oh yeah? From who?"

Paul realised he had given the game away that he had been to see Luke and Jane.

"Oh, I don't remember. Somewhere on Facebook,

I think. You know how quickly these things get around."

"It was just one of those things, you know?" Jason went on. "You know what it's like with women. But it was a mutual decision. She's upset, obviously, but she'll get over me."

"How about you? Will you get over *her*?"

"Get over her? Sure. Like I said, one of those things. I'll find someone else. But Claire's free and single now. Perhaps you should make a play for her."

Paul forced a smile before Jason said:

"Nah, she's not your type, is she? I wonder what your type is."

He didn't have to say any more. Jason knew that something was going on, and Paul realised that things were about to get worse. He needed to warn James that somehow Jason had figured things out, and that the shit was about to hit the fan whether they told him or not.

2

Paul had texted James before classes started to let him know what had happened on the way in to school. They arranged to meet behind the cricket pavilion, as they had done before. James was worried all morning that Paul was somehow just going to try to forget about what had happened at the weekend. Paul had buckled in the cinema the year before, so what was to say he wouldn't do it again?

"Luke didn't come to school today," Paul said. "I guess he wasn't feeling well enough."

"Luke can look after himself," James replied. "This is about Jason. We can't let him get the better of us."

"I don't know what we're going to do."

"Why has the plan changed, Paul? Why can't we just do what we planned? Just let him find out. What's he going to do that he hasn't done already?"

"I don't know."

"What good did doing what he wanted do you? You went to his party, and he had planned to screw you over. It's only because of Luke that he didn't manage to go through with it. You're no safer doing what he wants than just walking away."

"I know that."

"Then what is the problem?"

"I'm scared!"

"I'm scared, too. For the whole of the last year I've been scared. Every bloody day. But you came to me, remember? You were the one who came to my house last week and told me you wanted things to be how they used to be. You were the one who got us together over the weekend. It felt right. Didn't it?"

Paul didn't reply.

"*Didn't it?*"

Paul nodded.

"Yeah, it felt right," he said quietly.

The bell sounded in the distance to signal the end of lunch break.

"I'd better be going," Paul said.

He started to walk away, but James called after him. Paul stopped and turned back towards him.

"You need to make your decision," James said to him. "If you're changing your mind, I want to know now. Otherwise there's no turning back. Now, are we going to do this or not?"

Paul hesitated for a moment and then walked up to James and kissed him.

"Yeah, we're going to do it," he said. "I'm not changing my mind. I promise."

3

Andrew Green was in a defiant mood. His weekend had been good – better than any for some time, not least because he hadn't spent it alone.

Something was happening between him and Jonathan. He wasn't sure if a long-lasting relationship was going to take place between the two of them, but at least *something* was going on, and that "something" was the nearest he had ever got to having a relationship with another man.

However, his day had been marred by the constant reminder that he had to speak to Jason Mitchell at some point about the situation with James Marsh. He wasn't sure how he was going to tackle it, but he knew that he had to, as he realised that The Head was never going to budge on the issue. Their meeting the previous week had been proof enough of that. He had been surprised that he hadn't had a visit from him given the fact he had now talked to all but one of his classes in year ten or above. Each one was easier than the last, not least because he was well aware that word travelled fast, and everyone already knew what he was going to say. He had explained to them that he was doing it because there were rumours he wanted to deal with, and because he was aware of homophobic bullying within the school. He knew that it was putting his job on the line, but, at this stage, he didn't really care. If things didn't change at the school, he was probably going to leave anyway. Something had to give.

When he had been on morning break duty, Andrew had found Jason (back at school for the first time after the notorious party) and asked him to come and see him after school. He could have seen him during lunch break but wanted him to sweat it out for a while. Andrew thought he might as well make the little bastard suffer if he could. He might as well get a little of his own medicine.

Ten minutes after the end of school, Jason strolled into Andrew's classroom. He wore an amalgam of his games kit and school uniform, making Andrew wonder whether, if he hadn't asked to see Jason, James might have suffered the same fate after the day's games lesson as he had the week before. He tried to put the idea out of his mind.

Andrew looked up from his desk and wondered

how much of the mud clinging to Jason's legs would find its way on to the chairs and floor of his classroom. He was rather thankful for the cleaning staff.

"It would be polite if you knocked before you came in the classroom, Jason," he said, trying to sound as if he wasn't nervous about the forthcoming encounter.

"Why? You do stuff in here you shouldn't?"

Andrew ignored the comment. While Jason's class was the one group he had yet to talk to, he was well aware that word would have reached him already, and Jason was bound to use it against him whenever he could.

"And it might also be a good idea if you showered after games as well," Andrew went on. "I don't want that mud over my chairs."

"Want to join me in the showers, Sir?" Jason said, sneering.

Andrew slammed both hands down on the desk.

"That's enough," he said. "I am not willing to be sneered at and taunted in my own classroom by you. Do you understand? If you want to play games, then that's fine, Jason. But be prepared to lose if you play against me. Now, sit your arse down on that chair before I really lose my temper."

Jason tried to not look surprised at the sudden outburst from his usually placid teacher, and slowly pulled a chair up to the front desk, letting the legs scrape across the floor to make the maximum amount of noise. He turned the chair around so that the back was facing his teacher, and then sat down, his muddy legs straddling the seat and his shorts stretching to breaking point.

"So, what can I do for you, *Sir*?" Jason said.

"Turn the chair around and sit down properly," Andrew said.

Jason didn't move.

Andrew sighed, and opened the drawer of his desk. He took out a mobile phone, and started playing the footage that had been captured in the changing rooms the week before. He lay the phone down on the desk in front of Jason. Jason watched if for a couple of seconds.

"Nice phone, Sir." He leaned in towards Andrew. "But you really shouldn't have videos of naked boys on there, should you? People will talk."

Andrew snatched the phone back, and dropped it back into the drawer, and then slammed it shut loudly.

"One of my form brought that to my attention last week. He was kind enough to leave his phone with me today."

"Yes, that *was* nice of him, wasn't it? I'm sure that it's been very useful for you in here all alone at the end of the day." Jason lifted up his shirt and slowly scratched his stomach, grinning at Andrew as he did so. He was taunting him. "So, what did you want to see me about?" he said finally.

"Don't play games with me, Jason. You know damned well why I asked you to come and see me. I am not willing to sit back and tolerate behaviour like that."

"You think I had something to do with it?"

"So innocent, aren't you? I'm not stupid, but you might be. You took your face out of the video, Jason, but not your voice."

Jason realised Andrew was right. How could he have been so stupid? It was because Claire had been there, distracting him as always.

"Events such as those on that phone are not going to happen again, do you understand me?" Andrew went on.

Jason leaned forward, and started drumming his fingers on the table.

"Ah, so this is about old Marshy, huh? Nice kid, don't you think?"

"So what have you got against him, Jason?"

"Nothing, Sir."

"You call what's on that phone 'nothing'?"

"Not at all. You can't prove that's my voice. You shouldn't go around making accusations."

Andrew stood up and slowly walked around Jason until he was standing behind him. His patience was about to snap. He bent forward and whispered through gritted teeth into Jason's ear.

"If I had my way, you little bastard, you would be expelled here and now. In fact, if that happened it would be the highlight of my school year so far. Sadly, it's not going to. Instead you can have the pleasure of my company tomorrow, Wednesday and Thursday after school. Detention."

He waited a few seconds and then walked back to his desk. Jason stood up and pointed his finger at

Andrew.

"You can't get away with this. My Dad won't let you."

Andrew grabbed hold of Jason and pushed him up against the wall.

"I don't care how rich your dad is, Jason. He doesn't have any power here. Now, if you are not here for the next three nights, then what's on that phone gets back to him. And I'm pretty sure he won't be very pleased, Jason."

He walked away as Jason rearranged his clothing and walked to the door.

"You shouldn't have done that," he said, and walked out, letting the door slam shut behind him.

Andrew sat down at his desk. Jason was right, of course. He shouldn't have pushed him up against the wall like that. If he got reported, it would mean that he would be leaving the teaching profession whether he liked it or not. But, somehow, he thought that Jason would cut his losses. The last thing he would want was for his Dad to know what he had been getting up to.

4

Ironically, if Andrew hadn't detained Jason after school, he would never have bumped into James, who had gone out to the shop he went to regularly that dealt in records, old movie posters and memorabilia. He had the poster that Paul had given him in a carrier bag, and thought that Alfred, the old man who ran the shop, might be able to give him some more information on it, or maybe what it was worth – not that he would dream of selling it. He could have done the research himself on the internet, it wasn't difficult to do, but that would have prevented him from showing off his new prized possession, which was half of the reason why he was going to see Alfred in the first place.

The shop was about a twenty-minute walk from his house, and so James had hurried home after school in order to make sure he would get there before closing time. The familiar smell of decades-old records, books and posters met him as he opened the door to the shop as if he were an old friend. James wasn't surprised to see the store was devoid of customers. It really only ever got anything approaching busy on a Saturday and, even then, it was unusual to find more than two people browsing the shelves at any one time. James had noticed it had got less busy over the last couple of years. Other shops on the same road had closed down, and so there were less people walking past and being lured in by something that caught their eye in the window.

Alfred McKechnie, the owner of the shop, who James now regarded as a friend, looked up from his copy of *The Complete Sherlock Holmes* as James walked in. He had been reading the volume ever since James had started going to the shop a couple of years earlier, confiding in him that once he got to the end he simply started over again at the beginning. Holmes was an old friend who kept him company in the often-lonely days behind the counter, he had said. The elf-like figure smiled and stood up as James walked over to him.

"Master James," he said, "what brings you here on a school day?"

"Hey Alf. I've got a favour to ask," James said. "I've got a poster here that someone has given me, and I thought you might be able to tell me more about it. I think it's a special one."

"A special one, eh? Oh, I should think I could help you out there. I'm hardly rushed off my feet, am I? And it's not like I don't know what happens at the end of *The Musgrave Ritual.*" He patted his tatty volume of Sherlock Holmes. "So, what have you got?"

James handed him the hard cardboard tube and Alfred popped the plastic cap off from one end and peered inside.

"The problem with these blasted tubes is getting the poster back out again without tearing them. Especially the old ones. The paper tears so damned easily. And I'm guessing it *is* an old one. Am I right?"

James nodded as Alfred carefully prided the poster out of the tube and unrolled it. He stared at it for a few seconds and then looked across at James.

"Well, this is certainly interesting. And where did a young man like you get something as precious as this?" he asked.

"A friend gave it to me."

Alfred looked at him.

"A *lady* friend?"

James shook his head.

"No, not a lady friend, Alfred."

"Then a *very good* friend. You don't come across this kind of thing every day – and certainly not in this condition."

Alfred picked up his walking stick and manoeuvred himself out from behind the counter, shuffled across the shop floor and turned the sign on the door so that it read "closed" and then moved back to James.

"Let's have a cup of tea, and you can tell me all about where this little treasure came from."

James walked behind the counter and followed Alfred through a door that led into a small room which housed a small kitchen area at one end and stacks of records, DVDs and books at the other.

"I didn't see you on Saturday," Alfred said. "Did you do anything special?"

James suddenly felt a pang of guilt for not going to the shop at the weekend as he normally would.

"I just spent some time with a friend," he said, a little sheepishly.

"And so you should do at your age. The friend who bought you this?"

"He didn't buy it for me. He found it in his loft. It must have been left there by whoever lived there last."

"A very lucky find. So, what do you know about this poster then, James?"

"Not much. I thought you might be able to tell me something."

Alfred started making the tea.

"Well, I may be wrong, but *Mile-a-Minute Kendall* is a lost film, I think. You know about lost films, don't you?"

James nodded. For as long as he had been interested in silent film he had been intrigued about what were known as "lost films." He knew that as much as 90% of silent films were considered lost, with no copy of them being known to exist. Sometimes his Uncle David would tell him about a long lost film that had just been found somewhere, and said it was quite a big deal.

"So," Alfred went on, "this may be all that survives of this film. Not many of Jack Pickford's films survive, so I'm pretty certain it's lost. What do you know about Jack?"

"I know there was a scandal of some kind, but I don't know what kind of scandal."

Alfred brought the two mugs of tea across the kitchen and set them down in front of James.

"Yes, there was a scandal," he said. "Jack was the brother of Mary Pickford, you know that much. But he liked to party. Wine, women and song were what *he* liked. He married an actress called Olive Thomas when he was about twenty-one or so, and the story goes that they were on a kind of second honeymoon a few years later and in Paris. They had been out partying for the night, and, when they got back, Olive drank some poison by mistake. She died a few days later in hospital. Now, there were rumours at the time that Jack had a part in her death or that she drank the poison on purpose, to commit suicide. But nothing was ever proved. The newspapers played on the fact that Jack was a party-goer and blamed him for his wife's death whether he had anything to do with it or not."

"Did he?"

"No-one knows really. Probably not, I would say. He was just someone for the press to pick on. You know how they can be. Wasn't any different back then. But he died about thirteen years later, in his mid-thirties."

James frowned.

"That's not a very nice story to go with my poster."

"I won't tell you the rest, then."

"You mean there's more?" Alfred drank some of his tea. James watched him and said: "Go on, you might as well tell me now."

"Well, the director of the film in the poster is William Desmond Taylor, and he was murdered just a year after Olive died. No-one ever found out who did it."

James drank the rest of his tea and put the mug down on the table.

"Well, thanks for cheering me up," he said.

"Aww, that was all ninety years ago. There's nothing sad about your poster. I'm sure they had a great time making this film. You need to get yourself a nice frame and put it on the wall."

"Yes, I'll get one as soon as I can."

Alfred thought for a moment.

"I might have one here," he said.

He got up from his chair and disappeared into what James thought was a cupboard, but turned out to be the entrance to a staircase. James watched as Alfred tottered up the stairs. He reappeared a minute later.

"Yes, I've got one you can have," he said. "But it's very big. You'll have to get your Mum to come and pick it up with you in her car."

"That's great, Alf. How much will I owe you for it?"

"Oh, no need to worry about that," Alfred said. "In fact, I was wondering…you're going to stay on at school aren't you? In sixth form?" James nodded. "Well, why don't you start working here for a few hours a week during the summer, and then on Saturdays when you go back to school in September? It will give you a little pocket money – I can't pay you much, but something's better than nothing, isn't it? And I'm not getting any younger, either. It's either find someone like you to come in and help me, or shut the shop a couple of days per week – or sell up altogether. What do you say? Would you like to help me out a little?"

James felt like kissing him.

"That would be great!" he said.

"I hoped you might say that. Well, once your exams are over at the end of May we'll sort out when you can come in. But now you must let this old man go home. I get tired these days."

They went back into the main area of the shop. Alfred rolled the poster up, put it back in the tube, and then passed it to James. The two of them walked towards the door. Alfred opened the door for James.

"Thanks for everything, Alfred," James said.

"Thank *you*."

James walked out of the door, and then turned and smiled at his elderly friend. The old man waved at him through the glass of the door, and then James started the walk home. It had been a great visit. His poster was a real rarity, and now he had a part-time job, too. What with that and what had happened at the weekend, things were definitely looking up – until he saw Jason walking up the road towards him.

James contemplated running off and hiding somewhere until he had walked past, but he realised it was too late, for Jason had already seen him. James tried to look unflustered as he approached, and then tried to pass, Jason. He thought he had managed to pass him without incident until Jason grabbed at the poster.

"Well, well. What have we got here?"

He pulled the poster tube from under James's arm and waved it around in the air.

"A present for me?" Jason said.

James moved towards him.

"Give it back, Jason. It was a present! I've had enough of your shit."

Jason stared at him, surprised at James's courage, and then started to walk in circles around him.

"Do you know what I've been doing this afternoon, Marsh? I have been talking to that queer teacher that you like so much. He likes you, too, doesn't he? Not too keen on me, though. *Somebody* had shown him what happened in the changing rooms last week. I think it gave him quite a hard-on when he saw it. I think he had one while I was there, too. Now, the person who showed it to him wouldn't have been you, would it?"

"It wasn't me, Jason. Why would I show him that?"

Jason grabbed hold of his ear and pulled it hard.

"If I find out that it was you, then you and me are going to have a little falling out. And that's not going to be very pleasant for you, I promise. You think you've had it bad already, but you will wish you hadn't been born. Believe me."

He let go of his ear and pushed James away.

"Now," he said, "let's see what this is a poster of. A naked man, I bet. You like naked men, don't you?"

"Not as much as you do!" James replied, saying the words before he thought about what he was doing.

"What did you say, you little bastard?"

Jason took a swing with the poster tube and it smacked into James's arm. James shouted for Jason to stop, but he hit him again before taking the top off the tube and peering inside.

"Don't do anything to it, Jason. It's worth money."

Jason stopped and looked across at James.

"Well, that's very useful information, Marsh. Perhaps I'll take this and see what I can get for it. That sounds like a very good idea. See if I can make some money out of you. It will at least pay me for my time in detention over the next three nights, won't it?" He poked James in the chest with the poster. "Either way, you won't be seeing this again," he said, and walked off down the road, waving the poster in the air.

5

They had finally kissed. On Saturday night, when Jonathan was about to go home, and he and Andrew were saying their goodbyes at the front door of the flat, Jonathan had leaned in and Andrew hadn't run away. Andrew had known all night that it was going to happen and had prepared himself. And it *had* happened. And now, two nights later, the pair had to overcome an even bigger obstacle – making Andrew forget about work. Considering everything that was happening at the school, it was hard to do, and Andrew was only used to forgetting about it through drinking enough wine to send him to sleep. With Jonathan there, that wouldn't be an option.

Jonathan had positioned himself on the sofa so that he was sitting behind Andrew, and massaging his shoulders through his shirt. He was trying to relax him while the teacher told him about his eventful meeting with Jason after school.

"He sounds like a little bastard," Jonathan said, when Andrew had finished speaking.

"He is. A *spiteful* little bastard, but I have no idea why. I'm not sure even he does."

"Blame the parents."

"Perhaps, but if the parenting is that bad then you have to feel sympathy for the kid – and I don't feel any sympathy for Jason Mitchell right now. No matter what goes on at home, he knows right from wrong."

"You think he has other problems?"

"Such as?"

"I don't know. I just wondered if there was something else going on that you hadn't thought about?"

"Not quite sure what it could be. All I know is that the school is failing if it can't keep him in check. And if the school is failing, then it means that I am, too. And I find that difficult."

"You did all you could," Jonathan said. "You can only do so much. You can't bring down the system – or even a gang of bullies - all by yourself. It doesn't work that way."

"Don't I know it. But he's such a cocky little bastard. He's the only kid in all these years that I have really wanted to strangle! But I don't want to strangle him as much as I do The Head."

"Enough about work," Jonathan said. "Relax."

Andrew leaned back while Jonathan continued to rub his shoulders. "Hmm, that feels good. Where did you learn to do that?"

"It's a gift." He lowered his voice. "Comes in useful from time to time, if you know what I mean."

"I can imagine. And it depends where you massage, too, I'm sure."

"Do you have any suggestions?"

"Plenty, but not any that I would say out loud."

Jonathan sighed, disappointed. This was harder work than he imagined it would be, despite everything he knew about Andrew.

"It would be a bloody sight easier if you took your

shirt off. I can't grip through this." Andrew tensed up. "Ok, I know, I know. But it's got to happen at some point. And I'm not exactly asking for you to get your willy out...yet."

Andrew pulled away from Jonathan's hands and stood up.

"Coffee?" he said.

Jonathan smiled.

"You are the master in the art of changing the conversation, you know that?"

"Except when I'm talking about work, right?"

"Yeah," Jonathan said. "Too damned right."

"It's a gift. Comes in useful from time to time!" Andrew said, beaming.

Jonathan stood up and put his arms around Andrew.

"OK. A coffee," he said. "But first a kiss?"

"I think I could manage that."

They put their arms around each other's bodies as they kissed, touching and caressing through their clothes.

"Hmm," Jonathan said at last, "from what I could feel down there just then, it seems that you like this whole kissing malarkey."

"I'll put the coffee on," Andrew said, and went through to the kitchen area.

"You'd make a good politician if ever you do leave teaching. Never give a bloody straight answer to a question."

"Thanks. I think!"

Jonathan left Andrew to make the coffee and went through to the bathroom. He had no intention to make Andrew do anything he didn't want to. This was, after all, new to him. But at the same time, he was well aware that Andrew would need some encouragement to put himself outside his comfort zone. This was a middle-aged man who hadn't kissed a guy until a few days earlier, let alone got naked with them, or had sex. Both men knew that this was a now or never moment for Andrew. If it wasn't going to happen with Jonathan, then the likelihood was that it would never happen at all.

When Jonathan came back from the bathroom, his shirt was in his hand. He walked slowly and quietly turned towards Andrew and then put his arms round his waist from behind. Andrew turned and saw that Jonathan was naked from the waist up.

"And what's the meaning of this?" he said.

"I was getting hot. And I've got you kissing, so getting you to take that shirt off is next on my list of firsts for Andrew Green."

"Oh, is that so?" Andrew put his hands on Jonathan's chest, not knowing quite what to do next. He liked what he saw. Jonathan clearly liked to look his best. He was in no way over-groomed, but there had clearly been some hours put in the gym in recent months, perhaps, Andrew thought, to take his mind off the split with his last boyfriend. His chest was smooth, probably shaved or waxed; it seemed difficult to believe that a guy like Jonathan would be completely hairless.

"Somebody's been busy at the gym," Andrew said.

Andrew tensed up as Jonathan's fingers fumbled with the top button of his shirt. As it came open, Jonathan tenderly kissed the small area of chest that it revealed. His fingers moved down to the next button, and Jonathan repeated the procedure.

"Are you Ok?" he asked.

Andrew nodded slowly.

Jonathan pulled Andrew's shirttails out of his trousers and continued to slowly undo the buttons, looking at Andrew regularly to make sure that he was comfortable with what was happening. Finally, the teacher stood there with his shirt wholly undone. Jonathan slowly pulled the shirt off completely, letting it drop to the floor.

"It's all going to be OK," he said, quietly.

Andrew looked into Jonathan's eyes, put his arms around him, and cried.

CHAPTER TWELVE

1

Jason was tempted not to go to school, especially as he was expected to stay behind for the first of his detentions that evening. What was that fag, Green, thinking of? *Nobody* had ever put him in detention and, with only a few weeks left before he was totally rid of school, he wasn't about to let someone do it now. He simply wouldn't show up for the detention. What were the school going to do about it?

His dad would sort things out just like he always did. However, he had heard through the grapevine that Luke was finally returning to school for the first time since the fight at the party, and Jason was just too curious to see what would happen and if Luke would, indeed, show up. He was meant to go back to school the day before but hadn't. So, Jason would go in to school and leave at the normal time, and to hell with the detention – after all, he had some business to attend to elsewhere.

Jason, Badger and Smithy were standing in their normal position in front of the school gates as they waited for the bell to signal the beginning of registration. With just five minutes to go, there was still no sign of Luke. James had already walked past them ten minutes earlier, and looked visibly unnerved that they didn't try to block his path or trip him up as they normally would. But, for now, Jason was interested in Luke, and Luke only. James was to have a brief respite, and Jason thought he should perhaps make the most of it.

Eventually, Jason spotted Luke walking up the hill arm in arm with Jane. They were walking painfully slowly and Jason knew that he would be late for registration himself if he waited for them to arrive – not that he had anything planned for his ex-friend. Not yet anyway. He wanted to take his time and give Luke a false sense of security. He felt a pang of jealousy as Luke and Jane exchanged a kiss. What he would give to have her himself. Perhaps one day he would. What better way was there to get back at his ex-friend?

Then he noticed, to his surprise, that Claire was with them. Jason wasn't sure why this bothered him so much. Perhaps it was the fact that they had seemingly teamed up so quickly – or maybe they had been teaming up against him all along, and it was only now that they felt able to do so in public. He hoped that they stayed out of his way and not try anything clever for their own sake. Despite what had happened, Jason wasn't keen on hurting Luke physically any more than he already had done. He was still more than a little taken aback at his own willingness and ability to hurt those around him. It made him nervous and uneasy.

When it became clear that the threesome had seen Jason and the others waiting for them, Jason simply signalled for everyone to go into the school grounds and on to registration. He just wanted to make sure that Luke knew that he would be there, waiting, in case he was to try something. However, considering how much of a struggle it clearly was for Luke to walk, he wasn't likely to be picking any more fights in the near future if he could help it.

2

As the first class of the day filed out of the door of Andrew Green's classroom, The Head pushed his way into the room, seemingly not having the common sense to let the twenty-five pupils leave the room before he tried to get in. Andrew, who was pushing the few chairs under their desks that the class had been left untidy, looked up. He wasn't surprised to see his visitor

"Hello there, Headmaster," he said.

"Mr Green. I was wondering if we might have a chat?"

Andrew closed the classroom door and then perched on his desk.

"Of course," he said. "Sounds very serious."

It was going to take a lot to dampen his mood. The previous evening had been a night of "firsts" for him, to say the least, and Andrew Green was finding it very difficult to suppress his smile. The class that had just left had looked at him with a bunch of bemused expressions as he cracked jokes and bantered with them while they tried to get to grips with *Lord of the Flies*, a book that, for the most part, he was fed up to the back teeth of teaching year after year. But not today. Today was different. In a way, his new demeanour had won over his class in a way he probably hadn't done for several years.

The Head didn't appear to be in such good form, however. He scowled at Andrew as if he was a naughty schoolboy. This would normally have pissed Andrew off, but on this occasion, he simply thought it was quite amusing and felt like telling the Head to lighten up a bit.

With the scowl not leaving his face, the Head said:

"Jason Mitchell's father called me this morning."

Andrew raised his eyebrows.

"Oh yes? Perhaps he gave you some explanation for his son's behaviour?"

"It appears that you have decided to give his son detention for three evenings in a row."

"That's correct."

"Three detentions on successive nights is, as far as I'm aware, unheard of. Might I ask why you gave him such a punishment?"

Andrew would very much like to have told him that it was because Jason Mitchell was an arrogant little prick, but instead said:

"Swearing in class, making threatening comments to both myself and his classmates, making abusive comments."

"What kind of abusive comments?"

"*Unacceptable* abusive comments."

"I see. And did these comments warrant after school detentions?"

Andrew stood up, walked around his desk and began to pull out of his briefcase some marked work that he had to hand back to the next class.

"What would you suggest?" he asked. "I'm only following guidelines set out by yourself."

The Head sighed, and sat on the table closest to him in the front row of the classroom. The table groaned under his weight and he quickly stood up again.

"I don't think I need to point out to you, Mr Green, just who Jason Mitchell is."

Andrew stopped what he was doing. This was getting ridiculous, and he wasn't willing to keep quiet about it any longer.

"If you are referring to the fact that he is the son of a governor and, so you might say, friend of the school – as well as your own drinking buddy – then, no."

"I would prefer it if you didn't bring personal matters into this situation."

"And Jason's Mitchell's father being your friend doesn't make it a personal matter for you? I don't think Jason deserves special treatment just because of his parents."

"Quite. On that we are agreed, Mr. Green."

"I'm glad to hear it."

Andrew was expecting the Head to leave at that point, but clearly he wasn't finished. He obviously had an agenda which he was determined to see through.

"Do you think *any* pupil should have special treatment?"

Andrew knew where this was leading, and he didn't like it one bit, but he had no intention of giving in to the man in front of him. He had made his decision the previous week to do what needed to be done, and he wasn't about to back down now.

"No," he said. "No pupil deserves special treatment."

"Except this James Marsh."

"As far as I'm aware, he hasn't received any special treatment. On the contrary, I would say that his needs have been largely ignored by the school."

"And what needs are they?"

"The need to have his bullying sorted."

"Bullying does not take place…"

"Bollocks. I think we have had this conversation before." Andrew knew it was best to simply walk away. He grabbed hold of his briefcase and walked to the door. "I don't think we have anything left to discuss Headmaster." He walked out into the corridor, pulling the door shut behind him. The Head followed him out of the classroom.

"I believe that you are giving James Marsh special treatment," he said.

Andrew stopped in his tracks.

"Why don't you just spit it out? What exactly are you trying to say?"

The Headmaster walked over towards him. This had turned into a confrontation about which Andrew was beginning to feel very uncomfortable.

"What I am trying to say is that you know *who* Jason Mitchell is – and I know *what* you are. In fact, thanks to your comments to your classes last week, the *whole school* knows what you are. Did you not think you should have run your plan to announce your homosexuality to the school by me first?"

"No, I did not. I asked that the school started giving our LGBT pupils the support they deserve and require, and you laughed me out of the room. And so, if I have to give them the support myself, then I will. And, before you carry on down this line of conversation, I should warn you now that you are dangerously close to a discrimination complaint being made against you."

Andrew was visibly shaking, and had shocked himself at his outburst – and the fact that he had just threatened the head of the school.

"Teachers are not in the habit of telling pupils about their private lives."

"So, you have never let a class know that you're married? Or brought your wife and kids to a school social event?"

"That's not the same thing at all."

"They know just as much about your private life as they do mine."

"If you value your position here, and I hope you do, then I would suggest you lay off Mitchell and ignore Marsh."

Andrew stood in shocked silence. He tried to calm himself, but when he spoke, his voice trembled with anger.

"Are you threatening me?" he said quietly.

"You've already threatened me," came the reply.

"Do you realise I could sue you for this? And James Marsh could sue the school?"

"I think that is unlikely to happen."

Andrew smiled.

"Don't bet on it," he said. "I didn't become a teacher in order to have this type of conversation. I'm sure the local press could be interested in this."

The Head stepped closer to him and pointed his finger.

"Don't try it, Mr Green."

"Then don't force me, Headmaster. Jason Mitchell is a menace to the other pupils at the school. He and his friends are supplying drugs to kids on and off the school grounds, as I'm sure you are aware. His violence and attitude towards others has reached a totally unacceptable level and he should no longer be allowed to attend this school. In the last week, he has stripped another pupil, filmed it, and posted it online…"

"You have no proof of that."

Andrew ignored him.

"…and he has put another pupil in hospital," he went on. "And you're turning a blind eye because you're drinking buddies with his Dad, and because you think the school is a business that needs the support of Peter Mitchell as one of our governors. Well, we have a duty to protect out pupils, Headmaster, no matter who or what they are. And if you're not willing to do something about this situation, then I am."

The two men stared at each other. War had been declared, albeit inadvertently.

"I am going back in my classroom," Andrew said. "And you are not going to follow me. Next time we speak I would like to have a witness to the proceedings. I assume you won't object."

Both of them had said more than they had intended to, and more than they should have done, but Andrew wanted to make it clear that he was not going to be pushed around. The Head took a deep breath and walked quickly down the corridor. Andrew watched him, and then went into his classroom and closed the door quietly. He walked back to his desk at the front, sat down, and looked out at the empty classroom. He wondered for how much longer the classroom would be his.

How far would the Head go? And what was he getting at when he referred to Andrew giving James Marsh special treatment? Was he simply talking about how Andrew was trying to sort out the kid's problems, or was he insinuating that something more sinister was taking place? Andrew tried to put the thought out of his head.

3

A trouble-free day. Considering what had happened the day before when the poster was stolen from him, James was almost in shock when the bell rang to signal the end of school and found that Jason & Co. were not lying in wait for him outside the school gates. He had no idea why he'd had a sudden reprieve. He was still really upset at losing the poster, but was thankful for the lack of a follow-up from Jason, all the same. Sadly, he was also well aware that the reprieve was unlikely to last. He was also concerned that he had yet to persuade Paul to be as open about their new relationship as he had said he would be just a few days earlier. He understood why Paul was hesitating but, at the same time, he knew that it would get more difficult the longer they left it. He had asked Paul to walk home from school with him, but he had made an excuse not to. James began to wonder whether he should tell Jason himself.

When he got home from school that night, James found a post-it note stuck to the door of the fridge.

> ALFRED RANG.
> HE WOULD LIKE YOU TO GO AND SEE HIM.
> MUM x

James opened the fridge door and took out the carton of milk. He unscrewed the cap and gulped down a few mouthfuls before putting it back in the fridge and wiping the white residue from around his mouth with his hand. He ran upstairs and pulled off his school tie and then changed into jeans and a t-shirt and went out the door again to visit the shop that he had gone to the night before. He wondered what Alfred wanted, and realised it was more than likely something to do with the work that he had offered him for the summer. But why couldn't he have talked about that on the phone? Perhaps he had changed his mind, and wanted to tell James face to face. Well, even if that was the case, James hadn't lost anything, although he had been looking forward to working in the shop part-time. It had been the only good thing to come out of his visit the day before.

He wondered whether he should tell Alfred about what had happened to the poster that he had brought in. If Jason hadn't trashed it, it was probably now listed on eBay and about to earn him about a hundred pounds or so. If he had the one hundred pounds himself, he might have even offered it to Jason just to get the poster back. He was still wondering whether to tell Alfred when he reached the shop and opened the door.

What he saw shocked him.

Loads of DVDs had been taken off the shelves and simply thrown on to the floor. Alfred prided himself on the often-pristine condition of his stock, but now there were many with torn packaging. Much of the vintage sheet music that the shop stocked was torn in half, and some of the records had been taken from their racks and thrown around the shop. The sleeves were torn and the records damaged. Film posters from around the shop had been torn down and, worse than this, Alfred's personal pride and joy, a lobby card signed by the silent film star Lon Chaney had been damaged. The frame was broken, and the glass from it was scattered over the tired carpet. The card itself was still in one piece, but it had been trampled on and the beautiful (and expensive) collector's item would never look the same again.

James was so busy surveying the damage to the shop itself that he hadn't yet taken notice of the seventy-three-year-old shopkeeper.

"It's a bloody mess, isn't it, Master James?"

James looked over to the shop counter and saw Alfred sitting in his usual place, gazing out over the mess, clearly not knowing where to start in the clean-up operation. It was now clear that it wasn't just the shop that had been damaged, but Alfred too. There was a gash on his forehead, which James thought might well need some stitches, and there was a swelling along his cheekbone.

"Shit, Alfred. What happened?" James said quietly.

"What happened? I forgot I was an old man is what happened. I thought I could be some hero when some bloody hooligans came here, and now look at the place. If I had kept my mouth shut, none of this would have happened. I'll never learn."

"Who did this?"

"A couple of young men who came in around lunchtime. I wouldn't give them what they wanted so they said they would give me something to remember them by."

"Did you call the police?"

"Nope. What would they do? Nothing. Their finances are nearly as bad as the shop's."

"Is the shop doing that badly?"

"It's ticking over. Nothing to worry yourself about."

James picked up the Lon Chaney autograph and put it on the counter, trying to flatten it out as he did so.

"Alfred, I am so sorry," he said.

"Well, don't be sorry," Alfred said, standing up, "what the bloody use is being sorry going to do? We need to clear this place up so that we're ready for the morning. Come along, give me a hand. That's why I left the message with your mum. I just couldn't face doing all of this on my own."

"But Alf, you need to see someone about that gash on your head first."

Alfred felt his forehead and looked at the blood on his fingers.

"Huh, I didn't even know that was there."

"Did they hit you?"

"No, but I think Lon Chaney did when he came down off the wall."

James tried to stifle a giggle at this unexpected comment, but couldn't manage it. Soon, Alfred was laughing with him and they set about their work, picking all of the items up from the floor one by one and seeing if they could still be salvaged. Surprisingly, the damage to most was relatively minor and Alfred said he would start a sale rack and knock a couple of pounds off each one for any scuffs or tears that had occurred to the sleeves or artwork. Most of the DVDs only had damage to the plastic case, and Alfred said he would order some the next day and just replace them.

James tried to get through the job of putting the shop back together as quickly as possible, but Alfred took his time, picking up items and carefully examining them, or telling James the story behind them. Some of them had been part of the old man's personal collection. James realised for the first time that this was Alf's home far more than the house he went to after work to sleep. His life and memories were in the items scattered about. At one point, Alfred shuffled across to the counter and took a record out of its sleeve and put it on the turntable.

"I figure I might as well educate you while you're here, Master James. Silent film isn't the be all and end all, you know." He placed the stylus on the record and a bluesy trumpet solo emerged from the speakers mounted on the wall. "Benny Carter. *Jazz Giant* LP," he said. "And he certainly was. I saw him play once. I saw many of the greats play back when I was living in London. This song is called *I'm Coming Virginia*. I'm not even going to suggest how that track got its name."

He winked at James and laughed. James smiled back, but wasn't sure whether he should admire rude jokes coming from someone in their seventies, or be freaked out. Alfred sat behind the desk, staring out across the shop, unaware of anything except the music. A tear fell on to his cheek as the track neared its conclusion.

"My wife loved this," he said. "It was her favourite album. She's been gone five years, Jim. I was about to give up the shop when she died. A heart attack in her sleep, they said. She just went to bed one night and didn't wake up. It's the way to go, I suppose. She'd have preferred that to living for years with a cancer or something slowly eating away at her. I think, perhaps, that most of us would. Now the shop's all I've got. And some little bastards come in here and try to break the whole place up. Well, sod 'em. We can't let them win, can we Jim-lad?"

Alfred was the only person who had ever referred to James as "Jim-lad," and he thought it made him sound like a pirate. Normally, Alfred said it as a joke. Today, the joke was half-hearted; an attempt to make light of the situation. James walked over to Alfred, and put his hand on his shoulder.

"How about a cup of tea, Alf?" he said. "I think you need it."

Alfred put the record back in its sleeve.

"Yes, I think I do," he said. "Why don't you go out back and put the kettle on?"

James went through to the back of the shop where he had been for the first time the day before. Nothing had been touched out there. The boxes upon boxes of vinyl, magazines and memorabilia were still stacked high, but did nothing but bring back happier memories of his visit a day earlier. Sometimes James wondered what things of interest might be tucked away in those boxes, and that, perhaps, Alfred should look to selling some of the stock in the backroom online. Perhaps that was something that James could help with when he started working there in the summer – especially if the shop was struggling to keep afloat.

James walked over to the kitchen area and filled up the kettle and started to make two mugs of tea. Alfred came through from the shop and sat down. James turned to face him.

"Are you going to tell me what happened, Alf? Who did this? Why?"

"I suppose I will have to tell you anyway." Alfred sighed. "Two young men, about your age I should imagine, came in this morning with something to sell. Now, I know when something's stolen and when it's not, and I've never bought stolen goods in all the years I've had this place – and that's a long while, I might add. So that's what I told them – that their item was very nice but that I wouldn't be able to buy it from them. When they asked why, I told them: Because I believed it to be stolen. When they asked me how I would know, I said that I happened to know the young man that the item belonged to."

James's face drained of colour as he realised what Alfred was telling him. Jason and either Smithy or Badger had done this to his friend. He watched as Alfred reached down and picked up James's poster, still in the tube it had been in the day before.

"But, if nothing else, I got you your poster back, Jim."

James turned away from Alfred and looked out of the window, tears streaming down his face. Alfred walked up to him.

"Don't cry, Jim-lad. It's not worth it. Nobody got badly hurt, and there's not really that much damage, is there? Just a bit of a mess, that's all. Nothing that can't get cleaned up."

James turned back to face him, his whole body shaking as he cried.

"But it's my fault," he said.

"Nonsense. It's not your fault. And don't you think that it is. It's *their* fault. I don't know who they are or what they have been doing to you, but it's their fault. And you're going to tell me all about it. I know something has been bothering you these past few months and now you're going to sit down with a cup of tea and tell me everything. And then we'll decide what to do next. There is always a way to sort these things."

It was Alfred who finished making the tea while James tried to calm down and pull himself together.

"You really want me to tell you everything?" he said.

"Of course."

James sat quietly for a few moments, trying to decide whether he could actually tell Alfred the whole story. Alfred was an old man; he might not be as understanding as James might need him to be. But James knew that he would eventually have to tell *someone*.

"It's not very straightforward," he finally said. "One

of the guys who did this to you today was Jason Mitchell."

James then spoke about what Jason was like, what had happened the summer before between him and Paul, and how Jason had made their life hell ever since. Then he told Alfred about what had happened over the last ten days, from the bullying in the changing rooms to the weekend with Paul and how Jason had run off with the poster the day before. Alfred simply nodded at appropriate moments during James's story, and slowly sipped at his tea. When James had finished talking, Alfred stood up and walked over to one of the kitchen cupboards and opened it. He bent down to pull out a tin, opened it and took a knife out of the kitchen drawer. He walked back over to James.

"Cake?" he said.

James was slightly bemused at Alfred's reaction to what he had said and declined the offer.

"What's the matter?" Alfred said, "You think I shouldn't offer you a piece of cake because you tell me you're gay? Or perhaps you think I should make a fuss about it. Let me tell you something, I don't give a damn what you are, my boy, as long as you're happy. Now, have a piece of cake."

James smiled and dipped his hand into the tin and took out a piece of swiss roll. Alfred took a piece for himself and sat down.

"I was in the Forces in the 1950s, you know?" he said. "On national service. Something that this Mitchell lad of yours could do with, I might add. That would teach him a thing or two, I can tell you. But that's just an old man talking. We always think things were better when *we* were young. Now, let me tell you something. I was only young; eighteen or nineteen I suppose, something like that. Me and a group of friends had gone to some bar – I don't even remember where it was anymore. The old memory is giving up on me now. Perhaps that's not such a bad thing. Anyway, me and the lads thought we'd have a good night, get drunk and see what else we could get, if you know what I mean."

James nodded, not too sure of where the story was going.

"After about an hour or so – and after quite a few brandies – this woman comes up to me and starts chatting me up. I thought she was one of those girls who liked a man in uniform, as they say. I thought my luck must be in. We started kissing and cuddling in the bar and then she suggested we went outside around the back of the pub. Well, that could only mean one thing, so off we went and we, well, continued where we left off, so to speak. I wasn't exactly much experienced in such matters at that time, if at all, and so I didn't notice anything unusual until she leant back against the wall, and her hair somehow managed to get caught in something and appeared to move. The next thing I know, she's hitching her skirt up and I find out she's got a willy!"

James started laughing.

"It was a *guy*?" James asked. "Oh God! What did you do?"

"Well, I'm not ashamed to say it, this man (as he obviously was) was the most beautiful *woman* I had ever come in contact with – well, after a few brandies at least. I was drunk and thought to myself 'in for a penny' and so we just carried on. And, I have to say, I didn't regret it then and I certainly don't regret it now."

He paused to take a bit of his cake, and washed it down with some tea.

"So, what I'm trying to say," he went on, "is that not everyone is going to act like this boy and his friends. Most people won't give a damn. Especially these days. And that's the way it should be. It's not about what *they* think about it – it's about what *you want*. And if you like this boy, as you clearly do, and if you want to be in a relationship with this boy, then you must do everything in your power to make it happen – because fifty years down the line, you might lose him forever, and then you will regret every single day that you weren't together."

James sat in silence, trying to take in what Alfred had said to him. He was the first adult with whom James had been completely open about being gay and wanting to be with Paul. James wondered how much Alfred had already figured out for himself prior to their conversation. No matter what, Alfred had done his best to protect James, and now it was up to James to fight for what he wanted.

"Now, if you've finished your cuppa, let's get on and finish out front," Alfred said, matter-of-factly.

It took James and Alfred another hour or so to get

the shop looking somewhat respectable again. Some stock had been ruined completely, but not much of it, and nothing of great value, other than Alfred's signed lobby card. Alfred said he would sort out the rack of sale items the next day, and put things that had been damaged in there but, by the time James and Alfred left the shop at half past seven, the place looked almost as if nothing had happened. Posters that had been torn down had been replaced, the floor had been cleared of glass and other debris, and the front desk looked just as it had the day before when James had visited – even down to the volume of Sherlock Holmes stories sitting in its usual place.

James offered to walk Alfred home, worried that the old man was nervous after what had happened, but he protested that he was as strong as an ox – and James didn't really doubt that. As James walked home, he wondered what it all meant for *him*. Was this a sign of things to come? Just how far would Jason go?

CHAPTER THIRTEEN

1

It was something that the old man had said that made Jason suspicious. Something about how he knew that the poster belonged to a young man who had been in the shop the day before, and that it had been given to him by a friend. A *friend*. James Marsh didn't have any friends! Except Paul. Paul was the only person who would give James a present.

He wondered if the pair had made things up, maybe even spent time together at the weekend – which would certainly explain why Paul didn't answer his phone when Jason tried to call him. And Smithy had said something about Paul wanting to find out where everybody was and what they were up to when Jason was out of school the week before. Perhaps they were meeting up somewhere at school and thinking nobody knew. Was the great romance really back on? Surely James wouldn't forgive Paul for everything that happened over the last few months? Jason had to find out exactly what was going on.

Jason spent the next couple of days keeping low…and watching. He discovered that, while James and Paul made sure they weren't seen in public together, neither of them were especially discreet about their so-called secret rendezvous behind the cricket pavilion each lunchtime. Jason was, in many ways, hoping that they were cleverer than that; it would give him a tougher nut to crack.

He could do with a challenge – something to take his mind off all the weird things that had been going on lately, from the break-up with Claire to the fight with Luke. He didn't regret either of them, but something about his own behaviour had unnerved him. He had spent less time with Smithy and Badger, preferring his own company, staying in his bedroom and sketching to take his mind off things. Drawing seemed to be the only thing that relaxed him these days.

It seemed that catching James and Paul in the throes of passion was going to be easy after all. Every lunch time, without fail, James would run over to the pavilion and make his way around the back and then Paul would follow suit about ten minutes later, giving them twenty minutes or so together before they had to get back to the main school building for the afternoon's classes. Catching them would be simple. What Jason should do with them once he had caught them was the difficult part. Each time he saw them kiss he wanted to vomit.

It was something he had plenty of time to think about during his detentions at the hands of Mr Green. He had told his dad about them and said that the teacher simply had it in for him. He knew his dad was able to get him out of anything he wanted. There were distinct perks of having a parent friendly with the headmaster and on the board of governors. His father had rung the school and spoken to The Head, and was told that he would have a word with the teacher in question and he was sure that it would all be sorted out. When Jason came home from school and told his father that the detentions remained in place, he said that he must have deserved it and that he had to do them. It was the first time that he could remember when his father had failed to sort things out for him, and he wasn't pleased, but his father didn't seem pleased that he had done something bad enough to get the detention in the first place, and the fact that some valuables had got broken during the fight at the party hadn't helped matters.

Mr. Green watched him with contempt as he sat at his desk for an hour after school each night. The teacher had tried to engage him in conversation in the beginning, asking him why he picked on Marsh and whether he realised the harm he was doing. It was like listening to a self-righteous vicar prattling on. Jason didn't give a shit, and refused to speak and so Andrew Green read while Jason sat there in silence. Jason preferred it that way; he didn't like being watched by someone like that. On the first night, he started texting and playing games on his mobile phone until Green confiscated it until the end of the session. After that, Jason just sat there, drumming his fingers on the table in the hope that it was annoying his teacher. The teacher refused to be distracted, however – in fact, he seemed remarkably happy all week - and the hour seemed to go even slower for Jason on the second night. Now there was just one session left.

Although catching James and Paul was at the forefront of his mind, there was something else that was bothering him. Luke. He hadn't come through with his talk of revenge after the beating at the party, and he and Jane had apparently not even spoke to Smithy and Badger since Luke's return to school, keeping to themselves. But Luke always seemed to be there. If Jason was walking across the school playing field, he would see Luke out of the corner of his eye, hiding behind a tree and spying on him. When they shared lessons, Jason would turn around and see Luke just staring at him. Even when he couldn't see him, he had the feeling that he was there all the same, waiting and watching like a deranged stalker. Perhaps he was just trying to unnerve him and, if that was the case, he was succeeding brilliantly. He knew that, at some point, Luke would make his move.

But he was about to make a move of his own. On James and Paul.

2

Notwithstanding the stealing of the poster and the incident at the shop, James's week had been uneventful compared to the previous one. Jason and what was left of his crew had essentially ignored James all week, and he wasn't going to complain. The more they pretended he didn't exist the better, as far as he was concerned. To start with, James had been somewhat wary of the quiet, but as the week progressed he had slowly put aside thoughts that Jason was planning something for him. Perhaps he realised that, with the attack on the shop, he was getting himself into an altogether different territory that would involve a criminal record if he got caught. Or perhaps Alfred had finally decided to report the incident to the police and they had caught up with his Jason, and so he was being on his best behaviour – although James thought that Alfred would have let him know if this was the case.

On Friday, as with the rest of the week, James had managed to pass Jason on his way through the school gates without incident. He made his way to his locker to retrieve a textbook he had left there the night before that he would need for his first lesson. As was usual in the few minutes leading up to registration, the bank of lockers was busy with people trying to get things they would need for the rest of the day, and it took a minute or so before James could even reach his own. When he opened the door, a small piece of paper fell to the floor. James bent down to pick it up and unfolded it. He grinned as he read the note:

SAME TIME, SAME PLACE
P xx

It was the first time that Paul had left a note for him like this, but perhaps he thought it was safer than trying to seek him out before lunch in order to make the arrangements. James and Paul also had to sort out what they wanted to do over the coming weekend. They had talked a day or two before about going to the cinema to see the latest horror movie remake, and perhaps go for a pizza either before or after. Wherever they went, they both knew it had to be somewhere they were unlikely to bump into Jason or any of his gang. Paul was going to try to find out what their plans were for the weekend, so they would be avoided.

The first lesson of the day, history, passed slowly with the teacher going over ground that they had only covered a few weeks earlier. James knew that this was because of the upcoming exams, but he still wasn't keen on learning the same things twice. He would much rather be given practice questions for the exam than hear again about Hitler's rise to power in the 1930s. The teacher finished talking after half an hour or so, and then showed them a section of an ancient BBC documentary that basically retold the information she had just given them. They would probably have had time to watch the whole of the programme if the teacher had learned the art of switching on the television and pressing play on the video recorder. James couldn't believe that some people were still using VHS tapes. Mr. Green seemed to be the only adult in the whole school who was capable of basic technical expertise. James wondered how the teachers managed in the real world. If they couldn't get a TV to work, how did they manage to drive a car?

The last lesson before lunch was English with Mr. Green. This was also a revision lesson, but *Lord of The Flies*, which they had studied a few months earlier, was far more interesting than the Second World War. At least, it was to James. They had watched a black and white film of the novel before, but now they were shown parts of a colour remake and Mr. Green encouraged them to talk about the differences between the novel and the two film adaptations. The hour passed quickly, with even Jason joining in with the lesson on occasion. James assumed that this was because Jason could identify with the bullying antics of the kids marooned on the island.

When the bell rang to signal the beginning of lunch break, Mr Green sent the class on their way, winking at James as he made his way down the room to the door. James smiled back, hoping that he wasn't going to get stopped on his way out, as he wanted to meet Paul as soon as he could. He watched as Jason and his friends walked off down the corridor towards the dining hall, then, thinking he was safe, walked out of the building and started to run towards the pavilion.

The sun beat down on his back with a strength not

previously witnessed that spring and, by the time he reached the pavilion, sweat was gluing the shirt to his back. There wasn't any sign of Paul as yet, and so James sat down on the grass in the shade of a tree. He pulled the wet shirt from his back, loosened his tie and lay back in the grass.

"Is that your come-and-get-me pose?"

James hadn't heard Paul creep up on him, making him wonder if he had dozed off momentarily in the hot sunshine. He opened his eyes and looked up at his boyfriend.

"Something like that," he said.

Paul grinned and sank to the grass beside him.

"That's what I was hoping." He kissed James on the cheek, and then lay back, with his head resting on James's chest. "So, you OK?"

"Yeah," James said. "Just tired. You?"

"Yeah, I'm cool. Looking forward to the weekend. What do you want to do tomorrow? We could still go and see a film if you want. Jason and the others are going to the Odeon in the afternoon, so if we go to Vue, we'll know we'll avoid them."

"Sounds like a plan. But I want to go to the shop first. I want to check on Alfred, and make sure he's OK. I want to introduce you to him."

"OK," Paul said.

"Cool. What's on at the cinema? What did you want to see?"

"I dunno. I'm still quite keen on that horror film. I know it's meant to be shit, but there's always gorgeous guys in films like that.

"I thought you had a gorgeous guy?"

"I do. But there's no harm in looking, is there?" He leaned over and kissed James. James broke away. "What's up?" Paul asked.

"I thought I heard something."

"Like what?"

"I don't know." James walked slowly away from Paul and looked out from behind the pavilion. There was no-one in sight. "I'm just hearing things. You got me spooked talking about horror films. Next thing, I'll be dreaming about Freddy Kreuger."

3

Jason watched as Paul made his way over to the cricket pavilion and then, when he saw that he had met James there, walked unseen towards them and took a position about fifty metres from the two boys. He watched as they kissed and then lay across each other on the grass, with Paul's head resting on James's shoulder.

The sight of the two boys together repulsed him, and yet he was also almost envious. He had never been happy with Claire in the way that the two boys appeared to be now. There was something that seemed entirely natural when the two boys were together. They had probably had more sex than he had too. He couldn't believe that they would make out at the school where they could be caught. They could at least do it in the privacy of their own home! For one brief moment, Jason thought about just walking away and leaving them to it. He had no idea where such an idea came from. Perhaps he was just tired or bored. Or perhaps, just for a second, he questioned his own motives.

Jason quickly put the thought out of his head. He took his phone from his pocket and rang Smithy, telling him and Badger to come over to the cricket pavilion and meet him there. When Smithy started asking questions as to what it was all about, Jason simply disconnected. He couldn't risk being heard by James and Paul, and couldn't be bothered explaining things. Sometimes his friends were nothing more than a useful nuisance, even if they were the only ones that had stuck with him over the last week.

He carried on watching James and Paul. He had, of course, known all along that Paul had been lying about how James had come on to him in the cinema, and wondered if Paul would come up with the same excuse in a few minutes time. Surely he wouldn't do the same thing twice?

By the time Smithy and Badger arrived, James had pushed Paul against the side of the building and the two boys were kissing each other, unaware of anything that was going on around them. Jason motioned for Smithy and Badger to take a look at them, and then signalled for them to follow him. The two boys were taking it too far now. Kissing each other and being happy was one thing; full-on snogging was something else entirely. If Jason had had any doubts a few moments earlier about what he was going to do, then they were quickly pushed aside now.

Jason, Smithy and Badger came out from their hiding place and strode towards James and Paul. Jason stopped and watched as the boys continued to kiss.

"Well, well. Isn't this nice and cosy?" he said. "You too have obviously kissed and made up, haven't you?"

James and Paul stopped kissing and stared at Jason and the others. Paul pushed James away from him and James fell to the ground.

"The bastard came on to me again!" Paul cried out.

"Not literally, I hope," Jason said as he walked towards them. "Wouldn't want to make a mess of your school clothes, Paul. Daddy wouldn't like it, would he? How is you dad these days?" He squatted down beside James. "You know, if you'd behaved yourself I might have been convinced that you weren't a little fag. Screwed that up, didn't you? Can't even stick to your own kind, can you? You had to go after young Paul here." He stood up and spat at James. "You disgust me."

James looked up at Paul.

"Tell him the truth, Paul. This is your chance. Think about everything we talked about."

Paul looked down at the ground, afraid of both options before him. Either he saved himself and let down his friend, or he told the truth and feared ending up in a similar state to Luke.

"I have told the truth," he said, eventually.

"You lying bastard!"

James tried to get up and lunge at Paul, but Jason pushed him back.

"I think you're the one who's lying, Jim-boy. Don't you? What happened, Paul?"

"He told me to meet him here as he wanted to talk to me. Then he came on to me. Just like before. He pushed me up against the wall and tried to stick his tongue down my throat."

"Yeah, right. What did I do? Kidnap you and bring you out here?"

Jason stood over James and glared down at him.

"Now, what *are* we going to do with you, Marsh?"

James saw his chance and kicked Jason in the balls and then got up from the ground and started running. He had never run away from Jason before, but he knew that it was his only chance to escape whatever Jason had planned. Jason told the others to stick with Paul and then he ran after James, and found himself catching up with him quickly.

James headed across the playing field towards the main building. He didn't look behind to check on Jason, but knew that he would be closing in on him quickly. Once inside, he knew he had three choices. He could go into the dining hall, the toilets or the changing rooms.

As Jason entered the main building, there was no sign of James. He ran quickly towards the dining hall, not stopping even when told not to run in the corridor by a teacher. He opened the door to the dining hall, but there was no sign that anyone had run through the long hall. No teachers were standing up, and no kids looked as if they had been nearly knocked over by someone rushing past them.

He went into the toilets. Two boys were standing at the urinals, neither of which were James. Only one cubicle had its door shut. Jason kicked at it and the door burst open, revealing a boy about four years younger sitting on the toilet. Jason walked away without apologising.

There was only one place left. The changing rooms. Jason opened the door and the familiar smell of deodorant and sweat hit him. He stood just inside the door, perfectly still, listening to see if he could hear any noises. He started walking around the empty rooms, looking first in the shower area. There was no sign of James in there. Pity. It would have been quite apt for him to have chosen that as a hiding place given what happened the week before. He went through to the little cubicle reserved for teachers getting changed, but the door was padlocked.

He knew there was only one place left: the little alcove next to the changing room toilets, where various pieces of games equipment were kept. He walked quietly towards it, and saw the toes of a familiar pair of worn-out shoes sticking out from behind the bollards and athletics equipment. Smiling, he went back into the main area and texted Smithy, telling him where he was. They would join him soon. Until then, he would just wait it out, and let James get more and more nervous. He wanted him to suffer.

James knew that Jason had spotted him; that would

be the only reason why he hadn't walked past him and gone out through the far door. He was tempted to make a run for it again, but knew that Jason would catch up with him no matter where he went. Part of him just wanted the whole thing to be over. His only hope was the bell to signal the end of lunch break, but he didn't think that was going to be heard for another quarter of an hour or more, despite the fact that it felt like he had been standing in that alcove for hours. And there was a good chance that Jason wouldn't care about whether he was present for afternoon registration or not.

James realised that there was still a chance that the other person in the changing rooms wasn't Jason. It could even be a teacher, but he wasn't pinning his hopes on anything. After a couple of minutes, he heard the door to the changing rooms open again, and a couple of more people came in. Then he heard Jason speak.

"So, you came along too, Paul? Nice one. That's what I like to see. Good lad."

Jason, Smithy and Badger walked slowly over to where James was hiding. Paul tagged behind, clearly not wanting to be there, knowing that if he didn't do as he was told, Jason would turn on him too. Jason swaggered up to James, and stood at the front of the small alcove, giving James no chance of escape.

"Well, well. Here we are again, eh, Marsh? I have to admit, you can run quicker than I thought you could. To be honest, I thought blokes were normally running away from you, not you running away from them. Now, where were we?"

James instinctively shuffled back further away from Jason, although he knew that there was nowhere for him to go. A secret door wasn't going to open up behind him and allow for a last-minute escape. Jason was standing in front of him, his arms stretched out so that his hands were touching each side of the alcove. The fingers of the bully's right hand drummed against the wall.

"So," Jason said finally, "you like kissing blokes, do you, James?"

James stared at him. It didn't matter what he said. He could swear that he wasn't gay, but Jason would never believe him or leave him alone. It was too late for denial, and James wasn't sure he even wanted to deny things any more. It wouldn't even help matters if he did. For the first time, he admitted who he was to someone at school other than Paul.

"Yes," he said eventually.

Jason raised his eyebrows and turned to his friends, seemingly impressed by James's honesty.

"Well, I've got to give it to you. Never thought you'd admit it. Doesn't help you, of course. But at least we both know where we stand." He moved in closer towards James and whispered to him. "Why don't you kiss me?" James had no idea where this was going, and he again tried to back away, although there was nowhere to go. "What's the matter, am I not good enough for you?"

Jason suddenly lunged his head towards James and pressed his lips forcefully against his. James tried to jerk his head backwards, but he was already up against the wall. He thought he was going to be sick. Badger, Smithy and Paul watched on, not certain of what Jason was trying to do.

Jason wasn't sure what he was doing, either. The idea had come to him, and he had just gone with it, not thinking of how it would look to his friends, or how it would make him feel. The fact that he didn't find it as disgusting as he thought he would made him draw away quickly. He wiped his mouth with his sleeve, and then spat on the floor in an effort to demonstrate to the others how much he had hated what he had just done.

"You're not much of a kisser, James," he said. "Even Claire was better than you."

Jason moved away and walked over to Paul and ruffled his hair.

"You like *him* though, don't you?" he said to James

He laughed as Smithy walked over to James.

"You can kiss me if you like, batty boy," he said, with an exaggerated lisp. He turned around and mooned at James. "Why don't you *kiss my arse*?"

Jason, Smithy and Badger laughed as Paul watched on. Jason walked back over to where James was standing. He picked a basketball off the floor and started to bounce it as he spoke.

"The problem is, James," he said, "this is the second time this has happened. What are we going to do to make sure it doesn't happen again?"

He stood still and looked James up and down, and then threw the basketball at him. It hit him hard in the stomach, winding him. James bent over, trying to catch his breath.

"Sorry, James. I thought you liked balls." He turned to his friends. "So, guys, any suggestions?"

"Cut his dick off!"

"Now, there's an idea, Smithy."

Jason walked back up to James and grabbed hold of his crotch, squeezing James's balls hard. James winced in pain.

"What do you think, Jimbo? You don't mind me calling you Jimbo, do you? Would that be a suitable punishment, do you think?" He squeezed harder. "Should I do it?" James shook his head and started pleading for Jason to let go. "Perhaps not."

He let go of James's crotch, and James looked across at Paul.

"Tell him the truth, Paul. Please."

Paul looked away guiltily, and James realised that there was going to be no last-minute reprieve. Jason motioned to Smithy and Badger.

"Hold him still," he said.

Smithy and Badger walked over to James and held him still against the wall as they had been instructed. Jason turned to Paul.

"Well, Paul, as you seem to be James's favourite person, perhaps you should do the honours."

"What do you mean?"

Jason walked over and put his hand on Paul's shoulder.

"Well, we can't let him get away with this again,

now can we? I mean, being made out to be queer once is one thing, but this just keeps on happening. I think you should show him just how much you hate him, don't you? He might get the idea a bit more if you beat the crap out of him instead of me."

The colour drained away from Paul's face, and he suddenly looked more scared than James.

"Go on, Paul. You know you want to. That little fag was shoving his tongue down your throat. Next time he'll be trying to shove his cock up your arse. Or has he done that already? Just think what a disgusting little queer he is. Hit him, Paul."

James cried out.

"Don't do it, Paul! We can sort this! Think of what we've been talking about!"

Paul looked across at Jason and then back at James, and then at Jason once again. He had nowhere to run, and he was in a no-win situation.

"I told you to hit him!"

Paul gulped and then walked slowly over to James.

"Now, Paul. We haven't got all day."

Paul mouthed "I'm sorry" to James, and then punched him lightly in the stomach, barely making contact with his friend.

"You can do better than that, Paul. Just hit the little shit."

Paul thought he was going to throw up. He even wondered if that might get himself out of the situation that he found himself in. But he could feel Jason's breath on the back of his neck, and he knew he had no choice but to do as he was told. Paul hit James again, a little harder.

"Again. Harder."

He punched James again. This time he hurt him.

"Again."

He kept hitting him, tears rolling down his face as he did so, but with each punch getting harder as he forgot about who he was hitting, and just used the punches as a way of venting his frustration. James started sobbing and, finally, Jason pulled Paul away.

"You see?" he said to James. "That's how much he *really* likes you. Now, just one little thing and you can go."

Jason took a small penknife out of his pocket.

"It won't hurt much," he said, as he ran the blade lightly across James's face. James began to think that he was going to slash his face open. Instead, Jason moved the knife down his chin and on to his shirt, with it coming to rest behind the first button. He paused for a moment and then flicked the knife down and the button dropped to the floor. "Oops," he said. He moved the knife down to the next button and did the same thing again. He snipped off the rest of the buttons and James's shirt fell open. He put the point of the knife on to James's chest and applied a little pressure.

"What we have to do," he said, "is something that will always remind you of what you are. So a message on this cute little chest of yours might just do the trick. It's only three letters, so it won't hurt much."

A trickle of blood ran down James's chest as Jason

pulled the knife quickly down in a straight line. James cried out in pain, and struggled to get away, but Smithy and Badger's hold was too tight.

Paul watched on for a few seconds, but then couldn't hold back any longer. He grabbed Jason from behind and pulled him away from James. Smithy and Badger let go of James, and watched as Jason broke away from Paul's grasp and swung around to face him, the knife held out towards him at arm's length.

"You're going to regret that, you little shit!" he said.

"Put the knife down, Jason," Paul replied, shaking with fear that something terrible was going to happen.

Luke came into the changing rooms. He stopped and stood still when he saw what Jason was doing.

"What the hell are you doing?" he said.

Now, Jason turned his attention towards Luke, the knife held out in front of him. As he stopped moving, a drop of blood fell to the floor from the end of the knife.

"None of your business, I'm afraid, Luke. Now get the hell out of here before I use this on you instead of Paul."

He lunged at Luke with the knife, stopping just short of his former friend so as not to jab him. Luke didn't move.

"Drop the knife and get out of here, Jason."

Jason laughed.

"You think I'm going to do something just because you tell me to?"

"No, but Greeny is on his way."

"Yeah, sure he is."

Jason jabbed at Luke again, but Luke lunged at him, grabbing him from behind and pulling him away. He threw him to the ground just as the door to the changing rooms opened again and Andrew Green ran in. Jason got up quickly, picked up the knife that had fallen from his grasp, and held it out in front of him as he backed up and ran out of the rear door. Andrew shouted after him, but knew that Jason wouldn't stop and he had no chance of catching him unaided. Smithy and Badger released their hold of James and quickly made for the same door as their leader.

Andrew, Luke and Paul watched as James appeared to black out and collapse to the floor, almost as if in slow motion. Andrew ran over to him, pushing Paul out of the way. He turned to Paul and Luke.

"Go to the front office. Tell them there is a student on campus with a knife. Now!"

As Paul and Luke left, James began to come around.

4

Luke and Paul went to the office and gave them the message, which led to the secretary quickly running up the stairs to the staff room to inform The Head. A quiet but quick and intensive search for Jason Mitchell took place, but Jason had gone from the changing rooms and straight out of the school grounds. He knew better than to be caught on school property with a knife.

Jason wasn't the only one to leave the school. While Andrew went to get the first aid equipment, James slipped out of the changing rooms and stumbled out of the school gates. He knew he would have to kill an hour or so before he could go home and that he would have to be careful to get to his room unseen by his mother in order to avoid questions regarding the cut on his chest and his ruined shirt. He felt guilty about walking out on Mr. Green like that, especially as he had always been so kind to him, but he would have wanted to take him to see The Head and call his mother, and James felt that he couldn't cope with all of that. Not today. He could apologise to Mr. Green tomorrow - if he ended up going to school tomorrow.

As he walked towards the park, James mopped at some of the dried blood on his chest with a tissue. The wound had finally stopped bleeding, and the cut was clearly not as deep as he originally thought it was, but he still felt dazed after what had happened – not just because of Jason, but because of Paul, too. Perhaps things had been going too well. Not only had he got back Paul's friendship, but he had become his boyfriend as well. And now where did they stand? He had finally forgiven Paul for letting him down like that once, but what was he to make of Paul today? First he saved his own ass again, just as he had before, and then he risked getting slashed with a knife to stop Jason cutting James. Nothing was ever simple.

An hour or so after leaving the school, James walked up the front path towards his house. He opened the front door quietly and slipped inside, the door clicking shut behind him. He was hoping that his mother hadn't heard him come in; he wanted to go upstairs, shower and change before having to face her and explain why he was home early. However, she called through from the kitchen:

"Is that you, James? You're early."

He started walking up the stairs.

"Yeah. Is Rachel in?"

"She's in her room."

"Ok, I just need to see her. I'll be down in a bit."

He ran the rest of the way up the stairs and then crossed the landing and knocked on Rachel's bedroom door. She called for him to go in. He opened the door. Rachel was lying on the bed, reading. She looked up from the book as James walked in and shut the door.

"What the hell happened to you?" she said, taking her earphones out.

"Help me, Rachel. I need to get cleaned up before Mum sees me."

Rachel got up off the bed and walked around to where James was standing.

"What happened, Jim?"

"I got into a fight."

"You? In a fight? Yeah, right."

"I got beaten up."

He was fed up with trying to hide what was going on.

"At last the truth."

"Don't start, Rachel. Not today. I'll tell you what

happened later. Everything. But I can't right now. Are you going to help me?"

"Ok. Go and get out of those things. Get showered and changed. I'll make sure they get washed when Mum isn't here so she doesn't know what state they're in. We'll have to chuck the shirt out though, by the look of it. How can you lose all the buttons on a shirt?"

"You don't want to know."

"Believe me, I do. Mum probably won't miss a white shirt, though; you've got plenty. And then you're going to tell me exactly what happened."

"I will. I promise. Thanks."

James slipped out of Rachel's room and went into his own, getting a towel out of his wardrobe. He went into the bathrooms and then stripped out of his clothes, letting them fall to the floor in a heap. He turned the shower on and turned the heat up high. He winced as he stepped into the shower and the near-scolding water beat down upon his body, stinging like mad where Jason had cut him.

While James showered, his mother walked quietly up the stairs and tapped on Rachel's bedroom door.

"Is James alright?" she asked. "He's home really early today."

"I don't know. He said he wanted to pop in for a chat after he'd changed."

"He's in the shower."

"I know, Mum. It's hot outside. I reckon he wanted to freshen up."

"Ah, ok."

Rachel and her mother stood in silence.

"That's a cue for you to go back downstairs before he comes back, Mum."

"Oh, yes. Sure. I'll see you downstairs in a bit, ok?"

"Yeah, Ok."

As she walked back downstairs, James's Mum shot a glance at the closed bathroom door.

James was still in the shower, washing shampoo out of his hair. It ran down his face and into his eyes. It stung like hell, but he was beyond caring. He sank to the floor of the shower and sat down, letting the water pulsate down upon him, in the vain hope that it would somehow wash away not only the cut and bruises, but also the memories of what had happened earlier. Eventually he hauled himself out of the shower, wrapped the towel back around his waist, and opened the bathroom door to make sure his mum wasn't around. He didn't want her to see him half-dressed when he was cut and bruised. Seeing that the coast was clear, he made his way back to his own room. He pulled on a clean pair of boxer shorts and the jeans that were lying on the floor beside his bookcase. He took a clean T-shirt from the chest of drawers and carried it through to Rachel's room. He knocked on the door and walked in. Rachel looked up and saw for the first time the bruises and cuts to his chest.

"What the hell did they do to you, James?"

James avoided the question.

"Can you sort this cut out for me?"

"Yeah. Sit down on the bed. I'll be back in a

minute."

"Thanks."

James sat down and looked around the room. A poster of Ed Sheeran stared down at him. He thought that his sister's taste in men was dubious at best, something even more noticeable by the string of boyfriends she had brought home to meet her mum over the last few years. James smiled to himself, thinking that his own boyfriend had hardly been perfect.

Rachel came back into the room carrying some antiseptic, bandages and some cotton wool.

"Ed Sheeran?" James said, looking at the poster. "Is that the best you can do?"

"Hey, he's still alive. More than can be said for the people you like. Now, you want my help or not?"

"Yeah."

Rachel sat down beside him and dipped the cotton wool in the antiseptic.

"God, James. This is getting serious."

"I know."

"This is going to sting a little." James winced as Rachel gently dabbed at the cuts that Jason had made with his penknife. "Don't worry, I'll get your clothes sorted out for you without Mum finding out. I think she should know what's going on, though, but I won't tell her unless you want me to."

"OK. But not yet."

Rachel put the cotton wool to one side and cut off a piece of bandage.

"It's going to be OK, you know?"

"Is it? I don't know any more."

James sounded desperate. Rachel taped the bandage to his chest. She had never seen her brother in this state before, physically or mentally, and she knew that things needed to be sorted out once and for all.

"So, why did this happen?" she said.

"I don't know."

She raised her eyebrows.

"You've got no idea why they're doing this to you? You expect me to believe that?"

"If I did, I could do something about it."

"You can do something about it by telling the teachers."

"It's not worth it. It will only make things worse."

"Can it get any worse? I mean, look at the state of you. If Mum knew about this, she'd be up the school causing all kinds of hell."

"That's not going to help."

"Neither is you not telling me what's going on here. There's more to this than you're letting on. I'm not stupid."

"I can't tell you, Rachel."

"I'm not going to freak out."

James watched as Rachel put the bandage back in its packet and stood up.

"You know, don't you?" James said.

"I don't know. I've got a good idea of what's going on, Jim, but I may be wrong. It's easy to put two and two together and come up with five."

"I can't deal with this now."

James got up and made for the door. Rachel quickly blocked his path, determined not to let her brother pass until she had finished what she had to say.

"You're going to have to deal with it sometime soon, James. Or this isn't going to stop. This isn't just bullying. You could get the police involved. You know that, don't you?" James nodded. "Perhaps the school will make it a police matter anyway. Something's got to be done because I don't know how far they're willing to go."

"I don't want to find out."

The telephone downstairs started to ring. Rachel and James heard their mother answering it. She shouted upstairs.

"It's for you, James. It's Paul."

James opened the door and shouted back downstairs.

"Tell him I'm not in, Mum. I don't want to speak to him." He turned back to his sister. "I've got some revision to do. Thanks for everything, Rachel."

5

Paul put his mobile phone in his pocket and started to shake. What had he done? Why couldn't he just have stood up to Jason in the first place like he was planning to if anything like that were to happen? He was such a shit. No wonder why James didn't want to talk to him.

He would probably never speak to him again, and who could blame him? It wasn't even as if Jason believed him anyway. He never had. He knew that he and James were an item. *Had* been an item. Paul was guessing that they weren't anymore. But at least he had pulled Jason away when he had the knife. That was something he had done right.

What was he going to do?

He walked along the hallway and slowly mounted the stairs to his bedroom. He glanced at the clock as he walked in. Nearly five o'clock. He would have to hurry up if he was going to get his dad's tea ready in time. It had been James who had pointed out when he stayed over less than a week before that it shouldn't be Paul's job to cook and clean for his dad and often-absent mum. Paul knew that he was right. But what could he do about it? If he didn't do as he was told, he got beaten.

It was no different to James's situation with Jason.

He sat down on the edge of the bed and pulled off his school trousers, tugging on a pair of jeans instead. He took off his shirt and dropped it on to the floor beside his trousers. He got up and walked over to the wardrobe, taking out a pile of dirty washing from inside and took it, along with his school trousers and shirt, downstairs to put in the washing machine. They had no tumble dryer (not one that worked, anyway) but they would easily get dry before the thunderstorms forecast for the next day. Once he had loaded up the washing machine and switched it on, he went outside to take in the washing from the day before. Most of it belonged to his Dad, and he folded it carefully and put it in the small airing cupboard. One of the T-shirts was his own. He was about to pull it on, but then decided that it was too hot to even wear that and so he opened his bedroom door and tossed the shirt on to the bed.

Back downstairs, he went to the freezer and opened the door. He had been planning to put a pie in the oven for his dad's tea, but it seemed pointless making the house even hotter by putting the oven on when he knew there was still a pork pie and some salad in the fridge that needed to be eaten up. He got together what he needed, and set about getting it ready, not that he himself was hungry after what had happened earlier in the day.

He was so wrapped up in his own thoughts about James and Jason that he didn't hear his father come in. He stood in the doorway to the kitchen, watching his son preparing the salad for his tea.

"Look at the state of you," he finally said. "Not a bloody ounce of meat on you. And your mother's got more muscle than you have. I sometimes look at you and wonder if you're mine."

Paul felt himself tense up as his father spoke. It was always the same when he saw him like this. He had planned to cover himself up before his dad came home from work. As his dad scrutinised him, he felt more naked than merely shirtless.

"Look at me when I'm talking to you."

Paul slowly put down the salad and turned around to face his Father. The stench of alcohol had already travelled across the kitchen from his dad's mouth to

Paul. He could tell that this was going to be the perfect end to the day.

"What the hell are you doing anyway? Salad? Do I look like I want a bloody salad after I've been at work all day?" Paul doubted that his dad had been anywhere near work. "If I wanted a limp lettuce all I have to do is look at you. Now, best you start cooking, son, and quick."

"But it's nearly thirty degrees outside, Dad. It's too hot to put the oven on."

Mr Baker staggered into the kitchen and walked around the dining table towards Paul. Paul tried to back away, but knew it was pointless. Within seconds, a hand slapped his face.

"Put *something* in the oven, or I'll put *you* in there."

"Yes, Dad."

Paul held back his tears and moved back to the freezer to get the pie out for his dad's tea.

6

Jonathan Lewis turned over to face his boyfriend. It was gone 2am, and he'd virtually had no sleep so far – not helped by the hot, humid weather or the man lying beside him.

"Are you going to tell me what's bothering you, or are you just going to keep sighing all night and keep me awake?" he said. "If not, I think I'll just go home and sleep there."

Andrew turned his head and looked at Jonathan.

"I'm sorry."

Jonathan leaned over and kissed Andrew's shoulder and ran his fingers down his cheeks.

"What's up?"

"The usual. Work. What do you expect?"

"What happened?"

Andrew told him about what had happened at the school with James, and how he had caught Jason with him in the changing rooms. He was just thankful that Luke had gone and fetched him in the first place.

"Did you report it?"

"Of course I reported it. All The Head was worried about was whether news would get out that there was a kid on school property with a knife. I just hope the Marsh kid is OK. Why would he just walk off like that when I was trying to help him?"

"He probably just wanted to get away from the school. Wouldn't you if you were in his shoes?"

"I guess. I really don't know."

"But you can't bring this stuff home with you, Andy. It's not good for you. You're just going to land up more and more stressed."

"I know, I know." He rolled over on to his back and stared up at the ceiling. He paused for a few seconds, and then said: "I've decided to quit at the end of term."

"Really? You sure? What will you do?"

"I don't know. I don't really care. But if I'm going to resign, my plan is to take The Head down with me."

"Is that wise?" Won't it affect any other job you go for?"

"I suppose so. I don't know. Too bad if it does. I've got to do what my conscience tells me. I'll give in my notice just before half term and that will allow me time to make some noise. But I need your help, Jon."

Jonathan kissed him tenderly on the lips and played gently with his hair.

"I'll do whatever you want, and whatever it takes."

CHAPTER FOURTEEN

1

Nothing changed – nobody really thought that it would.

Jason was suspended from school for a couple of weeks, but it seemed to be a hollow gesture on the part of the school. Many of the kids, and even more of the teachers, wondered why he hadn't been expelled permanently for bringing a knife to school.

When he returned, Jason was unrelenting in his torment of James. The severity of the attacks had lessened, with nothing as orchestrated as those James had been subjected to in the first few weeks of school after the Easter holiday, but then Jason was clever enough to keep a reasonably low profile considering the knife incident. However, if the bullying had got less severe, it certainly hadn't got less frequent – and there was always the feeling that it could spiral out of control again at any moment. Each day resulted in James being given a dead arm, being pushed or shoved, being passed a threatening note, or being at the receiving end of insults, name-calling or promises of what Jason and his friends were going to do in the future. Luckily the things Jason mentioned in the threats didn't come to fruition, for which James was thankful. Most of them had been over-the-top and outlandish, but James never knew where Jason would draw the line or if there was one drawn at all.

Luke, Jane and Claire had appeared to have made their own little group and stayed completely away from Jason with apparently no repercussions – or none that James knew of. All three of them spoke to James, and Luke often reminded him to let him know if things got out of hand with Jason. James thought it was odd that Luke never apologised for the times when he had joined in with Jason in the past, though. Perhaps the offer of help was his way of doing things. It was better than nothing, and James appreciated the offer. It appeared that Jason's group of friends was getting smaller and smaller. Now there was only Smithy and Badger left.

James didn't tell his sister any more about what had been happening. He figured that he might as well just stick it out. There was no need for her to find out about the on/off friendship with Paul and how he had been betrayed. It would only make her worry more than she already did – or make her go and see Paul, which was the last thing James wanted. He just wanted to forget about him. At least he hadn't needed to go to her to be patched up after a beating from Jason again. James was hopeful that the incident with the knife would be the last time something like that was going to happen.

James and Paul avoided each other completely; James because he felt he couldn't forgive Paul for what he had done, and Paul because he was too embarrassed to see James and apologise. Paul had decided that it was best to just leave James alone; he had screwed up their friendship twice and so couldn't blame James for not wanting to have anything to do with him. It was only natural. But they both knew that it wasn't completely over between the two of them. If James couldn't forgive Paul for betraying him again, he also couldn't forget that it was Paul who had risked everything to make sure James didn't get cut any further with the knife. He could easily have been stabbed himself.

For Paul, things had gradually gone from bad to worse at home. More and more he seemed to be not up to the task of pleasing his Father, and each time that happened, he felt the force of his dad's fist. His dad seemed to be drinking virtually every night for no reason that Paul knew of, unless it was because his mother hardly spent any time at home now. Paul assumed that a divorce was on the cards. He wondered if, perhaps, a divorce might actually help things.

Some nights, Paul literally barricaded himself in his room, pushing a chest of drawers in front of the door, and didn't come out, not even to go to the bathroom. He just used that time as constructively as he could to finish off any outstanding coursework and to prepare for the forthcoming exams. He knew he wouldn't do as well in them as he should because of the situation at home, and the situation with James, but he would still do the best that he could.

Life was shit, and he knew it was likely to get worse. He just didn't know how soon.

2

When Jonathan walked through the school gates, he realised it was the first time he had been near Smithdale Academy since he had been a pupil there. Not that it filled him with fear; his school life had been relatively happy, but it still felt strange to be back, especially considering the reason for his visit.

The small car park at the school had been full, and so he had parked on a side street about a quarter of a mile away and walked briskly through the drizzle towards the main building. The school office was still where it used to be and he rapped lightly on the glass to attract the attention of one of the secretaries who, cursing silently to herself, got up from her seat and walked over to the window and slid it across.

"Can I help you?"

"Hi. I'm Jonathan Lewis. I have an appointment with Mr Brownlow at 2 o'clock."

"Ah, yes. Sign in, please."

A book was thrust towards him, and Jonathan signed himself in, with the sour-faced woman giving him an already-prepared badge with his name on it in exchange. He hated wearing such things, but had got used to it after being a journalist for three years. The secretary emerged from the side door of the office and told him to follow her. With no sign of either a "please" or "thank you", Jonathan wondered how, with so many people unemployed, someone with such a lack of people skills had got the job of school secretary.

Jonathan followed her down the corridor until she stopped at a door and knocked. She didn't wait for a reply, but instead opened the door and announced that Mr. Lewis was here. The secretary walked back down the corridor as the door opened fully and Jonathan found himself face to face with the man he had heard so much about.

Kenneth Brownlow seemed like the perfect gentleman, and had a considerably different demeanour to that which Jonathan expected. He had expected him to be a dour, discourteous man with an air of superiority about him, but it certainly was not apparent as yet. After introducing himself, Brownlow offered Jonathan a seat and a coffee, both of which Jonathan accepted. He poured from a coffee machine on the far side of the room and, as he passed him his drink, The Head asked Jonathan about the reason for his visit.

"Well, over the summer we are going to be running a series on schools in the area," Jonathan said. "Their successes, their failures, and any initiatives they may have set up in order to overcome a specific problem they might have had. Basically, a profile of each school, and how they are managing in the current difficult climate.

That kind of thing."

"You mean with finances stretched?"

"Yes. In part."

Brownlow leaned forward.

"And we are the first?"

Jonathan thought it was less a genuine question, and more an accusation. He nodded.

"Yes. As I'm the one doing the interviews for the series, I thought it would make sense to start with my old school, and perhaps show how it has changed in the years since I left. For the better, I'm sure."

"How long since you came here?"

"About eight years."

Brownlow smiled.

"Long before my time, then. This will be the end of my third academic year here."

Jonathan smiled.

"Perhaps you could tell me what about changes have occurred here since you took over as headteacher? I'm sure there are some ideas and initiatives that you brought here that you are proud of and that you would like our readers to know about."

"Indeed. There have certainly been some significant changes since you were at school here, Mr Lewis. Some challenges, too, of course. But we have been very keen to face up to them and to implement the changes needed."

"What kind of challenges?"

"Oh, just the ones that I'm sure you already know about. We had an issue with discipline at one stage.

Hardly surprising given the…" He paused for a moment to choose the right word. "…*background* of some of our pupils. I'm sure you are aware of some of the issues linked to the local housing estates."

Jonathan thought it was rather ironic that Brownlow had gone down the route of placing the blame for the lack of discipline on the poorer families in the area when someone like Jason Mitchell was part of one of the richest.

"So what has the school done about these issues?"

"Tighter rules, in the main. Letting both the pupils and their parents know what is and what is not acceptable."

"I seem to remember that was quite controversial."

"Virtually everything is, these days, Mr. Lewis. One person has a gripe, and they go on Facebook about it, and suddenly you have a riot on your hands."

The Head stood up and walked to the door and opened it.

"Why don't we go on a little walk around the school and I can show you some of the improvements which have taken place."

"I would like that very much. Thank you."

Jonathan quickly finished the rest of his coffee and then he and Brownlow left the office and started their tour of the school.

3

Andrew Green turned and looked around the restaurant. It was far from busy, but Andrew wasn't sure whether this was to do with it being a Tuesday (hardly the busiest night of the week for such an establishment) or because, when people were given their food, they could look at it on their plate for hours and still not be too sure exactly what they were eating. Andrew watched as a waiter brought the food to the next table. A rather rotund middle-aged man was given a plate upon which was clearly a beef-based dish, but Andrew thought it a shame that the ovens in the kitchen were no longer working, for the beef looked not just rare but raw, roughly the same colour as that which he would buy at Asda to roast for his Sunday lunch – if he could ever be bothered to do himself a Sunday roast.

He turned his attention back to Jonathan and smiled weakly before poking gingerly at the food on his plate that, his boyfriend had told him, was venison in a sauce of some kind. He wondered why he felt guilty about eating venison but not pork, for example. He presumed it was because the animal was nice to look at when alive and seemed, almost, innocent – unlike a pig that ate from a trough and rolled around in the mud.

"You're not going to eat that, are you?" his boyfriend said, dismayed.

"Hun, I'm not sure what it *is*."

"I told you what it was."

"I know you did. And it's very sweet of you to take

me out for my birthday. I do appreciate it. But, the truth is, I'm nervous. I'm not used to eating in posh places like this, and this tie is going to strangle me at any moment."

He tugged at the knot of the tie, loosening it slightly.

"It's not the tie, it's the fact that the shirt is years old and probably a tad too small for you."

"I know, I know. Don't remind me. I've put on weight. It's alcohol that did it."

Andrew sipped at the mineral water in front of him.

"And I'm very proud of you for trying to give it up," Jonathan said. "I know it must be difficult."

"You have no idea. I could *so* do with a drink right now. But I think I'd drink the bottle."

"Not with me around you don't! You've done that too many times. Look, you can still forget about the whole thing. You know that. I told my editor that you needed a day or two to think about it."

Andrew put a small amount of food on his fork and put it in his mouth, chewing as quickly as possible for a few seconds before realising that he actually quite liked what he was eating.

"Hmm. This isn't so bad."

"I knew you'd like it."

"Smart-arse. And thank you, but I don't need to time to think. My mind is fully made up."

"Andy, you're possibly throwing your whole career away here."

"I know. But if I were interested in myself I

wouldn't even have considered doing this in the first place, would I?" He rolled his eyes. "Listen to me. I sound like such a martyr!"

"I don't know about that, but you're sounding camper when you come out with comments like that."

"Bastard! Perhaps I am doing it for me, anyway. Seeing that school exposed for what it is will give me some satisfaction."

Another waiter walked past them, making his way through the obstacle course of tables with apparent ease. Andrew watched as he and his firm backside, contained in trousers that were just that little bit too tight (rather like his own shirt), made his way to the far end of the restaurant. He leaned over towards Jonathan.

"Tell me, is there such a thing as a straight waiter?"

"Not sure. I don't know of any. But stop changing the subject, and stop eyeing-up the waiters! You're not meant to look at them when you come out with me. It's not done in polite society."

"Sorry, I'm really not used to polite society. Look, I know you're worried about me, and I know you're concerned, but I know what I'm doing. I know what I have to do. I've thought long and hard about this, and you can print the story. I just hope that it does some good in the long run."

"Do you think it will?"

"Well, I'm guessing Brownlow will have to resign, at least."

"That's the first time you've ever referred to him by his name."

"Oh, I refer to him using all kinds of names."

"I've noticed."

"Mitchell will be off the board of governors, too. Neither men will be of any great loss to the school, although I think Peter Mitchell is relatively unaware of what has been going on regarding his son."

"Is The Head popular with the other teachers?"

"Some. If you don't bother him then he won't bother you. But others see him for what he is."

"Which is?"

"A spineless prick."

Jonathan raised his eyebrows and picked up the glass in front of him, drinking the rest of the water. He, too, would like to have had alcohol but knew it would be unfair to drink when Andrew was trying to give it up.

"You have such a way with words," he said, placing the glass back on the table. "The school might get worse people in."

"You can never know that. That's a risk you always have to take with these things, isn't it? But I can't see how the devil you know is the better option in this case."

"That's true. Are you going to try to find another teaching position?"

"I don't know. If the right one came up. If they'd have me."

Jonathan watched as Andrew started tucking in to the food in front of him, having gotten over the fear of trying something new.

"Well, we're assuming that this is all going to go against you, but we don't know that for sure. It might go completely in your favour. Some places like people who stand up for their morals. You might be viewed as a hero!"

"I doubt that. I think most places like to have employees who keep quiet, get on with their jobs and mind their own business. Robots, I guess. It's the easier option. But if I were planning to stay in teaching I'd make sure it was many miles from here. Where I'm not known."

"You want a clean slate?"

"Well, I don't want a history, if that's what you mean. Not least because I don't want the kids knowing all my business, and they will if I get a local job after what is going in the papers."

"There's nothing to say this is going to stay a regional story, though."

"You think it will blow up?"

"I don't know. But it's a possibility don't you think?"

Andrew ate the last of his main course and laid down his knife and fork on the plate.

"I don't know if people care enough for that to happen," he said. "Either way, the story will be forgotten quickly elsewhere. It's here that it's likely to linger a while. That's why I would want to get a job in another part of the country. Besides, I've come out at school. I think I knew when I took that decision that I wouldn't be hanging around."

"You mustn't forget that there are probably hundreds of gay teachers out there, many of them completely open about it. You could be a role model to the gay kids in the school. In fact, I'm sure you *are* a role model to them right now."

"I don't want to be a role model. I just want to get on with my life."

"But if you walk away, find another position and keep it quiet again surely you're giving in to the type of things that you're standing up to now? You shouldn't have to hide who you are just because somebody might not like it – whether it be a colleague or a kid."

"Jonathan, I just want to teach and have a quiet life when all of this is out of the way. If I can't teach, then I'll do something else. It doesn't matter. Now, I think we should get the dessert menu, although I'm sure you're going to tell me they don't have vanilla ice-cream topped with hundreds and thousands!"

Jonathan laughed and set about getting the attention of a waiter, who handed them dessert menus. Andrew faked a gasp as he looked at his copy.

"I haven't got a clue what some of these things are!"

"You're a sarcastic old sod."

"That's me."

They both ordered a portion of chocolate fudge cake, with Andrew getting quite excited at the normalcy of it after the rather adventurous (for him) main course.

"The thing is," he said once the waiter had walked away, "I don't know if I want to move away at the moment, even if a teaching job did come up."

"Why?"

He glared at his boyfriend.

"Why do you think?"

"Because of *me*?"

"Yeah, because of you." He rested his hand on Jonathan's. "Don't get me wrong, this relationship thing is completely new to me. It's still early days and it might not come to anything, but I'm not getting any younger and I'm having my first serious relationship. I've got to stick around and see how it pans out."

"I'd like you to stick around."

Jonathan rubbed his leg up against Andrew's under the table, quickly moving it away as the waiter came back with their desserts.

"That was close."

"I like it that way. Just to warn you," Jonathan said, "I probably won't see you tomorrow with all of this going on."

"That's OK. I understand."

"This story is a big piece for me."

Andrew started tucking in to his cake.

"I can cope with big pieces," he said.

"I meant the story."

"I know what you meant."

"If this is going in Monday's edition, then I need to try to get an interview with Brownlow tomorrow."

"He won't give you another interview. Not when he realises the real reason for your visit to the school last week.

"I know. But I've got to try. Or at least be seen to try."

"Now, this is real food," Andrew said. "With cream

too."

Jonathan leaned forward and said quietly "It's a pity we can't take the cream home for use a little later tonight."

Andrew grinned and realised that, no matter how difficult the coming days were going to be, he wasn't going to get an early night in order to prepare. And for that he was grateful.

CHAPTER FIFTEEN

1

Water pistols, stink bombs, eggs and flour were all part of the traditional mayhem on the day that the Year 11 students finished school prior to their exams. James expected to be the victim of many of these pranks but, remarkably, had managed to avoid everything, although he had seen plenty of others who hadn't been so lucky. One poor kid about three years younger than him had been absolutely soaked with giant water pistols, and was destined to walk around the school all day in wet clothes. James just tried to stay away from places where he might get caught up in such frivolity, spending his lunchtime and break in the library where the soon-to-retire school librarian ruled with a rod of iron. There would never be any stink-bombs let off in there, and it was one of the few places at school where James knew he would be safe from Jason. Even Jason was scared of Mrs. White.

As the bell sounded to signal the end of school, James waited for his classmates to leave their final lesson and then he made his way through the rabbit warren of corridors to Mr. Green's room. He felt that he needed to say goodbye to him, the one teacher who had always done his best to look out for him. He even knew deep down that Mr. Green had come out at the school because of what had been happening to him. He breathed deeply and knocked on the door and a familiar voice told him to go in.

When James entered the room, he found it virtually unrecognisable. The familiar film and theatre-related posters that had adorned the walls ever since he had started at the school had been taken down and lay strewn across several desks. The bookcases had been emptied and the contents packed into a number of cardboard boxes that were stacked up on the floor just inside the door. Mr. Green himself was in a cupboard at the far end of the room, packing up yet more boxes. James walked a little way into the room.

"Can I have a word please, Sir?"

Andrew Green walked out of the cupboard. His dark suit was full of dust, his shirt was hanging out of his trousers and his hair was dishevelled even more than usual.

"James. Yes. Sure. Come in. Sorry about the mess." He dumped another cardboard box beside the stack already on the floor. "Are you not celebrating your last day with your mates?"

As soon as he had asked the question he wondered

if James had any mates to celebrate with.

"I'm not into the whole party thing, to be honest," came the reply.

"I don't blame you. I'm not much into it myself."

"I'm trying to avoid the flour and the eggs."

"You and me both, James. Why do you think I'm hiding in here? Not all of my esteemed colleagues are looking quite so clean as when they came in this morning. Mr. Ives is walking around looking like he has been filming an advert for Homepride. It looks like we have done well to avoid everything." He perched on the edge of a desk. "So, what can I do for you?"

"Well, it's the last day of school, and I just wanted to come and say goodbye, that's all. And say thanks."

"Thanks? For what?"

"For letting me know that you'd be there to help if I decided to take you up on the offer. For looking out for me."

"That's what I'm here for. It's my job. I'd do it for anyone."

"You might, but not all of the teachers would. It means a lot."

"Thanks."

There was an awkward silence. They hadn't really spoken outside of a lesson since Andrew had walked in on Jason cutting James's chest. Neither of them had talked about how James had left while Andrew had gone to get the first aid kit. Andrew decided to broach the subject.

"How have things been for you the last few weeks?"

he said.

"Better than they were before. Not great, but better. Thank you."

"What are you going to do when you leave?" Andrew asked. "Are you coming back here to sixth form?"

"Yeah, probably. If my grades are Ok."

"I'm sure they will be."

"I hope so."

"What subjects are you going to do?"

"I'm not sure yet. Certainly English and drama. I've always enjoyed them both. So, you'll probably be teaching me again."

Andrew stood up and walked slowly to the window and looked out. He turned back to James.

"Look, I shouldn't say this, James, as it's not my place or my job. But have you thought about doing you A-levels away from here? At college?"

"Not really. You think I should?"

Andrew leaned against the window-sill.

"It's not up to me. But at least it would give you a fresh start away from this place."

"Yeah, I think I could do with that sometimes."

"It's been a hard year for you, hasn't it?"

"Yeah."

"A hard year for both of us."

"But next year will be different. Some people will have left."

James looked around the classroom and down at the boxes in front of the door.

"Why are you packing, Sir?" he asked. "Are you moving classrooms?"

Andrew sighed. He thought he would be able to get away without any of the kids asking him what was going on, but that wasn't to be.

"No. I'm leaving."

James was taken aback. He couldn't believe what he had just been told. The school wouldn't be the same with Mr. Green, he was one of the reasons why he had wanted to take English and drama at A-Level.

"Oh. I didn't realise. There wasn't any announcement or collection or..."

"I made the decision quite recently."

"Why?"

"I can't really say. The reasons are personal. I'm sorry."

"I understand."

The teacher smiled.

"Actually, I can say. It doesn't matter anymore. There were things I wanted to do here that I wasn't allowed to – and there were people that I wanted to help that I was told not to. I'm leaving because I can't work here and do what I came into teaching for. I handed in my notice yesterday and planned to work up until the school holidays in July, but I have been suspended – I guess you would call it that, anyway. I've got the local papers involved, James. My partner is a reporter and is exposing what's been going on in this place and, no doubt, other schools too. I'm sure you'll see the shit hit the fan, so to speak. It might mean I won't teach again, but it will hopefully mean that this place will have a new Head, some new governors and some new ideas when next term starts. I'm just sorry it didn't happen while you were here."

James wasn't sure what to make of what he had just been told. The fact that his favourite teacher wouldn't be around to teach him during sixth form would certainly make him think hard about the option of college that had been suggested. He hardly dared ask the question which was at the forefront of his mind.

"Is this because of me?" he finally asked.

"No, it's to do with the fact the school refused to do anything about what was happening to you. This isn't your fault, James. None of this is your fault."

"I don't see how the school would have the answers."

"It probably hasn't. I'm not sure if anyone has. But it doesn't have a right to turn a blind eye to what you've been going through either. Kids are meant to be safe here. And they could be if it wasn't for certain people. I put ideas forward that might have helped, but they were turned down."

"Is this going on the telly?"

Andrew Green smiled.

"Well, in the papers anyway. After that, I'm not sure. It depends if this whole thing blows up." He sighed and looked around the empty classroom. "I've got to finish packing," he said. "I'm going to miss this place. I've worked in this classroom for a long time now. I've had good times here."

"The school will miss you too, Sir. I'm sorry for holding you up."

"Don't be silly. It was nice of you to come and say goodbye." He held out his hand, and James shook it. "I hope things go well for you in the exams and after, James – whatever you decide to do. It was a pleasure teaching you."

"Thank you, Sir."

Andrew Green smiled and half-waved as James opened the door of his classroom.

"Goodbye, Sir."

James closed the door and walked down the corridor as he had many times before. But this time was very different. He had finally left school and never had to go back again if he didn't want to, and it was a great feeling.

2

As Paul walked out of the school gates on his last day of compulsory schooling, he saw Jason, Smithy and Badger on the other side of the road. Jason and Smithy, their shirts wholly undone and scrawled upon by classmates in traditional last-day-of-school style, had stripped Badger to his boxer shorts and were taping him to a lamppost using gaffer tape. A small crowd of fellow school-leavers watched, cheered and jeered as Jason and Smithy pulled various items out of their school bags.

Jason laughed as he smashed three eggs on the top of Badger's head and they started to run down his face.

A couple of local residents came into their gardens to see what the commotion was about, and looked on dismayed, shaking their heads at what was happening outside their homes – not because of sympathy towards Badger, but because of the mess that would be left behind.

Smithy picked up a squeezy bottle of tomato ketchup and tucked it down the waistband of Badger's boxer shorts. He squeezed it repeatedly, pumping the sauce down the inside of his shorts and, within seconds, it was trickling out the bottom of them and making its way down Badger's legs.

Paul watched from the other side of the road, glad that it wasn't him on the receiving end instead of Badger. He was surprised that it wasn't. Badger tried to take it all in good humour, but his smiles and laughter were clearly strained. Jason and Smithy weren't laughing at all. This didn't seem to be a prank or last-day-of-school high jinks to them. This was something else. The humiliation of their less-than-bright friend wasn't fun; it was almost a *need*. Someone had to be the butt of their jokes.

Next up for Badger was a bag of flour, tipped over his head by Jason, and sticking to his face, body and legs where remnants of the egg and ketchup remained. Jason then grabbed hold of Badger's boxer shorts, as if he was about deliver the ultimate humiliation and pull them down. But he appeared to think better of it, and let go of them at the last minute. Paul then watched with amazement as Jason and Smithy simply walked off, their job done, leaving Badger tied to the lamppost. Within seconds, the small crowd of onlookers who had gathered to watch the ritual dispersed, none of them caring enough to release the victim from his bonds.

It was then that Paul realised that Badger's problems had only just begun. The gaffer tape with which he was secured to the post was wrapped across his bare chest and arms, and removing the tape was more than likely going to remove a fair amount of skin and hair at the same time.

Badger looked across the road and made eye contact with Paul. He smiled hopelessly, and mouthed the words "help me" to Paul. For the first time, Paul realised that Badger was no different to himself. Jason wasn't on his side at all; he had got Badger on board in order to humiliate and take the piss out of him. The only difference between the two of them was that Jason had controlled Badger for much longer. Now, on his last day of school, he had been ridiculed in front of everyone and finally been made aware of his position in Jason's circle of friends – the jester and a pawn.

Paul hesitated, and then crossed the road, walking up to one of the residents still in their gardens and asking if he could borrow a pair of scissors or a knife. The old man said nothing, but nodded and went back into his bungalow, returning with a Stanley knife. Paul thanked him and went over to Badger.

"Why did they do that?" Badger asked as Paul

walked towards him.

"Why do you think?" Paul replied.

He slipped the knife between Badger's arm and the lamp post. He slowly cut through the tape, releasing his arm. Paul then moved across and gingerly cut the tape between his arm and chest, repeating the process on Badger's other arm. He moved away from the post and thanked Paul, and started picking at the tape still stuck fast to his body and arms. He winced as his first attempt removed a bunch of hairs from his arm.

"How am I going to get this off?" Badger asked.

"No idea, mate. Sorry."

Badger looked at Paul.

"He'll pay," he said eventually.

With that, Paul walked away, handing the Stanley knife back to the old man and then starting on his way home.

He wasn't sure how he felt about helping Badger. Perhaps he should have helped him more, or at least tried to comfort him after his ordeal. But Badger was, after all, one of *them*. The problem was that so was *he*. He was no better than Badger – in fact he was worse, even; Badger was so gullible that he would have believed anything Jason had told him, but Paul had known exactly what was happening all the way along. Luke had even got himself beaten up and taken to hospital in order to help him. In return, Paul had beaten up James at Jason's request.

Paul walked up the path towards his front door and put the key in the lock only to find that the door was unlocked. He opened the door and went into the entrance hall, throwing his school bag down in the corner. Something was wrong. He had assumed that his father had forgotten to lock the door when he went out that morning. It wouldn't have been the first time. But there was an atmosphere in the house. His dad was home for some reason, and that could only spell bad news.

Paul walked over and slowly opened the door into the lounge. The curtains were drawn across the window and it was almost dark in the lounge. It took his eyes a couple of seconds to adjust to the lack of light, and then he spotted his dad in the armchair furthest from the door.

"Are you going to stand there all day or are you going to come in here?" his dad said. He was drunk. At four o'clock in the afternoon. Paul wasn't surprised. "Come on, then."

Paul shut the door and walked further into the lounge.

"You're home early, Dad."

"Yes, I am, aren't I? Well, actually, no I'm not. Because I haven't been to work today."

"Oh. I didn't realise you had a day off."

"I didn't. I just didn't go in."

This wasn't good. Yet another sign, as if he needed one, that his dad was going through what his mother rather inadequately referred to as "a bad patch".

"You'd better sit down, Paul. We need to talk."

Paul went over to the armchair opposite the one in

which his Father was sitting, and sat down.

"Good. That's better." He finished off the drink that he was holding in his hand. "Your mother sent me a letter from her brother's. It arrived this morning. She wants a divorce."

"Oh, shit."

"Yes. Oh shit, indeed. Her beautiful letter informs me that she can no longer cope with my drinking habits and the way that I beat her. I don't ever remember me hitting her, do you?"

"No, Dad," Paul lied. His dad might not *remember* hitting her, but he certainly had done so, and hit Paul too, on more than one occasion.

"Good.

"So, I rang your mother this morning to tell her what I thought about the whole idea. I don't think I was very…*polite*…about the whole thing to be honest. But you can understand why, can't you? I mean, the slag has no right to leave me like that. But, do you know what she said, Paul? *Do You Know What She Said?*" Paul shook his head. "She said that she didn't want anything to do with me or her *fag son*." He thought for a couple of seconds. "Yes, that is the term she used. *Fag son*. You wouldn't happen to know what she meant by that, would you, Paul?"

Paul shook his head slowly. He felt like running, but for some reason he seemed totally rooted to the chair as his dad went on. His world was about to come crashing down around him. All of the time he had feared his dad, often with good reason, and now it was his mother who had betrayed him.

"Well, I asked her what she meant. And she told me to open my eyes. Open my eyes. So that's what I did. I went upstairs into your bedroom and looked. I knew she had to be wrong. No son of mine would ever be queer. I pulled open all your drawers, opened all your cupboards and found nothing. Nothing."

"That's *my* room, Dad."

"And it's *my* house. Don't interrupt. I found nothing. Nothing. Until I lifted up the mattress and put my hand underneath to make sure you weren't hiding any fag porn under there. And guess what I found, Paul. Just guess what I found!" He reached down the seat of his chair and pulled out a copy of the Gay Times and threw it at Paul. "I found this."

Paul couldn't believe it. It had taken him ages to pluck up the courage to go into town and buy the magazine just after he had got together with James. He had gone to the counter in the newsagents, expecting a dirty look or a snide remark from the shopkeeper. But they said nothing. Paul wasn't sure if the shopkeeper even realised which magazine it was. Perhaps he didn't care. Either way, it was the only one he had ever bought. He realised there wasn't much in there to interest him and so didn't buy one again.

"I'm sorry," Paul said quietly. He stood up and edged himself around the back of the armchair.

"Sorry. Is that all you've got to say? I want you to tell me why you've got that filth in my house."

Mr. Baker stood up and started slowly walking to

Paul, who backed away from him.

"No son of mine is ever going to be queer. You hear me?"

Mr. Baker threw his empty glass across the room at Paul. Paul saw it hurtling towards him just in time and ducked, causing the glass to smash loudly against the wall behind him.

Paul bolted towards the lounge door, with his dad lunging after him. He escaped up the stairs but came to an immediate stop when he came to his bedroom. It looked as if it had been hit by a tornado. The mattress was on its side leaning precariously up against the wall, but that was the least of the problems. The chest of drawers had been emptied, with the contents thrown haphazardly on to the floor. His small stereo appeared to have been thrown across the room and was now in pieces.

He turned and saw his dad reaching the top of the stairs. Before he could try and get away, his father's hand was hurtling towards him, slapping his face hard. This was followed by a blow to the head that sent Paul to the ground. He fell against the bed, the wooden frame cutting into his back.

Paul yelled out in pain and screamed at his dad to stop, but a foot was already speeding towards him and hit him hard in the chest. Paul tried to back away, but there was nowhere to go, so he rolled himself into a ball and did his best to endure the series of kicks and punches that landed on his legs, face and torso, knowing that he probably wouldn't be able to get past his father even if he did manage to make an effort to get out of the house.

He started to become worried that his dad was never going to end the attack, and tried to stand up in an attempt to escape. As he manoeuvred himself into a kneeling position, he saw too late his dad's foot coming towards him, and heard the crunch as it made contact with his nose. Paul thought it was broken and it throbbed intensely as blood dripped out of his nostrils and onto his school shirt.

Perhaps the sight of the blood scared his father, for the punches and the kicks stopped suddenly, and Paul watched as his father walked towards the bedroom door.

"You've got ten minutes to get your stuff and get out," he said, as he went out of the door and stumbled down the stairs.

Paul stayed on the floor for a minute or so, trembling and crying – not out of pain, but out of sheer terror. What was he to do now? He was being chucked out of his house and had nowhere to go. There were no other relatives in the area – certainly none that would put him up even for a few nights. He didn't even have any friends. He thought briefly about going to James's house and trying to apologise for everything that had happened, but he just couldn't do it. He still couldn't forgive himself for what he had done, so there was no way he could ask somebody else for forgiveness.

The only thing he could do was pack a bag with as many clothes and belongings as he could and go to the park for the night and sleep there. He had some credit on his mobile phone, and perhaps he would think of somebody to call later on when he had calmed down a little.

His chest and back had begun to throb, and Paul grabbed at some tissues to try and stop his nose from bleeding. He knew that he had to get up off the floor and pack a bag or he would be thrown out with no belongings at all. He wouldn't bother about food, knowing that he had about a hundred pounds in his bank account. He would go to a cash machine and get a takeaway later on. Paul certainly didn't feel like eating at the moment – in fact, he felt like he was going to throw up.

He got up and started to fill his sports bag with clothes. He wasn't sure what he should pack, or how long he would be gone for. Was he really being chucked out of the house for good? He had no idea. He wasn't sure if it would be a bad thing if he was. As long as he found somewhere to stay, he certainly wouldn't miss living with his dad who was getting drunk more and more as time went on.

Paul wasn't really upset about being thrown out. He thought it probably hadn't sunk in as yet, and would probably hit him later. He was more upset that his mum had let the cat out of the bag that she knew he was gay. How she knew, he wasn't too sure. Why she told his dad he had no idea. Perhaps she didn't care about him either. Why else would she leave him there all those weekends alone with his dad? As Paul zipped up his bag, he realised he had a sudden hatred of his mother and the fact that she had abandoned him. At that moment, he hated her even more than he hated his father.

3

As he walked out of the house with the crammed sports bag slung over his shoulder, Paul realised that if he had to spend any nights outdoors then this was probably the time of year to do it. There was no forecast of rain for at least three or four days, and the temperature had fallen no lower than to around fifteen degrees over the last few nights. It would probably be more comfortable outside than in, but he had stuffed a blanket into his bag nonetheless. It was the dangers of sleeping rough that worried him more than the practicalities.

Paul walked slowly towards the park, still trying to come to terms with what had happened – and on his school-leaving day, no less! He wondered whether he should go to hospital and get himself checked over to make sure nothing was broken, but decided against it – although it might have been a way of getting a bed for the night. But he didn't want to have to answer the questions they would ask about how he had landed up in such a mess. He had enough problems without the police getting involved. He had no idea what they might do to his father if he got reported – or what would happen to himself. He didn't need any extra worries.

He decided to make a small detour in order to take

in a McDonald's, which would do for his evening meal. He knew he had enough cash in his pockets to cover that, so he wouldn't have to visit a cash machine on the way.

He sat inside the restaurant and ate his meal slowly, watching people come and go for a good half an hour after he had finished eating. He had nowhere else to go. A few of the customers were from his year-group at school, and he guessed that they were eating there before going out and celebrating their last day at school. None of them spoke or acknowledged him, but he wasn't surprised and didn't really care.

By the time he picked up his bag and continued on his way to the park, he had come up with something resembling a plan. He would first find somewhere nice and secluded so that those using the park as a short cut after leaving the pubs and clubs of the city wouldn't spot him. The last thing he wanted was any more trouble. Then he would use his mobile phone to ring James's house and try to speak to Rachel and perhaps arrange to meet her the next day. He just prayed that she was at home, for she was his only hope.

CHAPTER SIXTEEN

1

Rachel sat at a table in the corner of the café. The place seemed surprisingly quiet for a Saturday morning, with just her and then two other customers sitting closer to the counter. She took a sip of her coffee and then looked out of the window, wondering why Paul had asked to meet her in the park cafe, rather than somewhere closer to home, and why he had asked to meet her at all. It was James who was his friend, not her.

She finally saw Paul in the distance walking towards the café. He came in, spotted Rachel and walked over to her. He put his bag down on the floor and sat down.

"Hi, Rachel."

"Hello, Paul. I got you a coffee."

She pushed the mug of coffee towards him.

"Thanks."

He tasted the coffee and then looked around the café and then back at Rachel. He smiled.

"You look like shit," Rachel said.

"I know."

"You don't smell much better."

"Thanks."

He wasn't surprised by Rachel's comment; he had always known her to be what might be called "forthright" with her opinions. And he didn't doubt that he *did* look like shit. He hadn't been exactly nervous spending the night out, but it was disconcerting, and he found that he hadn't been able to relax enough to get any worthwhile sleep. He reckoned that he had only slept an hour at most. He also hadn't found anywhere to wash since he had woken up. The public toilets in the park were normally closed at night, but were closed all the time at the moment due to vandalism. Paul had wondered at the time if Jason had been a part of that too, but then realised that he couldn't blame him for everything, no matter how much he might have wanted to.

"So, what's all this about, eh?" Rachel asked. "I don't like being asked to meet people behind my brother's back. Especially when I know that they have upset him."

"He's told you?"

"No. But it wasn't difficult to work out, Paul. I've seen how James has been acting and then, with you turning up out of the blue the other week, it didn't take too much of an effort to work out that you were part of the equation. You *are* part of this, aren't you?"

Paul nodded.

"Yes," he said.

Paul had thought that this wasn't going to be easy, and he wasn't wrong. He had forgotten how protective of her brother Rachel was. Not that it was a bad thing; he wished *he* had a sibling who could be protective towards him. It might have solved all sorts of problems.

"Look, I feel awful about asking you to meet me like this," he said, "but I didn't know who else to talk to. James doesn't want to speak to me and I don't blame him. But I wanted to see you so that you could pass a message to him, or something."

Rachel leaned back in her chair and sighed.

"This isn't making any sense. Why don't you start at the beginning, Paul, and then we'll take it from there. All right?"

Paul hadn't planned on having to tell Rachel the full story of what had happened. He knew that James wouldn't want her to find out from someone else, but, then again, he also knew that, right now, he didn't have much choice. He needed Rachel's help and there was no one else he could turn to.

"Me and James have been friends for years, you know that."

"Of course. You used to be at the house all the time until last autumn, when you must have fallen out or something."

"Kind of. Last summer, we spent almost every day together at your house. It was really great. It was nice for me to get away from my parents, and me and James had fun."

"Go on."

"Well, things happened at the end of the school holidays."

"What kind of things?"

Paul hesitated, unsure of how much he should say. James was going to hate him even more for telling Rachel what had been going on, but what choice did he have?

"We…well we…"

"Just spit it out, Paul."

"We became boyfriends, I guess."

"*At last.* I guessed that something like that was going on. So, why didn't you speak for so long?"

"There's a guy at school, Jason Mitchell. He's the ringleader of a group of kids in our year. He caught us together. At the cinema. We were holding hands – or kissing. I don't remember which. It was dark and so we thought no-one would see. But Jason turned out to be right behind us. We had no idea. He confronted us in the foyer of the cinema. I pushed James away and said that he had come on to me and that it was all his fault. Since then he's had trouble from Jason and I was forced to hang around with him in order to protect myself. I even joined in with the bullying. I tried not to, but…it was difficult, you know? Then, a month or two ago, I thought Jason had gone too far and I was feeling guilty, and that was when I came around to see James and make up with him. To try and sort things out. We made up and he came and stayed with me that weekend."

Rachel smiled to herself. She had wondered who

the "friend" was that he had gone and stayed with that night. James wasn't well known for his abundance of mates.

"We had a really good time," Paul went on. "We were just going to be open about it. Take the wind out of Jason's sails. Then the next week, before we could do that, Jason found out about us and, when he caught us, I did the same as I did last time. I told him that James had come on to me. I didn't know what else to do. He made me hit James, and then he did other stuff too, with a knife. I pulled him away from James then, But it was too late. I had already betrayed him again."

Rachel leaned back in the chair. Finally she was hearing the whole story. In many ways it was so much worse than she thought. She'd had a good idea that James was having trouble at school – he had near enough admitted it himself – but she hadn't imagined anything this serious.

"I feel like a shit," Paul said.

"You *sound* like a shit."

"I'm sorry."

Rachel finished the last of her coffee.

"It's not me you need to apologise to, is it?"

"I know. But James won't see me."

"Can you blame him?"

"No. But I really do want to see him. I was wondering if you would tell him I'm sorry. I just wanted someone to tell him that before I went."

"Before you went where?" Paul didn't reply. "What's going on here, Paul? What is the *real* reason we're here?"

"My Dad. He found a copy of a magazine in my room. A gay magazine. Under my bed. He was drunk when I got home from school yesterday. He beat the shit out of me and chucked me out. I've got nowhere to go."

Rachel wasn't sure if Paul was telling the truth or not. She wondered if he was just telling her he had been chucked out in order to get her on his side. But he *did* look awful, and she could remember James saying how Paul's dad used to treat him.

"Where are you staying?"

"Nowhere."

"Are you sleeping rough?" she asked.

"Yeah. Until I sort something out."

"You can't do that. It's not safe."

"I don't have a choice. I found a quiet spot in the park last night, out of the way so people wouldn't see me. It wasn't too bad really. But I didn't really get to sleep. I was too nervous."

"What about your mum? What does she say about all this?"

Paul looked out of the window and Rachel watched as tears welled up in his eyes.

"She's as bad as he is," he finally said. "I didn't realise it until yesterday. But I don't think she gives a toss about me. When things got bad with Dad she would just get up and stay at my uncle's for a few days – weeks sometimes – but she used to leave me behind. But apparently, she told Dad yesterday that she wanted a divorce, and told him that I was gay, too. I don't know how she found out. I thought James was the only one who knew. She told him to look in my bedroom if he wanted proof. That's what he did. He'd turned the place upside down by the time I got home from school. And he found what he was looking for."

Rachel wasn't sure what to say. What *did* you say to a story like that?

"Are you going to be OK?" she said.

"Yeah. I hope to find somewhere to stay within a couple of days, but I don't know where. But I'll sleep in the park until then."

"There are people who can help you, Paul. Social services and that kind of thing."

"Yeah, I know. I'll see about them after the weekend I guess. Until then, I'll just manage. So, will you tell James for me, please?"

"Yeah. But it's going to take a long time for him to get over this. He was hurt pretty bad, you know?"

"I know. But tell him he can find me in the park during the next couple of days if he wants to. My mobile will be on as I can charge it in the mall."

"I will tell him. I promise. But I don't know if he'll come and see you."

"I understand."

She left the café a few minutes later, buying Paul some breakfast and another coffee before she went. She made him take some money even though he said he didn't want or need it, but it was the least she could do. The biggest problem was going to be how to tell her brother about what had happened.

2

When, later that morning, James saw his sister looking at the window display of the record shop, he assumed it was because she was coming to say hello and give him some support on his first day at work. He had arranged with Alfred to work every Saturday throughout the year and on Wednesdays as well during the school holidays. Alfred said he might even leave him alone in the shop after a few weeks while he went and looked at large collections of records, posters and other memorabilia that customers wanted to sell him. In the space of less than twenty-four hours, James had left school and started work in his first job. He felt quite grown up, and glad to be able to get away from the school.

Rachel walked into the shop and smiled at her brother.

"Hey, Rachel," James said from the behind the counter.

"So, this is the famous shop, huh?" she said.

"Yeah. You like it?"

"I like it."

She walked towards the counter and James introduced her to Alfred.

"Alf, this is my sister."

Alfred stood up as Rachel offered her hand for him

to shake. He surprised her and kissed it instead. He was clearly quite pleased to have a pretty young lady in the shop for once instead of slightly nerdy middle-aged men.

"James, I'm sorry to come here to your work, but something's come up," she said. "Is there anywhere we can talk for a minute or two?"

Alfred suggested that James take Rachel through the back of the shop, promising him that he would be OK on his own. He *had* managed the shop for years, after all. He told him to put the kettle on while he was there. James was amazed at how many cups of tea the man could get through in one morning.

James and Rachel made their way through the door behind the counter.

"What's up?" James asked when they were out of earshot of Alfred.

Rachel wasn't quite sure what to say and so just came out with it.

"I know about you and Paul," she said.

James looked at her in dismay.

"Oh," he said. He was quiet for a few seconds and then said: "Are you mad at me?"

"Why should I be mad at you?"

"Just because…"

"I'm not mad at you."

"Does Mum know?"

"No. I haven't told her. But she's not stupid, Jim. I'd worked out roughly what's going on. I'm sure she has too. She'll be OK with it."

"I hope so. How did you find out?"

"I got a phone call from Paul. He asked me to meet him for a coffee this morning."

James flung his arms up in the air.

"And you went? I don't believe this! You shouldn't have gone. This is all his fault."

"He's living on the streets. His Dad chucked him out yesterday when he got home from school. He found a magazine in Paul's bedroom and all hell let loose, apparently."

James walked over to the sink and filled up the kettle.

"He deserves it."

"You don't mean that. No one deserves that, Jim."

James dropped teabags into some mugs and then sat down to wait for the kettle to boil.

"What did he want from you?" he asked.

"He didn't *want* anything. He just wanted me to tell you that he was sorry, that's all. I nearly offered for him to stay at ours for a few days until he got himself sorted but…"

"He beat me up, Rachel! He was told to beat me up and he did!"

"He was scared."

"What do you think I was? There were three of them beating the shit out of me!"

"Yes, but he also stepped in when Jason had the knife."

"This is screwed up."

As he finished making the tea, James said:

"We need to tell Mum. You remember Mr. Green

at school?" Rachel nodded. "He's been looking out for me a bit but the Head won't do anything. He's quit his job and gone to the papers. I think it's going to be in on Monday."

"Good for him."

"Yeah. But the shit's going to really hit the fan when the papers come out on Monday if Mr. Green has really done what he says he has. I just don't want Mum finding out I'm gay through gossip about the story."

"He won't have named you."

"That's not the point. She'll still work out who it's all about."

Rachel put her arm around her brother's shoulders.

"Ok then. We'll tell her. But don't be surprised if she already knows. But then you should go and see Paul. He's sleeping in the park."

James glared at his sister, but he knew she was right.

"All right," he said finally.

3

When Paul returned to the park later that evening, he found it transformed. A large stage had been erected at one end, with two beer tents towards the other. According to the giant banners, the park was the location for a council-funded concert featuring local bands. Paul realised that there was no way he was going to be able to stay there that night as there would probably be people clearing up until dawn. With that many people about, and no doubt a police presence too, he would be spotted and told to move on anyway. He walked away from the park to try and find somewhere else that he could safely spend the night, although he thought that he might return to the park a bit later to see what was going on. At least the entertainment would kill some time, and perhaps he would meet someone there that he knew.

He decided it would be better if he found himself somewhere a little out of the town centre, so that he wouldn't be disturbed by people leaving the bars and clubs later that night. The last thing he wanted was to be attacked by a violent drunk, like the guy he had seen on the local news a couple of weeks back.

He started walking back towards his own house, remembering a small alley that he had used as a short cut occasionally if he had been late getting home. He was pretty sure that it would at least ensure him a quiet night. Once there, he would text Rachel with the number she had given him earlier in the day and tell her where he could be found just in case she or James went looking for him. He knew that wasn't going to be likely, but he could only live in hope. Something good had to happen to him eventually.

The little alleyway seemed dingier than it had done before, but then he realised he had only ever seen it at night and so wasn't likely to notice the odds bits of rubbish on the floor and the weeds growing up between the paving slabs.

He decided that the best thing to do was to find a hiding place for his bag and leave it there so that he didn't have to carry it all the way back to the park if he decided to see what was going on there. He found a patch of ground a little way away that had been planted with shrubs. Paul could hide his bag in there and know that no one was ever likely to find it. He wouldn't be back late anyway. He took his phone and wallet and hid the bag in the bushes, covering it as best as he could. From the path, you would never know it was there.

On his way back to the park, he passed a sandwich shop and went in to get a filled baguette for his evening meal, but he knew that he could only really afford to get a takeaway again because of the money Rachel had given to him before she left the café that morning. This would be his last one. He had to stretch his money out as much as possible. He knew that there was a soup kitchen that set up a stall in the city centre every night to feed the homeless. He had seen it there sometimes. He had never in a million years thought he might have to use it, but now he realised he might have to go there for his main meals in the future.

A crowd had begun to appear by the time he finally got back to the park and a man was on the stage talking. Paul assumed he was the compere for the evening, although from what he heard of what he said (which wasn't much due to the excessive volume of the loudspeakers) the man clearly thought he was funnier than he actually was. Ten minutes later, the first band appeared. The Cormacks consisted of five middle-aged men in checked shirts and jeans singing a series of country covers. Paul hoped things would get better as the evening progressed, although he found the sight of five grown men singing *Stand By Your Man* a little odd and, if nothing else, entertaining.

The country band played a set of about twenty minutes and were followed, by way of the unfunny host, with a three-piece punk outfit which was even less to Paul's taste than The Cormacks were. An hour, and a rock and a jazz band later, Paul slowly started to make his way back to his makeshift bedroom for the night. The entertainment had been pretty awful and he was glad that he wasn't staying in the park after all. The last thing he wanted to do was to listen to more bad music.

His bag was still where he had left it. He dragged it to the alley and took out his blanket, covering himself with it after he realised that a cool wind cut through the narrow passageway. Paul made a pillow out of his jacket and placed it on top of the bag and settled down for the night, hoping that he might actually get some sleep this time around. He was hopeful; no sleep the night before and then walking around all day had started to take its toll and Paul was worn out.

4

As Rachel had predicted, James's mother took the news that her son was gay extremely well. As soon as James came home from his day at the shop and said that he needed to talk to her about something, she knew what it was that he had to say. The possibility that James was gay had also been something that she and Rachel had discussed on a number of occasions. Her reaction was simply the opposite to that of Paul's dad. She hugged her son and told him that she didn't care what he was as long as he was happy. That was the important thing. His being gay didn't change anything. She didn't cry, just told James that she loved him.

James took the opportunity to fill her in on what had been happening at school and the fact that the story was going to hit the local newspaper on Monday. She said that she remembered Mr. Green from the previous year's parents evening and, if she ever saw him again, she would thank him for everything he had done in helping James. Alice Marsh admired a man who stuck to his morals. She just wished she had married one.

James also told her about Paul. He started off by talking about what had happened the previous summer and finished with how Paul had betrayed him a few weeks earlier in order to save himself. Rachel continued the story and told her mother about what had happened that morning when she had met Paul and how he was sleeping rough after his Father had thrown him out.

"No matter what the boy has done, James, we can't let him sleep rough," Mrs Marsh said. "I'm not saying he has done the right thing at times but it seems that he's had other things to deal with, too, if his dad is as bad as you say he is. The three of us will go and find him later.

If he wants to talk to you, then I think you should listen to him, Jim. If things work out, then he can stay here until he gets sorted, but only if you're happy, OK?"

James smiled and nodded. He *did* want to make up with Paul, but he still wasn't sure if he could see past what happened when Jason caught them together for the second time. One time he could forgive, but two?

Rachel told them that she had got a text from him, saying where he would be from about ten o'clock. They agreed to have dinner and then the three of them would go and find him.

But when they went to see Paul, he wasn't there.

5

Paul slept only fitfully. He first stirred when some people walked past the end of the passageway, chatting noisily. Then, about half an hour later he awoke to the sound of scratching. He looked around sleepily to see what was causing the noise and saw a small rat running away from him. He shivered, somewhat disconcerted at the near-encounter and tried to settle down once more but found that he couldn't drift back to sleep.

A few minutes later he heard more people approaching the alleyway. Paul recognised the voices instantly. Jason and Smithy. He did his best to stay still and quiet, seeing no reason why they should turn down the alley and see him. Then he heard Smithy say:

"Hold up a sec, Jase. I need a piss."

He saw Smithy walk a little way down the alley and then start to urinate against the wall about ten feet away from him. Smithy belched, did up his fly and started walking back towards Jason. Just when Paul thought that he hadn't been spotted, the rat made a return visit and he kicked at it instinctively with his leg. Smithy turned back and sauntered down the alley towards him.

"Well, well. Look what we have here," he said. He called to his friend. "Hey, Jase, come here. You've got to see this!"

Smithy burped again as Jason made his way to where he was standing. This was the last thing that Paul needed, There was nothing to protect him from Jason now.

"Well," he said finally. "If it isn't our little queer friend."

Paul shuffled away from him.

"Sod off, Jason."

"Now, now. That's not very nice, especially after lying to me about James. Oh yes, we know everything now!"

Smithy crouched down beside Paul.

"Your dad chucked you out, did he? That's what happens to queer boys. Didn't your mum even stick up for you? Poor little queer boy!"

Smithy got up as Jason bent down and snatched away Paul's blanket. He held it up for Smithy to see.

"This is your bed, is it? Very nice. No room for James in there, though."

"Give it back, Jason."

"Come and get it, my friend." He threw the blanket to Smithy but Paul remained seated. Jason kicked at him. "I said come and get it *queer boy*."

"No. I've seen all this before. Is that the best you can do? Throwing stuff around? I can't be bothered with it."

Jason turned towards Smithy in a mock frown and shrugged his shoulders. He threw the blanket back down over Paul.

"Oh dear," he said. "He's not playing, Smithy. He must be really pissed off."

"Just go home and sober up, Jason."

"And what if we don't want to?"

Paul knew he had two choices. He could run off, but knew that he would have to leave his bag where it was or he would never have a chance of getting away from Jason. If he did that he would probably lose everything that was in it. Jason would tip it out on the floor, trample on the breakables, and tear the clothes. His other option was to stay and try to finally stand up against him. He stood up and Jason walked towards him; his breath reminded him of his Father's.

"Get away from me," Paul said.

"Wouldn't want to come near you, mate. You might try and shag me."

"You think too much of yourself, Jason. You're both quite safe, believe me."

Jason took another step towards him and started to feel himself through his trousers, rubbing his crotch in what Paul assumed was meant to be a provocative manner.

"You hungry? Bet you'd like a piece of my meat, wouldn't you?" Jason said. He moved closer still to Paul and then pushed him to the ground, his taunting becoming yet more outrageous. "You want to suck me off, Paul? Is that what you want to do? I heard on the grapevine that it's what you like."

"Willingly, Jason. It would give me the opportunity to bite it off."

Jason turned to Smithy.

"No one ever told him that cocks are for women and pissing, not for shagging men with." Smithy and Jason laughed. "Talking of which, I could do with a piss."

He walked over towards Paul's blanket and bag and straddled them.

"Don't you dare, Jason."

"Or what?" He gave Paul a sudden kick to the stomach and Paul curled up into a ball in pain. "That's what I thought."

Jason undid his fly and urinated over the blanket. He shook and put himself away. As he did so, he said:

"By the way, not very sporting, you know. Beating up your boyfriend. Probably not the best way to go about having a long-lasting relationship. But, then again, who'd want one with you?"

Jason walked back over to Paul.

"So, what now? Who is even going to know what happens to you? Does anyone really care anyway?"

Paul realised that he had no choice but to run. Jason was drunk, and Paul knew what he was capable of when he was sober. If Jason started kicking him or punching him, would he know when to stop? Besides, perhaps Paul could outrun him if Jason was drunk. He started backing away from him down the alley. Jason followed, but when he got too close, Paul kicked him in the crotch, then just started running.

He could hear Jason swearing behind him, and then begin to give chase, but Paul didn't look back. He had to get as far away from him as possible. He didn't think of where he was going, but once he was back on one of the main streets, he just followed it. All he was after was distance between himself and Jason. He managed it, but his legs soon began to tire.

He followed the main road, hoping that Jason wouldn't be stupid enough to start something where people could see him. But, once he was on the bridge across the river that ran through the town, Paul's legs gave way, and he stumbled to the ground. Jason and Smithy stopped about ten metres away.

"A fat lot of good that did you, Baker," Jason said, trying to catch his breath. "But I give you credit for trying. But now what are you going to do?"

Paul got up off the ground.

"If you don't back off, Jason, I'll jump."

"Yeah, right."

Paul wasn't even sure what had made him say it, but just in that instant the thought of it didn't seem so bad. He had screwed things up with James. He'd been chucked out of his own home. And he was about to be beaten by two drunken boys. Without thinking, he edged his way to the railings of the bridge.

"I'm not kidding, Jason."

"Does it look as if I care? Do what the hell you want."

Paul jumped so that he was sitting on the railings of the bridge, and then swung his legs over so that he was facing away from Jason and towards the river. A woman in a passing car saw what was happening, and pulled the car over and got out.

"What the hell's he doing?" she said to Jason and Smithy.

They both just looked on. Jason realised that this wasn't a game. Paul might actually jump, and it would be his fault.

"Get down, you idiot," he said to Paul, trying to sound calmer than he was. "You've made your point. We'll go. We'll leave you alone. Just get down. *Please.*"

Paul turned to look at them. He was standing on a small ledge on the side of the bridge, holding on to the railings behind him.

"You mean it?" he said.

"Of course we mean it. You'll never see us again. I promise."

Paul hesitated for a moment, and then the realisation of what he was thinking of doing hit him and he started to panic. The woman from the car saw what was happening, and she stepped towards him.

"Hi," she said. "What's your name?"

Paul didn't answer. He was breathing too hard, and his mind was working overtime. He was remembering the summer before with James, getting caught in the cinema, his dad beating him up, being forced to beat up James.

"His name's Paul," Jason said.

"Paul," the woman said. Paul didn't respond. "Paul," she said, louder this time.

Paul looked at her.

"Come back to this side of the railing, love," the woman went on. "Sit on the railing and swing your legs over. Everything's going to be OK." Paul continued just staring at her. "Everything's going to be OK," she repeated.

Paul nodded his head slowly.

He pushed down on the railings behind him, so that he could sit on them as the lady had suggested. But he lost his footing, his hand slipped, and he fell.

The woman from the car screamed.

Jason and Smithy went to the railings and looked over.

"Paul!" Jason shouted. There was no response. "He's gone," he said.

Jason looked at Smithy and the woman from the car.

"What are we going to do?"

"I'll call the emergency services," the woman said, and ran back to her car to get her phone.

"They won't be quick enough," Jason said to Smithy,

He pulled off his shoes and jacket, and climbed over the railings of the bridge.

"What the fuck are you doing?" Smithy shouted. "You'll drown!"

But it was too late.

Jason had already jumped.

CHAPTER SEVENTEEN

1

Three years later, when Andrew Green was in a counselling session, he compared what happened next with opening the lid of a bottle of fizzy drink after shaking it. You could shake the bottle as much as you liked and all the contents would stay inside – but as soon as the lid is unscrewed just a little, the contents come flowing out and make one hell of mess.

The newspaper story that Jonathan wrote about Smithdale Academy and the bullying that was taking place there was the equivalent of the opening of the bottle. Once the story was printed, it was followed by a number of others in the coming weeks, and they affected many different people.

On the morning of the printing of the original story, a bunch of reporters waited outside The Head's front door as he walked out of the house to go to school. Among the reporters was Jonathan Lewis. He held his dictaphone close to The Head as he followed him down his garden path. The man at the centre of the scandal was doing his best to act as though the whole thing was going to blow over within a day.

"Are you planning to stand down as headmaster of Smithdale Academy following the allegations this morning?" one reporter asked.

"I don't think that will be necessary, but, ultimately, that decision is not in my hands. It is up to the board of governors to decide."

Jonathan asked him "You don't feel you should resign?"

"I don't believe I have done anything to warrant a resignation."

"Are you saying that the allegations are false?"

The Headmaster stopped and turned to Jonathan.

"You're Jonathan Lewis, aren't you?"

Jonathan nodded.

"I commend you on your article in this morning's paper. It is a fine piece of creative writing that makes me proud to know that you learned your skills at Smithdale Academy. However, the allegations that you make are complete fabrication. If there was drug-dealing at the school gates, or students bringing knives to school, then I would be aware of that. We run a tight ship at our school. I am also happy to confirm that bullying is not an issue at Smithdale Academy. The allegations this morning are the result of an embittered ex-colleague – your boyfriend so I am led to believe, Mr. Lewis - and I am sure this whole unpleasant matter will be put to rest very shortly. That's all I have to say. Thank you."

With that, he finished the walk to his car, ignoring the rest of the questions fired at him. He got in and started the car as reporters continued to fire comments and questions at him. An egg, thrown by an enraged parent, hit the car as he drove down the street for what would turn out to be his last day in charge of the school.

2

Also making the news that day was the incident on the bridge that had happened the night before. It had occurred too late in the evening to make the morning newspapers, but it was reported in the later editions, although the link to the story about Smithdale Academy was not yet apparent. In fact, at first Jason Mitchell was hailed as a hero for jumping into the river to try to save another youth that had attempted to commit suicide. That narrative soon changed, however, when the truth became known.

Jumping into the river after Paul was the moment that ultimately changed everything for Jason. Unlike Paul, he didn't escape the fall unscathed, with his leg seriously injured as he hit a rock or some debris as he plunged into the water. He stayed in hospital for days while stories started to run in the local press about who he was, his part in the Smithdale Academy saga, and what really happened the night he jumped off the bridge.

When the stories started appearing, Jason's dad confronted him in the hospital.

"Is what they are saying true?" he said, waving the newspaper in front of Jason, and then throwing it on his bed.

Jason looked briefly at the newspaper, but said nothing.

"Jason. Answer me. Is it true? This business about selling drugs…"

"It's only hash, Dad!"

That wasn't strictly true, but this wasn't the time to reveal that.

"I don't give a damn what it is! And these stories of bullying and the rest of it. Are they true, too?"

Jason nodded his head.

"I needn't have asked. I've talked to the police already. They want to talk to us about the allegations, Jason. I've said I'll take you to the station when you get out of here, providing they'll wait that long. I'm not sure they will. Whenever you speak to them, I don't want to hear a single lie coming out of your mouth, young man. Do you hear me?"

Jason nodded. Jason's mum looked across at her husband.

"What's going to happen to him?"

"I don't know. Whatever it is, he'll deserve it, don't you think?" He turned back to his son. "What the hell were you thinking? You're an embarrassment to the family."

Perhaps it was those words that made Jason realise that things had to change. He had bullied, sold drugs, taken a knife to school, and lots of other things his parents would never even know anything about, and all they cared about was that he had embarrassed the family.

As he lay in the hospital bed, day after day, Jason decided that, in order to get out of the cycle of violence that he himself had begun to grow scared of, he would have to try to forget that his parents even existed. Jason wasn't sure he had it in him to force that kind of change upon himself. It was certainly going to be more hard work than it would be to carry on as he had been, but that course of action had landed him in hospital, in the newspapers, and talking to the police. Something had to give.

3

A few days later, the camp bed that had been set up in James Marsh's bedroom for Paul to sleep on was empty. Both of the boys were squeezed into James's single bed, with James's arm laying across Paul's chest. They thought that Alice Marsh wasn't aware that the pair of them cuddled up in the one bed at night, but she wasn't stupid. She would never let on, however. She liked to think that cuddling was *all* they would do while they were in her house! She thought her son knew better than to try to do anything more than that.

A chink of sunlight shone into the bedroom through a gap in the curtains. The sunlight landed directly on James's eyes and he awoke and turned over, looking up at the ceiling. Paul stirred next to him and he looked across at James.

"Hey," he said.

"Hey. You sleep Ok?"

"Yeah. You?"

"Like a dream."

Paul leaned over towards him.

"I love you," he said, and kissed James on the cheek.

James realised that waking up like this was something he could get used to.

There was a certain irony that Paul had got out of the river by himself, almost totally uninjured. He spent the next eight hours in hospital and explaining to the police what had really happened, before being released and returning to James's house, and he had stayed there in the days since.

James guessed that Paul probably wouldn't be staying with him forever. He had already said that he didn't want to impose on James and his family, and that he wanted to find somewhere of his own to live as soon as he could.

However, by the time James started sixth form in September, Paul was still living with him, and it had become clear that the arrangement wasn't going to change in the near future. Paul's parents didn't care where he stayed, and James was happy now that he and Paul could be open about being boyfriends, with their past troubles seemingly behind them – and that made Alice Marsh's decision to let Paul stay very easy indeed.

James had thought about going to college instead of sixth form, as suggested by Mr. Green, but decided against it, thinking that the school might be a different place under a new regime.

Things had definitely changed. Not only had the headteacher gone, but a number of other teachers who had been implicated by association in the newspaper allegations had resigned either voluntarily or forcibly. One of those was the head of the English department, and James was surprised to see on his first day back at school that she had been replaced by a familiar face who had been persuaded to take back his resignation and was now being treated as a kind of local hero for exposing what had been happening at the school.

The events of the previous six months had brought changes to everyone involved in them, both good and bad. But change could be hard to deal with, as they would all soon find out.

THE END

Also available!

Breaking Down, in which we catch up with James, Paul, Jason and Alfred two years after the event of *Breaking Point.* Sample the opening of the book on the next page.

CHAPTER ONE

James Marsh took a deep breath and then mentioned something he had wanted to talk about for the previous forty-five minutes.

"I saw Jason today," he said

"What happened?"

"I went into the newsagent's, just to pick up some milk for Mum. He had his back to me, so I didn't see him at first. It was a bit awkward when he turned around and we saw each other. He smiled at me, paid for his stuff, and left. I've seen him around before, in Tesco and that, but it's easy enough to avoid each other in somewhere like that. You just go down another aisle and pretend you didn't see him. You can't do that in a tiny newsagent's. You have to acknowledge each other."

James took a sip of water, and waited for his counsellor to respond.

"What do you think when you see him? Does it bother you?" she said.

"I still hate him, if that's what you mean. I don't think I will ever do anything else. I'm not about to shake hands and be best friends. But…"

James stared out across the room, his concentration lapsing for a moment. It wasn't an unusual occurrence.

"But what?"

James looked back at the counsellor.

"But he looks sad. And lonely. And I guess he probably is. And I know what that can feel like. And I don't wish that, even on him. I don't know who his friends are, these days. If he has any. None of the crowd he went around with at school. There was only Smithy left anyway, and I know Jason hasn't had anything to do with him since the night on the bridge. As far as I know, he just broke off all contact with him. With everyone, I think. It's weird. But perhaps that's what he felt he had to do to move on."

The truth was that James didn't know *what* he felt about Jason Mitchell any more, the boy who had made his life hell more than two years earlier. It seemed so long ago now, and yet those events still tended to dominate his life without him fully admitting it. The nightmares, the panic attacks, the distrust of other people. James was sure that Jason was to blame for all of that. And he was definitely to blame for James going to counselling sessions week after week. But, in his efforts to try and forget him, he talked about him for an hour a week. Sometimes it seemed like a backward logic.

"Do you feel sorry for him?" the counsellor asked.

"Sometimes." James smiled. "He screwed his life up. You only get one shot at it. That sounds stupid, right?"

The counsellor shrugged her shoulders.

"You feel what you feel. You've told me that you were lonely at school. It's only natural to feel empathy for someone else in the same position, isn't it?"

"I don't know. Not considering he ruined my life for over a year. But, after everything that he did to me and Paul, and others, over the years, he risked his life to save Paul that night. Why would he do that? Why torment someone for all that time and then jump into the river to save them? It keeps coming back to me, and I can't get my head around it. He ended up in hospital with a shattered leg, and he's not going to ever be able to walk as well as he did before, never mind run or do the sports that he used to. He made our lives hell, and then tried to rescue Paul. And all for nothing because Paul had got on to the riverbank by himself anyway. It's almost farcical."

"But he didn't know that at the time."

"No. That's true. But there is a certain irony, all the same."

James and his counsellor sat in silence for a few seconds. James couldn't think of anything more to say. The subject had been discussed at previous sessions, and he still hadn't been able to come to terms with the events of that night, and he struggled with things that didn't make sense to him.

"This is our last session, James. Next week you're

off to university. Is there anything else you want to bring up before we finish?"

James shook his head.

"I don't think so. I mean, I'm nervous about going. About leaving Paul behind. Whether I'll cope on my own. Whether *he'll* cope on his own. Whether we'll be able to stay in a long-distance relationship. But you know all of that already. We've talked about it for weeks. I feel it's time to move on. From school. From this town. I'm looking forward to that. To putting the past behind me. Or trying to. I have to do it. I feel like it's a case of now or never. Now or I'll go completely mad, even. I need to *escape.*"

"How difficult do you think that might be? To escape. Honestly."

"I have no idea. But it's probably going to be easier for me than it is for Jason. I haven't got a bad leg to remind me of my past, like he has."

"You have memories."

"Yes, and nightmares. Even a scar or two. Another reason why I can't just forget."

"Two years isn't such a long time in which to forget, James. Not for someone who went through what you did."

"I guess I'm frustrated. I don't want to be defined by what happened to me when I was at school. From that point of view, me and Jason are in the same situation."

"You seem more concerned for Jason than you do for yourself."

"No. Not really. It's just that I happened to bump into him, and it took me by surprise."

James sat back in the chair and closed his eyes, taking a few moment to get his thoughts together.

"But I don't like...I don't like the fact that sometimes I feel sorry for him," he went on. "It bothers me. I don't think I should be feeling that. But I guess I've come to realise that things aren't as straightforward as I thought they were. The most difficult thing at the moment is trying to get my head around the idea that nothing is black and white. I'm with Paul, a good guy who did some awful things to me during that last year at school. And then there's Jason, who I always thought was the spawn of the devil, and yet risked his own neck to try and save Paul – whose life he had made a misery for a year. A good guy that does bad things. A bad guy that does good things. It just screws with my head sometimes. I struggle with that idea almost more than anything else."

James glanced at the clock on the table.

"Time's up," he said.

CHAPTER TWO

1

James Marsh gently woke the boy lying next to him.

"You're going to have to move, Paul. I've got a dead arm."

Paul Baker groaned and turned over in bed so that James could move the arm that Paul's head had been resting on. He hated being woken up early in the morning, but today was even worse. It was the day that he had been dreading for months, and he had barely slept all night through thinking about it.

Paul had been living with James and his family ever since he had escaped from his fall in to the river. It had been a temporary, unofficial arrangement to start with, but Paul's parents hadn't seemed to care about what he did or where he stayed.

When his dad died suddenly a few months after Paul had left school, he had gone home to live with his mum, who had moved back into the house with her current boyfriend. It had been a disaster. The boyfriend was no better than his dad had been, and so, when that hadn't worked out, the Marsh family had taken Paul in permanently. It had been inevitable. It felt right.

The two years that followed had been the happiest of Paul's life. For the first time, he had felt wanted and accepted, and part of a real family. He had chipped in towards his keep once he had got a job, and the constant fear that he had suffered while living with his parents had evaporated.

And now, all of that was about to change.

This had been James and Paul's last night together for what could be three months. James was leaving for university later that day.

While James had gone on to sixth form, Paul had found himself a job in a local supermarket. He knew that James had plans to go to university, and would never have tried to stop him – no matter how much he might have liked to. He'd saved as much money as he could over the previous year and had already found himself a small rented bedsit which he would move into over the coming weekend.

James's mum had told Paul he could still live with her, but he didn't want to. It would remind him constantly that James was no longer around, and that their days as a couple might be numbered. Besides, James's family had already done enough. They had looked after him when nobody else had wanted to, and now he needed to try and stand on his own two feet. What he didn't realise was that James's mum viewed him as one of her own family, and could have done with the company now that she was going to be alone in the house with both her children at university.

James snuggled up to Paul, put his arm over his boyfriend's chest and gently kissed his neck.

"I need to get up in a minute," he said. "You can stay in bed if you want to."

"No. We've only got a couple of hours left together. We might as well make the most of it."

James laughed.

"I thought we did that last night."

"You know what I mean."

James kissed Paul again.

"I'm not going to the other side of the world, you know? You can visit. And I'm coming back."

"Yeah, I know, I know. But will you be coming back as my boyfriend?"

James propped himself up on his elbow.

"That again. We've been through this. What makes you keep thinking that I won't?"

Paul turned towards him. He had tried to explain his fears to James before, but they hadn't been taken seriously, and he was told he was worrying unnecessarily.

"You're going to university," he said. "Things are going to be different for you. You're going to meet new people, new friends. New *gay* friends. Ones that you might want to go out with more than me. I'm virtually the only gay person you know, James. You might find someone you like a lot more. It's only natural."

"Don't say that. It won't happen."

"It's true."

And James knew it was.

He was off to university, and realised that things were unlikely to ever be quite the same again. Things *were* going to change. He knew couples a year older than himself where they had gone to different universities, and they had pledged to make a go of it long distance, but it never worked out. Skype helped, of course, but even with a call each night it couldn't make up for seeing each other. Skype was for staying in touch, not for keeping a relationship going.

James hoped that he and Paul would be different, that their relationship would beat the odds, that they would somehow find a way, but he knew deep down that it wasn't very likely. And it wasn't just to do with not being with each other as much. He thought he could trust himself around other guys, but he didn't know about Paul. Despite the fact they had been a couple for the last two years, he hadn't forgotten how Paul had betrayed him in the past.

When they had been at school, James and Paul had been caught kissing by Jason Mitchell and his friends, and Paul had turned on James to save himself from the bullying – not once, but twice. James knew why it had happened, and even understood why Paul did it, but there was always that nagging feeling that it might happen again. He didn't think Paul would cheat on him, but he just couldn't be sure. There was that fear there would be a third betrayal.

James kissed Paul on the lips.

"We'll still be together when I come home at Christmas. I promise."

"I hope so."

"I *know* so. But now I need to shower."

Paul watched as James got out of bed, and padded naked across the bedroom, picking up his towel and wrapping it around his waist.

"I hope you're right about us still being together at Christmas," Paul said. "I don't want this to be the last time I see you with no clothes on."

James smiled at him.

"It won't be," he said. "I'll flash at you when I come back from the shower, too."

James walked out of the room and Paul listened to his footsteps as he walked along the landing to the bathroom. He turned over and lay on his back, staring up the ceiling.

He really didn't think that they could get through such an upheaval as this unscarred, and he even wondered if James was in the right frame of mind to try. Six months of counselling hadn't stopped him from having nightmares and panic attacks on a regular basis. Paul only hoped that going to university would help James rather than make him worse.

2

Since Jonathan's Lewis's newspaper article about the failings at Smithdale Academy had been published two years earlier, many changes had been made at the school.

The Head had lasted just one more day in his job before realizing that there was no way he could do anything but resign over the allegations that he had turned a blind eye to the bullying of James and Paul, and that he had allowed a student to get away with bringing a knife to school.   A number of other teachers who had been implicated had also left.

Andrew Green, Jonathan's boyfriend, who thought he would be treated as a pariah for his part in taking the Smithdale Academy story to the newspapers, had been approached by the new headteacher and asked to take back his resignation. He agreed, returning as the acting head of the department before his new position was finalized a few months later after a recruitment process for the job that nobody else was ever going to win. His fellow teachers (those that hadn't resigned) were pleased for him.

But it had been a difficult period, and being a local celebrity was not something Andrew had found easy. He couldn't wait for the attention to go away, but, by the time the story had died down at the end of the summer, it was time for the new school year to begin and he had to put up with yet more attention from both parents and pupils alike as they saw him for the first time since the newspaper article had been printed.

Now, two years on, Andrew sat in front of his first class of the day and stared at them. Not *at* them exactly, but through them. He felt as if he was separated from them in some way, like he was in a glass booth within the classroom, but one where the walls were built with invisible materials. And yet, despite this feeling of distance, Andrew could sense the unease coming from the twenty or so children that sat in front of him. It was palpable. It was only their third week at the school, and now they were faced with a teacher who was out of control.

They didn't speak, but many turned to each other, unsure of what to do. They hadn't ever sat in a lesson with a spaced-out, incoherent teacher before. Oddly, none of them appeared to find the situation amusing. There was no giggling, no joking, no messing around. This was a new experience for them and they found it to be unsettling instead of an opportunity to misbehave. An hour discussing the short story they had read for homework suddenly seemed an attractive proposition. Hell, even writing an essay would be better than this.

Beyond the haze which surrounded him, Andrew Green was well aware that he was losing it. Perhaps it was more than that; he had *already* lost it. No matter how much he wanted to, he couldn't snap himself out of his dazed state. He felt concussed. He felt exhausted – so exhausted that he just couldn't muster the energy to even open his mouth and find the words to apologise to his class, or explain that he was feeling unwell.

He knew that his current state might have been caused by his new medication, but he also knew that this was partly his own fault. Andrew had let things go too far.

The point of no return.

He had been like this before, even if it had been a long time ago, back when he was barely out of his teens. He knew the warning signs from back then, and knew he had ignored them for months before going to the doctors. Why had he left it so long? He had no idea. Sorting it just seemed like more effort than letting it get worse, and now here he was, unable to function at all, and the tablets that might eventually make him better were giving him side effects he could do without.

Not only was he spaced out, but he also felt sick and his stomach sometimes churned so much that he felt as if it was inhabited by a washing machine. He wondered if he would throw up in front of the class. The ultimate humiliation.

He hadn't been surprised that his ill-health had returned. There had been too much pressure. He couldn't live up to the image that had been painted of him after the newspaper story had come out.

He was no hero, despite what had been written about him. He had simply done what was needed to be done, and the stress of those months and the pressure to perform afterwards, to live up to his new reputation, had left him ill and worn out. Now he felt like one of the walking dead.

With the children staring at him, partly in horror,

partly in disbelief, Andrew knew he just had to get out of the classroom. He took a long deep breath, and then finally summoned up enough energy to lean forward in his chair and slowly closed the book in front of him. All eyes followed his every move, wondering why it was that their teacher was moving almost in slow motion, and watching intently to see what he would do next.

He muttered "I'm sorry", and then he stood up and slowly and deliberately put on his jacket. Picking up his briefcase, he forced the slightest of smiles at those in front of him, and then slowly walked out of his classroom.

He wondered if he would ever return.

Breaking Down is available in paperback and Kindle formats from all Amazon stores and other selected online retailers.

Printed in Great Britain
by Amazon

33411214R00209